Smart Girls Don't Trust Strangers

C.A. Larmer is a journalist, editor, indie publisher and the author of multiple crime series, two stand-alone novels and a non-fiction book about pioneering surveyors in Papua New Guinea. Christina grew up in that country, was educated in Australia, and spent many years working in London, Los Angeles and New York. She now lives with her musician husband, two sons and cheeky Blue Heeler on the east coast of Australia.

Sign up to her newsletter: www.calarmer.com

ALSO BY C.A. LARMER

The Sleuths of Last Resort
Blind Men Don't Dial Zero (Book 1)
Good Girls Don't Drink Vodka (Book 3)

The Murder Mystery Book Club
The Murder Mystery Book Club (Book 1)
Danger on the SS Orient (Book 2)
Death Under the Stars (Book 3)
When There Were 9 (Book 4)
The Widow on the Honeymoon Cruise (Book 5)
Gone Guest (Book 6)
Peril on the Indian Pacific (Book 7)

The Ghostwriter Mystery Series
Killer Twist (Book 1)
A Plot to Die For (Book 2)
Last Writes (Book 3)
Dying Words (Book 4)
Words Can Kill (Book 5)
A Note Before Dying (Book 6)
Without a Word (Book 7)

The Posthumous Mystery Series
Do Not Go Gentle
Do Not Go Alone

Plus:
After the Ferry: A Gripping Psychological Thriller

An Island Lost

A Measure of Papua New Guinea:
The Arman Larmer Surveys Story (Focus; 2008)

C.A. LARMER

Smart Girls Don't Trust Strangers

Sleuths of Last Resort
(Book 2)

LARMER MEDIA

Published by Larmer Media
Northern Rivers, NSW 2482
Australia

www.calarmer.com

Paperback ISBN: 978-0-6452835-4-9

Cover design by Nimo Pyle
Cover photography: Silhouettes from iStock & Shutterstock
(majivecka, Funkey Factory, Yurchenko Yulia, Kozyreva)

Edited by The Editing Pen
& Elaine Rivers, with thanks

For Dianne and Michael

PROLOGUE

She thought she was doing him a favour, a simple request, and she'd be on her way.

"Look, I know you're busy," he said, waving in the general direction of the oval she'd just circumnavigated. "I have a quick request, then I'll leave you in peace, I promise! I just need you to call my mobile phone for me."

He flashed the most adorable smile, then pointed at the phone in her hands, the one she'd been scrolling to get her walking tracks.

"Just a quick call," he pleaded, rattling off the number. "Just want to see if I've dropped it somewhere in this abomination of a car."

Then he nodded towards his enormous SUV, a shiny black Jeep Wrangler, the latest model with all the bells and whistles, and that sealed the deal. She loved his car. Had coveted one just like it.

"*Please, please, please,*" he added, hands prayerlike at his lips, eyes suddenly flirty. "I'm running late and I've looked *everywhere*. If you don't mind."

Sighing to show she did mind—very much indeed!—the woman scrolled for her phone's keypad and held it up. "Okay, but let's be quick. What's the number again?"

He sighed too. More a relieved exhale. "Thank you!" Then he repeated the number, and she quickly tapped it in and pressed the green Call button.

They both stood back and listened for a moment, hearing nothing but the soft tweet of butcherbirds overhead and the drone of a distant bus.

Then the ringing started, somewhere deep within the vehicle. They looked at each other, relieved. The man plunged into the front seat, scrambling about while the woman stepped closer, phone still at her ear.

She frowned. "I think it's back here," she said, moving towards the SUV's exterior where the tailgate was already open to reveal an

1

extended boot space. She saw it was cluttered with towels and wetsuits and something else. Something that should have sent her running if only she'd had a moment to think.

"You're right," she heard him say, his voice suddenly close. Too close.

Then, before she could move, she felt a violent smack across the top of her head. As she crumpled into the back, she began to lose consciousness, and very soon there was nothing left but the diminishing drone of the bus.

CHAPTER 1 ~
A FRESH INVITATION

Frankie Jo's almond eyes swept the lane like a laser printer, absorbing every detail—the graffitied walls, the overturned bins, the suspiciously dark patches across the grimy cobblestones— copying it all for later use, while her perfect button nose inhaled the rancid scent of rotting meat, booze-soaked urine. Death.

The man's body had been removed hours ago, but the true-crime journalist could see it all so clearly and feel it in the shiver that ran through her bones. Could imagine the sprawled legs, the bloody clothes, the blank, unseeing expression. His hair, once gelled smoothly for a night on the town, now dishevelled and flopping into his dead eyes, his pungent aftershave, daubed with such optimism (*who even wears Old Spice anymore?*), still lingering like a broken promise just above the stench.

"You okay, Frankie?" said the man beside her. "Not going to throw up all over the crime scene are you?"

"Oh piss off, Tagger," she replied, glancing across at him as her smartphone let out a loud *ding!* "The only thing that makes me sick around here is your sorry excuse for a tie. Channel Seven cutting back on stylists these days are they?"

The television reporter swept a hand down his paisley tie. "Hey, my wife bought this for me."

Frankie dropped her head to the side, her blond locks tumbling with it. "Okay, *now* it all makes sense. Smart woman you got there."

"Huh?" He blinked at her, confused.

"Who'd want to shag you with that on?"

She smiled innocuously as she slipped back under the police tape, then stepped towards an older man who was scrolling through images on a fancy digital camera.

"Get everything you need, Yang?"

3

The *Herald* photographer nodded, then followed Frankie's eyes back to the laneway. "Got any deets on this chap yet?"

Frankie knew he didn't really care. Just needed a name for his digital files.

"Press conference at four, just in time for the evening snooze— I mean *news*," she told him. "All will be revealed then. For now, let's call him Spice Boy."

"I heard he was older. Early forties maybe?" He'd missed her clever play on words. Missed the lingering scent, in fact.

She glanced at Yang sideways. "He was still someone's little boy, Yang," was all she said.

As they made their way back to their respective vehicles, Frankie sighed, thinking as she often did on a day like this how a few minutes of chaos would now ripple outwards, causing a lifetime of pain, and not just for the victim's family. There was another family who was about to be broken too—the family of the killer. And for some reason Frankie felt even sorrier for them. Because how did you reconcile bringing up a monster?

"Sometimes I hate my job," she said as she reached her blood-red Audi, and Yang gave a little snort as he kept walking.

"No, you don't," he called back. "You live for this shit, Frankie Jo."

And she didn't bother to contradict him because the thrill that was currently running through her veins would make a lie of that.

It was only when Frankie was finally in her car, checking her messages, that she realised one of them was from Verity Vine— personal assistant to a wealthy mogul who'd lost half his family in one violent, tragic night.

Talk about ripples of chaos…

Hey there, supersleuths, Verity's text read. *I have another favour to ask. Can you drop into Seagrave in an hour? Apols for the short notice, time is of the essence x VV.*

Frankie tapped her chin with the phone and thought about that. Had something happened to Sir George Burlington? Or was there something else going on entirely? Didn't really matter, if truth be told. Both options saw the petite blonde's veins go tingly again.

~

Meredith Kean read Verity's text and tried to muster some

enthusiasm, curiosity, anything! She just couldn't do it. Not today. Not this week. Not at this stage of her life.

Time is of the essence? Ha!

"You're telling *me*, Verity," she said aloud as she dropped the phone onto the kitchen bench and slipped into her eldest son's bedroom, her heart as empty as his closet.

Nudging her glossy pink spectacles into place, Merry waved her free hand across the loose coat hangers, which played a mournful tune in return. Then stepped back and glanced around.

Otis's walls once boasted massive artworks, his own clumsy designs, the desk his staggering array of devices, speakers, headphones, and the photos she had given him. One was of Merry at the last Cluedo championships in Vegas. Another of the day she earned her freedom—Lola, Archie and Otis surrounding her like a warm shawl as she held up a red provisional driver's licence, beaming. Well, she wasn't beaming anymore, and the photos were all gone, the walls now bare, the bed as naked as her grief, and she dropped down onto the mattress, grappling for his pillow and hugging it like a life vest.

Then Merry whipped off her glasses, pulled her knees up into the foetal position, and sobbed like a baby, for her baby.

And for the shocking, unexpected, visceral loss of him.

~

Earle Fitzgerald hugged his pretty floral coffee mug tight and thought about Verity's unexpected message. The timing was wrong, all wrong, but he couldn't be more relieved.

He needed to get out. Away from this.

Glancing across at the missus, he saw she was hugging a matching cup, lost somewhere in her own thoughts. So, too, Gruff. The old mutt's bushy eyes staring out across the neatly mowed lawn to Beryl's veggie patch and Tess's defunct treehouse and a past that couldn't prepare them for this.

Not them. Not this.

Where had they gone wrong? Was the treehouse not good enough? he wondered. Did the now-retired detective spend too much time focused on crooks and not enough on his crooked kid? He could predict a criminal's every move, yet he never saw this one coming.

"It'll be all right, love," came Beryl's voice across the patio, and he glanced back at her. Faked a smile.

"Course it will," he said, rubbing his white beard and trying not to shift his gaze inside to their daughter, who managed to be napping despite just dropping her bombshell. Despite just detonating their life.

"Yeah, course it will," he said again, more forcefully this time.

But he could say it till the cows came home. Wouldn't change the fact it was a lie.

He plonked his cup down and scooped up his phone, bashed in his slow and clumsy reply.

Happy... to... come... Verity. See... you... soon.

Then he glanced across at the wife again and felt like the captain of the *Titanic*.

~

Martin Chase read Verity Vine's text for the second time and frowned, giving his nose an angry rub. He thought he was done with Sir George Burlington and his diligent PA. That their business had been concluded many months ago when the lovely large cheque had finally cleared.

Although if there was more money in it...

The author's mind wafted back to that massive mansion, the garish yellow living room, the revelations that had unfolded that final, harrowing day. It would have made a good book, if he were still writing crime. Instead, he'd left Frankie to tell the story and been working on his first real piece of literature.

Or not working, as it happens.

Six months ago he'd sworn off crime fiction, determined to write something more lofty. Turns out, *lofty* was exactly as it sounded, not as easy or as enjoyable as he'd been expecting, and he kept resisting the urge to bump off a character and move the plot along.

Pushing away from the battered kitchen bench, he read the phone message yet again.

What could Verity possibly want now? Or was Sir George still calling the shots?

"Anything important?" came a voice from the stove, and he turned his eyes to the pretty woman holding a spatula. She could easily have passed for his sister, just the hint of feathery lines around her eyes to prove she was his mother. That and the fact she was cooking him banana pancakes for lunch. Like he was seven.

"Having you here has been a blessing, Braxton—I mean, Martin," she said, following it with a quick apology smile. Just could not get used to his new name, his *nom de plume*. "But you don't need to stay. You know that, right? I don't deserve that."

"You've got to stop beating yourself up, Olivia."

She flinched at both the sentiment and her name but let it drop as she'd been doing now for months. She wanted him to call her mum, he knew that. But it didn't feel right. His *mother* had walked out on him when he was just a few hours old. It was going to take a lot more than self-reproach and pancakes to get that woman back.

Standing up, he tugged his statement T-shirt (RELAX, JUST VAX) down over his ever-growing paunch and said, "Actually, I do need to get back. I've got an appointment. I can't stay for…" He stared at the pancakes. "That."

"Oh, of course."

She flicked off the gas flame, dumped the spatula and stepped towards him. "Will we catch up again soon?"

He took a step backwards. "Not sure to be honest. I'm trying to bash this new book out and also looking for new digs, so…"

A flicker of surprise. "You're moving? I didn't realise." Smile jittery, she added, "Will you at least give me your new address this time?"

Like she was asking for the world. And in many ways she was because she wasn't going to get it. Not this time.

But he nodded his head anyway, then slunk away like the snake he knew he was.

~

"The guy's a snake," Kila said as he dropped his phone to the desk, pushed his unruly black curls from his eyes and focused again on the woman in green. It was a pleasant sight. His client, Brittany, was a stunner. Knew it too, and that's why she was so pissed off. "You're better off without him."

"But how could he possibly *do* it?" she demanded. "How could he cheat on *me*?" Then she waved a hand down her voluptuous figure as if to prove her point.

She made a pretty convincing argument. While she was a

knockout, her husband was the human equivalent of a cane toad and punching so far above his weight he should never have been allowed in the ring in the first place. But that's exactly why he cheated. Kila had seen it so many times before. When a man didn't measure up, he went looking elsewhere for a better fit, usually to something a lot less worthy. It was about ego, not lust. He glanced at the photos he'd printed out—of the cane toad with a chubby redhead, another with a scrawny bottle-blonde, one more with a woman who looked old enough to be his mother. Each one showed him locked in a slobbery embrace, in broad daylight. Like he wanted to get caught.

"Take him for everything he's got, Brittany," he told her. "From what I've seen, you'll be set up for life."

"I don't want to take him," she said, her voice now whimpering. "I just want my Boo-boo back."

He sighed. Had heard that many times before too. And knew better than to try to talk her out of it. Or to take his own revenge. His days of stashing prawn heads in philandering husbands' cars were over. At least that's what he'd promised his lawyer.

"So what happens now?" Brittany asked as he gathered the images together and placed them back in the envelope.

"That's up to you and him, I guess. I'm just the confirmer of your worst fears. Now you have to present him with the evidence. Demand that he stops." He held the envelope out like it was a booby prize and added, "Or not."

Because he knew plenty of women who simply couldn't do it.

She nodded warily and took it from him, thanked him for his time and made her way out. And he knew she would fall in the latter category and the vicious cycle would continue. Bummed him out, but then he had better things to think about.

Like why Verity Vine had just sent a text message requesting his presence at her boss's family mansion and how happy he was at the thought of seeing the gang again. Or, more specifically, Frankie.

Talk about a vicious cycle…

Snatching up his phone, Kila tapped out his own text:

Hey, Sexy Reporter Girl. You get VV's mysterious message? Wanna go together? Maybe grab a drink afterwards?

It took just two seconds for her answer to come back. It was an emoji of someone weeping with laughter.

He replied with a broken love heart.

CHAPTER 2 ~
RETURNING TO SEAGRAVE

The house at the top of Harrow's Drive looked like it had not had a visitor in months, let alone a groundsman. Weathered newspapers lay strewn along both sides of the driveway, junk mail piled up in the wall-mounted letter box, and the shrubbery around the perimeter was overgrown and unkempt.

Merry frowned as she pulled her car up to the mansion gate and pressed the buzzer.

There was a long pause, then a crackle and the gate swept open, still as smooth as she remembered it. Once inside the property, things weren't much better—the gardens ungroomed, the exterior waterfall drained silent. If it wasn't for the collection of cars in the guest car park, she would have sworn she'd come to the wrong place.

Unlike her last visit—that day of shocking denouements—Merry was in the driver's seat this time, and her son Otis was far, far away. She'd swap her licence to have Otis back behind the wheel any day.

"Look at you!" called out Frankie as Merry pulled in beside her.

The journalist was leaning against her Audi, scrolling through her phone. Like she had all day.

Merry leaned out the window of her smaller, less flashy vehicle and waved. She'd resisted the urge to buy something fancy, but then she hadn't expected to be rubbing bumper bars with the rich and famous again quite so soon. Her bright yellow hatchback looked toylike now, wedged as it was between Frankie's luxury Audi and Martin's gleaming Aston Martin. At least they hadn't upgraded either, although what that would look like was beyond Merry. A Rolls Royce? A limo, perhaps?

As she stepped out of the driver's side, Merry felt more confident than she had last time and proudly straightened down her suit— the jacket matching the skirt this time.

"Nice threads," said Frankie, eyes still on her device.

Merry grinned. "This ole thing?" She giggled. "I came into a bit of money, don't you know?"

"Oh yes, it's been a bit of a treat, hasn't it? I got to pay off my mortgage in one fell swoop. My bank manager nearly had a coronary."

Merry giggled again, still nervous in Frankie's presence, then waved at the other vehicles. "The rest of the sleuths already inside?"

"Ooh, you're clever," said Frankie, looking up and towards the cars. "You should be a detective. How'd you figure that?"

Merry felt her smile begin to crumple, tried to scaffold it back up. She wasn't sure if she was being mocked but knew she wasn't up to mockery today. Not after the month she'd had.

Frankie didn't appear to notice. She was staring hard at Kila's new four-wheel drive. Something had caught her eye. It appeared to be a long, thin scratch down the passenger side.

Merry noticed it, too, but was more concerned with the state of Seagrave. "They've really let the place go, hey?" she said. "I guess that's what happens when nobody's at home."

"Quite the contrary," said Frankie. "Sir George lives here now and won't let anyone remove so much as a broken twig." Then she shrugged like that wasn't a strange statement and added, "Go in. I'll see you in there."

Then her eyes returned to Kila's vandalised SUV.

Sir George Burlington looked as neglected as his property and like he'd aged twenty years in six months. It broke Merry's heart to see it.

His once neatly trimmed grey beard was now long and shaggy, a little like his linen shirt, which hadn't seen the warm side of an iron in some time. And his wheelchair—once little more than an annoyance to him—now felt like the only thing keeping him upright as he steered himself shakily towards the middle of the Yellow Room where the rest of the sleuths had gathered.

The room was as fabulous as Merry remembered it though, with the dripping crystal chandeliers and velvet curtains and exquisite antique furniture. It was the last place the five sleuths had all met, each going their separate ways after the gruelling case, and Merry, for one, was feeling sentimental.

They had made a lot of money that last, fateful day, and it had changed their lives irrevocably. Or at least it was supposed to. Merry's grand ambitions hadn't quite come to fruition, but she didn't want to think about that now.

Instead she accepted the warm hugs being delivered by both Kila—"Hey, it's Merry Christmas time!"—and Earle—"Missed you, Mez!"—and then swapped polite smiles with Martin, Verity and Sir George.

"You still thrashing opponents in the Cluedo championships, Festive?" asked Kila, using a nickname she'd never heard before that sounded jollier than she felt.

Merry had made a career out of playing her favourite board game, one she was very good at. Now she just shrugged and said, "Haven't had a game in a while, no."

"Well, you're still busy with your kids," said Earle, and she nodded.

Truth was she was caught in a loop, one she couldn't seem to get out of.

"And you guys?" she said, changing the subject. "Kila, you're still busy with the investigations business?" He nodded. "And Earle? What are you up to?"

"I'm thinking of giving Kila a run for his money and starting a private detective agency of my own," the older man said, catching both of them by surprise, but before they could enquire further, Frankie was striding in and straight to Sir George, where she threw her arms around him and gave him a good, long hug.

Okay, that too was surprising.

"Looking good, you old dog," Frankie said as she stepped back, although everyone knew she was lying.

"I'm glad you could pull yourself away from that piece of drivel you call a newspaper," he replied, his voice, at least, still full of vigour.

Frankie chuckled and threw herself onto a sofa, legs tucked underneath her like she owned the place.

For her part, Frankie did feel so much more comfortable in the rambling mega mansion. And in George's presence too. They'd spent considerable hours together while she researched and wrote a series of articles on his family's murders and had become very close. She understood, as Verity did, that the old man's bark was so much worse than his bite.

"Well, I've got more drivel to write," she told him, "so shall we get on with it?"

George's eyebrows lifted, but then he just cackled some more and turned rheumy eyes to his PA, deferring to her as he'd always done.

Verity stepped forward now and looked exactly the same—curly red hair, smart but dull suit, deeply efficient expression in her eyes. But this time she was missing a wad of papers.

"No confidentiality agreement?" said Frankie, who never missed a beat.

Verity smiled. "Your discretion, however, would be appreciated."

Frankie wanted to object, but Martin was already intervening.

"What exactly are we being discreet about this time? Not another murder in the family I hope."

"A missing person," said George. "Chanel Chambers. And she's as good as family."

Frankie squinted, not recognising the name. Missing women were big news in her industry. Especially if they showed up dead, a suspicious husband lurking in the background. Forget stabbed men in stinky laneways, *this* is what sparked a media feeding frenzy, not to mention endless platitudes from politicians about the rights of women and the scourge of domestic violence. Yet nothing changed. A woman was still murdered every week in this country.

As common as Sunday brunch.

Before she could enquire further, Verity had one hand up and was pointing towards the buffet she'd set up on a side table. As always. "Shall we start with a refreshing beverage, then we can tell you all about it."

Like that's all this was, a relaxing chat over a tea and scone.

As she watched them load their plates with treats, then settle back into their seats, chatting amongst themselves, George's PA, Verity, couldn't help smiling. She'd missed this lot too. Had grown quite fond of them last time even if they had accused her of murder at one point. She couldn't believe it had been six months since they'd gathered here for that final, shocking revelation. Oh so much had changed since that horrendous day, not least of all her boss. She glanced at his shrunken figure and felt her heart lurch. The group's presence, especially Frankie, had brought him back to life, but it would be temporary. She knew that.

Shaking her shoulders out, she waited until things had settled a little, then said, "Thank you so much for coming and at such short notice. As George said, we have another case for you. If you're up for it, of course."

"The million-dollar kind, I hope," said Martin, eyes on the mining magnate.

Sir George dropped his head to the side. "No such luck this time," he replied, "but I don't believe any of you were doing it for the money then, and I don't think that's why you're all back. Am I right?"

He swept his steely eyes across the group, and despite everything, they all found themselves glancing away. Even the cocky reporter. He smiled. Like a shark. Added, "You will, of course, be paid handsomely for your time, and this case is just as important as mine. More so, I would suggest."

Then he gave Verity the nod, and so she began.

"As George explained, we're very concerned about a young woman called Chanel. Chanel Chambers. One minute she was taking a walk, the next she vanished. Chanel is the daughter of a family friend. She's just twenty-seven, is an admin assistant but is between jobs at the moment. Had recently moved in with her mother after breaking up with a longtime boyfriend. She told her mother she was heading off—she circles a local oval, just down from her mum's apartment. She's usually gone about an hour. After two hours, Prue—that's the mother—began to worry."

"Look," said George, holding a frail hand up to stall her. "Prue's a worrywart at the best of times. She was a good friend of my second wife, Pookie, and would panic if she broke a fingernail; that has to be said. But I think she has reason to be concerned. At least that's how it feels to me."

And he would know, thought every single one of them.

"The concerned mother approached you directly?" asked Earle

"Prue knows what I've been through. Perhaps she knew I'd take it seriously. Perhaps she just wanted my advice. In any case, I told her to call the police immediately and then dispatched Verity to see her."

Verity nodded. "She's beside herself. Has done her own search of the oval, the surrounding area. There's simply no sign of her daughter. It's like she's been swept away. We think you guys could help. If you can free some time up, of course."

The group glanced amongst each other, but no one said a word.

"Think about it," said George, wheeling himself back towards the door. He might have diminished in size, but he was still as big on grand exits as he was on pronouncements. "I've arranged for you to meet Prue at her apartment in an hour."

"Whoa, hold your horses!" said Frankie, causing him to stop in his tracks. "Where's the fire? I know the situation is tragic—a missing woman and all—but I've got a media conference scheduled in an hour and a story to write straight after."

George looked disappointed. "This is of the utmost urgency, Frankie. Once again, I'm asking you to drop everything on your plates and get started right away."

"But isn't this a cold case?" she asked. "What difference is it going to make?"

"It's not a cold case, is it?" said Earle, stroking his white beard carefully.

"Not at all," George replied. "It's still piping hot, which is why time is of the essence. I want you lot on it. Now. Before the trail goes cold."

"How hot?" persisted Earle. "When did Chanel go missing?"

The old man checked his watch and raised wet, red eyes towards them. "Six hours ago, and we don't want to lose another minute."

CHAPTER 3 ~
MULLING IT OVER

"*Six hours?*" said Merry under her breath to Kila. "I mean, I'm no expert in all this, but isn't it a tad early to be bringing in private investigators when someone's only been missing for six hours?"

"If your daughter had been missing for six minutes, wouldn't you pull out all the stops?"

This was George, who had overheard and was now back in the centre of the living room.

Kila could see Merry blush at that, dutifully slapped into place.

"How about I show you all what she looks like?" said Verity, like that was going to resolve it.

And for Kila, at least, it did.

As Verity handed around an A4 photograph, much like she had done last time—this one featuring just one woman looking sweet and soft and innocent—Kila's first thought was of his sister. This woman was older than Chili but had the same sporty look, make-up-free face, wide open smile, and that's when he knew he had no choice.

Chili had ended up lifeless in a laneway. He didn't want that to happen to anyone else.

"I'm in," he said, surprising them all. He was the most reticent last time.

"Me too," said Frankie, which wasn't surprising, but Kila suspected her decision was based on statistics as much as headlines, and she quickly proved him right.

Women's safety had become her new *raison d'etre*.

"I've done a lot of missing persons stories," she told them, "and I know for a fact that missing women are more likely to be victims of foul play than, say, kids—who often run away from home after an argument—or even older men who are more likely to be a suicide.

15

I don't blame the mother for being worried."

"Was Chanel the type to just vanish?" asked Martin.

Verity shook her head. "Prue says she's a devoted daughter. Would never just leave without notice. She's not answering her mobile. It just goes straight to voice mail. Has left all her belongings, including bag and bank cards at home. Prue is certain she's been abducted."

"What's the situation with the police?" asked Earle.

George waved a dismissive hand. "Too early is all they say."

"And they're right," said Earle. "Yes, Frankie, your stats are correct and they make terrifying headlines, but they're also misleading. Fact is, stranger abductions are very rare. Didn't you say Chanel had just broken up with her partner? She could be somewhere clearing her head. Or she might've slunk back to him. Here's some more stats you left out: over half of all missing people show up within the first twenty-four hours, the vast majority within the first week. Most of them are okay."

"There's always exceptions to the rule," she shot back. "My paper is littered with them."

"Prue has spoken to her daughter's ex," Verity said, getting them back on track. "His name is Colin Boyder. He hasn't heard from her either."

"*Or so he says*," said Kila. "What's he like? This ex?"

Verity nudged an eyebrow upwards. "Let's just say if Merry had her whiteboard in here, you'd definitely want to scribble his name up there somewhere. At least, that's according to Prue's appraisal."

"Dodgy was he?" asked Kila.

"More disinterested, I'd say. Prue had to leave multiple messages before he returned her calls, and when she finally spoke to him, just an hour ago, he dismissed her concerns outright. Didn't want to help her search, didn't seem to care one jot. I understand it's early days, but to us that feels a little"—a glance at George now—"*odd.*"

"Who else?" asked Frankie. "Who else should we look at?"

"Hang on," said Merry. "So we're going to do this? All of us? Together?" She wasn't sure she was ready yet to come out of her period of mourning.

"Yes, Merry!" snapped Frankie. "Do keep up, honey. I think we've all agreed on that."

"But how long do we have?" she asked. "And, well… what

happens if we don't find her?"

"Do we still get paid?" said Martin.

"Of course," said Verity. "As we said, you will be compensated for your time. But at a more reasonable rate." Another frown at her boss. "Kila, perhaps you can let us know what you think is fair."

He nodded, but he didn't really care. Money was always a side issue for the private eye. It was justice that drove him.

"How many weeks does she want to hire us for? Initially?" asked Martin.

"Seventy-two hours," said George, catching them all by surprise again.

George nodded towards his PA. "Verity knows a few stats herself, and that's the most critical period. The evidence is still there; witnesses still remember. We want to hire you for three days. How you use those three days is your concern. I want Prue's daughter found, and I want her found fast. I also want her found alive." He gave them another steely look. "I'm a betting man, people. Have been known to wager a million dollars on a horse. My money says, if we don't find Chanel within three days, we won't find her alive. So you need to get cracking."

Earle peered at George over the top of his spectacles. "There can be no guarantees in a missing person case, sir. Chanel might return this evening, or she might never be located."

"That is not an option," he shot back. "I have faith in you five. If anyone can do it, you can."

Merry looked emboldened by the compliment, but Earle felt it was hot air and bluster. Just like last time, the wealthy tycoon acted like everything was a business deal that could be pushed through with manipulation and money. This was a woman's life he was talking about, and it was far from their control.

Earle's thoughts turned to his own daughter, another life out of his control, and perhaps that's why he agreed to the job even though he didn't hold much hope of finding Chanel soon or alive. If she didn't waltz into her mother's apartment in the next six hours with some sorry excuse, he didn't expect her to ever waltz again. Frankie wasn't the only one who saw the exceptions. But she just reported on them. As the onetime head of Sydney's Serious Crime Division, Earle had to live them and breathe them and knock on the doors of the exceptions' terrified parents. The odds were in Prue's favour, but sometimes your luck ran out.

So he'd give George his seventy-two hours—and himself a handy distraction—then he'd hold up the white flag and return home to face the music.

"We can give no guarantees we'll find Chanel alive, let alone find her at all," he told George, his voice deep, trying to match the bluster. "But I can guarantee that I will give it my full attention for three whole days. Hopefully, we won't need it."

For his part, Martin hoped they would. He was also looking for a distraction. From a book that wasn't being written. From the woman who called herself his mother. And most of all from the mess he'd made of his life.

Better to immerse himself in someone else's mess for now.

"So, meet again in an hour?" Martin said, dusting crumbs off his tight skinny jeans, too tight for him these days.

"I simply can't!" wailed Frankie. "I have a media conference in…" She checked her phone. "Twenty minutes!"

"Then you could opt out of this," Martin replied. "Us four can do the job."

Frankie looked offended by that, even more so when George said to her, "Is this conference of yours about a woman who is missing? If not, I'd suggest my case trumps that one."

Frankie frowned and sat back. It wasn't quite that simple. She was still holding on to her newspaper job by the skin of her teeth. Her extraordinary exposé of the Burlington murders was keeping the shoulder tap at bay for now, but there were no guarantees in journalism anymore, and she'd already waved goodbye to too many retrenched colleagues.

Not even the awards she'd won for the Burlington story could offer any comfort.

Especially with the Boss still circling.

That was the nickname Frankie used for her best friend, Jan. Or, rather, her *ex*-best friend, because the two university pals had had a falling out during the Burlington case. The details now seemed irrelevant but not Jan's indignation and spite. Words were said, threats were made, and Frankie was waiting for the other shoe to drop. Or, more precisely, for her best friend's shoe to wedge in her door and turn her life upside down.

Because Jan knew all of Frankie's secrets, and not all of them were pretty.

"You'll regret this," were Jan's final words before she promptly vanished. Since then there had been hints of the woman but nothing concrete, and Frankie was glad of it.

Jan was one missing woman she didn't want found.

Misreading her expression, Verity stepped forward with a conciliatory smile. "I understand you are all busy and have your own lives and that it really is very early." She locked eyes with Earle. "Yes, the first few days are vital, but it is also true that Chanel could reappear at any moment. And wouldn't that be lovely? Which is why I'd like to make another suggestion if I might." Now she offered George a firm look, one Frankie had never quite mastered. "Let's give it the full twenty-four hours. If Nel is still missing tomorrow morning, let's all meet at Prue Chambers's house and take it from there. How does eight a.m. sound? Down at Balmoral Beach, the scene of the crime, if indeed there is one."

Because it sounded to Frankie like Verity was not convinced.

The PA added, "That will give you all time to get your affairs in order and be there early enough to meet Prue and then walk the route where her daughter was last sighted, at the exact time she walked it. At nine."

The sleuths all looked at George, waiting for him to explode. His PA had just contradicted him in front of others. Surely that was grounds for dismissal! Or more bluster at least. But the old man just slumped into his chair, his expression as defeated as his body, and so Verity clapped her hands together, like she was applauding herself, not the suggestion.

"Great, that's settled. Hopefully Chanel will reappear between now and then, and we can cancel this horrible job and you can get on with your lovely, busy lives."

What Verity didn't know as she handed out a printed card with Prue's address on it, what the sleuths themselves would never admit, was that most of them did not have lives they *wanted* to get back to, at least not anytime soon.

~

Frankie was the exception. The busy reporter was keen to follow up on the Spice Boy murder and was champing at the bit to hear what the police had to say at the first media conference, arriving just in time to see the official party stride in—first Detective Inspector Andrew Morgan, Earle's old friend and foe, followed by a man in a drab suit that Frankie didn't recognise, then the Force's public relations woman, a chirpy young thing, too chirpy for this conference.

Chirpy chick was dressed in a tight red jacket and smiling like she was posing for Instagram as she introduced drab man as John Kolleroy, acting head of the State's parole board, which was interesting in itself and caused a flurry of tapping from the press. Then she handed over to Morgan, whose growly look reset the scales. He provided the salivating journalists with the basics.

Identity of the Kings Cross laneway victim: Phillip Malcolm Weaver, age thirty-four, from Western Sydney.

Time of death: sometime between eleven forty-five p.m. on Tuesday night and two a.m. Wednesday morning.

Cause of death: fatal stab wound to the lower abdomen (weapon not presently located).

Current leads—sweet F-all.

Which was why he quickly handed over to Kolleroy, who cleared his throat and leaned towards the microphone, tapping it to check it was on and causing a loud squeak, which brought groans and eye rolls from the gathered throng.

"My name is Johnathon Kolleroy. I'm from the State Parole Authority," he began, like they hadn't just heard that, "and, er, Mr Weaver was recently an inmate of the New South Wales Corrective Services. He was released on conditional parole nine days ago."

That brought the tapping to an end—there was nothing less sexy or sympathetic than an ex-con, except maybe a dead one—but Frankie was intrigued. Convicted criminals were her forté. She shifted to a spare seat closer to the front.

"FYI," Kolleroy was saying, using those exact letters, "Mr Weaver was incarcerated on charges of aggravated robbery in 2016 but had also been incarcerated previously on charges relating to fraud and forgery, including two years for Obtain Financial Advantage by Deception." He paused to clear his throat again. "Mr Weaver served his time and was deemed low-risk upon release, and while we are currently looking through his last known movements and contacts during that period, at this stage we are not clear as to the exact circumstances surrounding his murder."

The man spoke as though it was personal to him, a fault somehow of his system.

"Could it be retribution related?" Frankie called out.

Kolleroy's eyes danced around to find who was speaking while Morgan leaned towards the microphone and spoke for him:

"We're keeping all lines of enquiry open, Frankie, and are just here to call for witnesses to contact our police hotline if they have any information that can assist the case. We also have some footage of his last known movements to provide you with."

Morgan gave chirpy chick the nod, and she picked up a remote control and waved it towards the large screen above their heads.

It took a moment to click in, then Frankie watched as black-and-white security footage showed a hooded man walking steadily down a busy, brightly lit street, a young woman beside him. The man was tall and lanky, his face hidden within the hood; the woman was half his height and twice his weight, and her face was much clearer. She looked young, maybe twenties, and was wearing a lot of make-up, her hair black and flowing around a faux-fur winter jacket. They stopped after just a few seconds and appeared to be talking, heads close together, before the woman suddenly turned and strode back in the direction they'd been walking while the man leaned into himself to light a cigarette. He stood on the street for a few more seconds, dragging on his smoke, before stamping it out with one foot and then walking back in the woman's direction, then out of sight of the camera. That's when the screen went black again, and Morgan continued talking.

"This footage was taken at approximately 11:40 last night, just down from the Bourbon Hotel in Kings Cross, not far from where the deceased was found. We'll get copies to anyone who needs it but ask that stations air some of this footage in their evening bulletin in the hope that someone might recognise the victim and come forward." He stared straight into the nearest camera, deepened his voice a little. "At this point, we're making a number of enquiries, but we are asking anybody who saw this man or this woman in the vicinity of Kings Cross last night to come forward or call Crime

Stoppers. Anyone who has any information that could help the case is also asked to phone the police hotline."

"And you have absolutely no idea who the woman is?" yelled out Tagger, the Channel Seven reporter, sitting in the front row, looking pleased with himself.

Morgan slapped him with dead eyes. "If we knew that information, we wouldn't be here wasting everybody's time."

Tagger slouched a little in his seat, and Frankie couldn't help sniggering. She loved when the smarmy TV guys got their comeuppance. Morgan's bad mood didn't perturb the others though, and soon they were firing questions like bullets, most of which he batted away as dismissively as he'd answered Tagger's, but it wasn't Morgan Frankie wanted to question, so she waited until the gunfire had steadied a little, then called out:

"Mr Kolleroy! A question please!"

The head of Parole looked startled and sat forward again, his eyes now locked to Frankie. She offered him her best *This won't hurt a bit* smile and said, "Which prison had Mr Weaver recently been released from?"

"Oh, okay…" He seemed relieved by the question, and she wondered what she *should* have been asking. "It was Silverwater Correctional Centre."

Then he frowned, confused, as Frankie's face lit up like she'd just won a prize.

CHAPTER 4 ~
AND SO IT BEGINS...

Kila awoke to the sound of the front door closing and glanced across to the empty space beside him. He sighed. Never could keep a woman for long.

Couldn't keep a woman.

Couldn't keep a sister.

He jumped up—no point spiralling down that rabbit hole again—and gave his thick curls a good scratch. Then he snatched up his phone and began scrolling through his messages as he padded out and towards the front door, opening it wide to fetch the newspaper.

The *Tele* was resting, as it usually was, on his ratty old doormat, but this time it came with a special little treat, a pile of fresh dog faeces.

Kila smirked, half wondering if it was a comment on last night's performance, then frowned and looked up. A woman was jogging towards him on the pavement, hair in a high ponytail, face in a fierce grimace that matched the suited man walking on the other side, although he had a touch of midweekitis about him, his shoulders hunched, his hands thrust deep into his trouser pockets. But there were no dogs to be seen. No errant dog walkers either.

He shrugged and kicked the paper back to the curb. He'd check the news later, online. For now he had a call coming through, and he leaned against the open doorframe and went to answer it, then realised who it was.

Speaking of dog turds, he thought as he tapped the Reject Call button.

"Hey Morea!" came a voice from across the road, and Kila looked back to find the young guy who lived next door, standing beside his mailbox.

"You piss someone off last night or what?" The man was pointing at Kila's brand-new Toyota four-wheel drive.

The PI frowned and walked towards him, careful to avoid the newspaper. "What are you on about, Macker?"

Then he spotted it, a long, shaky scratch down the right side of his vehicle, from the driver's side door all the way to the back. Someone had taken a key to it, and it wasn't the first time.

Okay, now he was getting grumpy.

~

Beryl Fitzgerald tried not to look grumpy as she watched her husband tie his shoelaces, preparing to head out. Again.

Another day, another distraction from the issues that needed discussing. At least it wasn't golf this time. Was a lot more important than that, and so she said nothing, just cleared his empty cereal bowl and wished him luck.

"It's going to take more than luck to find this lady," Earle told her, as if after forty years as a police officer's wife she was clueless.

"I know that," she said, her tone just the right side of snappy.

He caught it and tried for a warm smile. "I'll try to sneak back for lunch if I can manage it."

"Do what you need to do," she told him, shuffling away. "Tess and I aren't going anywhere in a hurry."

We're not ducking for cover. Like some.

~

Merry was hurling final instructions to the kids—"Don't forget soccer training tonight, Archie! Jack's mum will collect you at four! Lola, you've got that English essay due tomorrow, yeah? And for the love of God, get out of that blasted shower!"—then slammed the front door, pushed her pink glasses into place, and made a beeline for her car.

It was parked out on the road. They didn't have a garage. It was another bugbear of the house, but she couldn't think about that now. Her head was swirling and not with the current case.

Merry's ex-husband had called first thing, asked to drop over.

"I won't take much of your time," Darren had promised. "I just want to see how everything is going, you know, after Otis...?"

He'd dropped the *O* bomb. That had done it. And despite her better judgement, Merry found herself agreeing, telling him she'd message when she got back.

She was just unlocking her car when her elderly neighbour appeared, still in her floral dressing gown.

"Hi, Mrs B!" Merry called out, smudging her lips into a smile. "How are you today?"

"Oh *I'm* fine, dear," the older woman said, leaning now against the fence. "It's you I'm worried about. Ever since Otis… Well, you haven't been yourself, love."

Merry nodded, clearing the frog that formed in her throat every time her eldest son's name was mentioned. Waved her off. "We'll get used to it. Eventually."

Mrs Baxter dropped her head to one side. Squinted. "It's okay to be sad, love. It's natural."

"Yes, yes, I know." Merry's smile stiffened.

"Any more thoughts about moving?" the woman asked. "You know my grandson's a real estate agent. He tells me it's a top time to be selling. Your place would fetch a lovely price."

Mrs Baxter had good reason to ask. Merry had talked incessantly about moving since her windfall from the Burlington case. In fact, she'd wanted to flee this house long before that, the moment she'd returned home from the Vegas Cluedo championship to find Darren on the patio with his own Miss Scarlet. Merry hadn't used the patio since. Could barely look the marital bed in the eye. But she'd been too broke back then to replace it so had swallowed her pride and lived with the memory of Darren's infidelity. It was a literal take on the old refrain—you made your bed, now lie in it.

Six months ago she'd promised herself and the kids they'd move somewhere fabulous. But all she'd done was buy a king-size innerspring mattress with pocketed coils and a plush pillow top. Pity it was so large and empty.

"I'd better choof off!" Merry said. "But if you need a hand with that lawn of yours, Archie's looking to earn some extra pocket money."

"Oh, he's a good lad, isn't he? Must be quite a comfort now that…" And again she let the sentence drop.

Merry ducked for the comfort of her car before the tears began to stream out.

By the time she got to the harbourside suburb of Balmoral Beach, Merry's tears had dried up and her eyes were wide with wonder.

She couldn't recall the last time she'd visited, but what a pretty place it was!

She drove slowly along the beach-lined esplanade from one end, with its elegant white rotunda, to the other, where she spotted the residential building she was looking for, then parked further up and backtracked on foot. Aptly named Bellavista, the red-brick block of apartments certainly had a beautiful view of the glistening bay just across the road. It was no Seagrave, that's for certain, but it probably had a comparable price tag, judging by this upmarket location, and was certainly beyond Merry's budget, if she ever did find the energy to move.

The other sleuths had all beaten her there and offered a range of greetings before Verity led them through a latched gate to the building's front door, where she pressed the buzzer for apartment four.

The door was released without a sound, and they made their way in—through the well-lit entryway, up a series of graduating stairs to the first two apartments, then up a second set of stairs to the top level. The door to one apartment was shut; the other was just opening as they reached the landing, a plump sixty-year-old in woollen pants and a creamy cashmere sweater was peering out, her wide, haunted eyes showing them they'd come to the right place.

It was just on eight a.m., Thursday morning. Prue's daughter had been missing for twenty-three hours, and there was no comfort in that fact. Merry felt her heart bleed for the mother and tried to give her a warm, positive smile as Verity made the introductions.

"Thank you so much for coming," Prue said, leading them through to the elegantly decorated living room and on to a tan suede lounge suite set around a low mahogany coffee table. Compared to the chaos in Prue's eyes, the apartment was like an oasis, all soft hues and fresh roses, and the scent of vanilla and ylang-ylang.

It felt so incongruous.

"Did anyone want a cup of tea?" Prue asked, no enthusiasm in her voice.

"I'll do the honours," said the PA, standing up again. "While I do, Prue, why don't you tell the team a little about your daughter?"

As Verity headed through a side door towards the kitchen—clearly no stranger here—Prue gawped back at them like she had no idea where to start, so Earle jumped in to help her, pointing towards a collection of framed photos gathered beneath a large crystal lamp on a side table, most clearly of Chanel.

"Your daughter is twenty-seven, is that correct?"

Prue's eyes lost their haunted look for a moment. "Yes, she had her birthday two weeks ago. A few of us went out for dinner. She isn't much of a party girl."

That was obvious from the photos. Chanel was mostly dressed in sporty outfits—polo shirts, ski gear, gym wear—her dark brown locks swept up in high ponytails or top knots. There wasn't a lick of make-up on her tanned face, and she hadn't drenched her brows in black like most women her age. One image showed her in a graduation gown. A younger one in what must be her formal frock, but it was nothing like the tizzy, low-cut number Merry's daughter thought she was going to wear to her own formal later this year. (She wasn't.)

Offering an apologetic smile, Prue said, "Chanel was poorly named. Her father's idea. He thought it would elevate her, make her feel special. She hated it. Insisted we all call her Nel from a very young age."

"Then Nel it is," said Merry, offering another warm smile.

"And she's not working at the moment?" Earle continued. "Is that correct?"

"No, that's partly why she moved back with me. She had broken up with her boyfriend, you see? A fellow by the name of Colin Boyder, but she was also thinking about going travelling. Letting her hair down for a bit."

"Any issues with the ex-boyfriend? Animosity after the split?"

"Oh, no, nothing like that. I mean, it *seemed* amicable." Prue's haunted look was returning. "They were not well suited as it turns out. I think she'd finally worked that out."

"What about her employer?" asked Martin. "People at work? Any reason she'd left the job?"

"I don't believe so… She was just a bit bored, I think. Looking for something more in life. You know?"

Prue's eyes were on Frankie, the one closest in age to Nel, like she was beseeching her to agree. Frankie didn't bat an eyelash.

"Can you tell us about the last time you saw, er, Nel?" asked Earle. "That was yesterday morning, yes?"

She nodded, clutching the pearls around her neck. "It was just on nine o'clock. She was *fine*." Like someone was suggesting otherwise.

From her side of the lounge, Frankie wondered about all that. Yes, she was a similar age to Nel, so she understood that feeling of angst that creeps into your bones as thirty rapidly approaches. Finding yourself single, jobless *and* living with your mother at that age was like the holy trinity of dashed dreams for any woman, so *fine* seemed like a misnomer.

And sure, missing men were more likely to be suicides, but if Nel had even a whiff of depression added to the mix, it amplified everything.

Could she have acted out in a moment of despair? Thrown herself from a cliff somewhere? Waded into the sea…

It wasn't beyond Frankie to throw those questions at a parent, but she didn't need to. Martin was doing the honours.

"How can you be sure she hasn't left deliberately?" he asked. "Even self-harmed?"

He said it so casually even Frankie matched the scowl he was now getting from the others. But Prue was not perturbed, shaking her head emphatically.

"She wouldn't do that. She wouldn't leave me. Not after her father…"

Frankie held a finger up. "What happened to your husband, Mrs Chambers?"

"He died last year. Cancer. I've struggled; she knows that. That's partly why she moved in. She wouldn't let me struggle again… She knew how much that affected me. She's a very, very good daughter, very devoted, loves me to bits. No matter what was happening in her life, she wouldn't just up and leave. She just wouldn't *do* this! Not to me!"

Merry was nodding along with her, but Frankie wasn't convinced.

She was thinking of her past, of a suicidal politician and the aftermath of that. The reporter had seen enough, experienced enough, to know that someone's own personal struggles often trumped their thoughts and feelings for others. She didn't air that thought either because the clock was ticking.

"Can we get back to yesterday? Nine a.m.," said Frankie. "Nel left here for a jog, is that correct?"

"For a walk, actually. Her daily speed walk," said Prue, who clearly liked to get facts straight, which pleased the journalist. It was all about the facts for Frankie. "I was in the kitchen, making some breakfast. She popped her head around the door, said 'I'm off,' and then… that was it."

"'I'm off'?" said Frankie. "Not, 'I'm off for a speed walk'?" Again the inference that perhaps she wasn't really heading where Prue thought. Again, Prue was shaking her head.

"She had her usual walking gear on, including walking shoes and cap. No handbag or purse. I found those in her bedroom. She walks every morning at nine, at least when she stays here she does. If Nel was going somewhere different, then she would have said that."

"And she seemed happy?" asked Earle. "No indication that she–"

"She was fine!" the woman said again.

She would not have anyone suggest otherwise.

"I'll take you down to the local oval after this, show you the usual route," said Verity, who had now returned with a large teapot and a tray of matching cups. "We think that's probably where Nel, er… vanished." A quick worried glance at Prue. "Because parts of the oval are quite secluded."

"What exactly was she wearing?" asked Earle.

"What does it matter?" demanded Frankie. "You're not victim blaming or slut shaming, are you, Earle?"

He stared at her wearily. "I'm getting a thorough description so we can canvass the neighbourhood."

Frankie raised her chin and waved him on, but now Prue seemed irritated.

"Nel was wearing her black leggings, blue singlet with a yellow sweatshirt over the top. Um… she has black Nike trainers. Plain blue cap with a grey Nike swish." She sniffed. "It was her favourite."

Prue didn't hesitate as she recalled this, and Frankie wondered if she had a great memory or had checked her daughter's wardrobe.

"Height? Weight?" asked Earle.

"Um, just under six foot; she was tall for a girl. And I guess she was sixty kilos? But strong, yes? Not too skinny. I liked that about Nel." Now Prue's eyes had wafted to Merry, who tucked her short, shapely legs under the couch.

Earle felt a twinge of disappointment. Apart from the yellow sweatshirt, the rest of Nel's outfit sounded completely forgettable.

You wanted your missing person to stand out from the crowd—massively tall or obese, wearing something unusual or eye-catching, with a shaved head or bright pink hair. From what Prue was saying and the photos he could see, she was just a lovely, ordinary-looking girl. Brown hair, brown eyes, brown face.

If Nel had dressed up like a *slut*, they'd probably have more luck with witnesses, especially in this conservative neighbourhood. Not that he was going to say *that* out loud.

"Any distinguishing features?" he asked now. "Like a birthmark, perhaps?"

Prue played with her pearls again, clearly hesitating. "Well," she said finally, "she does have one of those dreadful tattoos." She swept a hand down the back of one shoulder. "But you never see it. She always covers it up, rarely wears anything revealing anyway. It's not her style. I know it was covered yesterday under her sweatshirt, so I wouldn't bother with that."

"Tell me about the tattoo," said Earle.

The ghost of a smile now. "It was a moment of madness. Got it while travelling on her gap year with friends. It's some silly line about peace and love or some such, written in some foreign language."

That made Earle feel sad, because chances were Nel did not meet with either.

"And her phone? She had that with her?" asked Kila, and she nodded, then thanked Verity, who was handing her a cup of steeped Earl Grey.

"I've tried it so many times my fingers are almost bleeding," Prue said. "Just goes to voice mail. Other than that, she had nothing else, no money, no keys, nothing..." Her voice cracked a little.

"Do we know if anyone saw her between here and the oval?" asked Earle. "A neighbour? A shopkeeper, perhaps?"

She blinked rapidly. Reached for the pearls. "Goodness... I... I'm not sure. I spoke to Les. He's the fellow down in unit one. But I didn't manage to... I mean I should have asked the others... Sorry, I didn't think."

"It's okay, Prue," said Verity quickly, "that's what these guys are here for."

Then the PA invited the others to help themselves to tea and condiments.

As Earle added milk to his own cup, he said, "I believe you called the police yesterday? Can you tell me who you spoke with?"

"No one!" said Prue, her voice rising, wobbling with emotion, her cup rattling along with it. "Just some young woman on the phone. She sounded thirteen! She took a few details, but I could tell she didn't think it was serious. Told me to wait by the phone and Nel was likely to call or show up any minute. If she was still missing after a day or so, to come down to the station and make a formal statement. I could tell she thought I was being melodramatic. But I'm not! And now, thanks to *her*, my baby has been out there, alone. All night!"

Prue's voice was now high-pitched, and fat tears were dropping into her cup.

Verity moved closer and rubbed her back gently.

Watching them, Earle felt heartbroken for the woman, really he did, but he also understood the police's hesitation. Because most missing loved ones showed up so soon, running around in the early stages was more often than not, a waste of police resources.

But he couldn't say that to a panicked parent.

"That's why I called George," Prue said, clunking her cup down on the table. "I'm desperate, don't you see? I'm not sure we have time for all this... this... chatter! I just want you to go out there. Find her!"

Just like George, thought Earle. Like they could click their fingers and it would all be sorted. "It's important we get our ducks lined up before we start running about, Mrs Chambers. We'll get some facts from you, and then we'll check the place over, starting with Nel's bedroom."

Prue looked horrified. "I haven't misplaced her under the bed!"

"No, but perhaps there's some indication in her room as to where she might have gone, or who she's been in touch with."

"Or maybe she left a note for you in there!" said Merry, trying to help Earle out and only flustering the woman further.

"Oh! I didn't look! I didn't think..."

"We'll do that first thing," said Earle. "Won't take more than a few minutes."

Verity pointed to a stairwell leading downwards between the front door and Prue's master bedroom at the back of the apartment. "She's in one of the rooms downstairs."

Earle nodded, eyes back on Prue. "Does your daughter own a

computer or laptop we could check out? In case there's some email or website or document that might indicate—"

"No. I mean, she had a laptop, but I know she left it at Colin's. She didn't seem to care, checks all her emails on her phone. It's glued to her hand, that thing."

Verity said, "The team will also retrace your daughter's steps, Prue. Can you show us the route that she—"

"I'm not leaving here! What if Nel calls? What if she reaches out?"

"Don't you have a mobile phone?" asked Frankie, but Prue was shaking her head.

"Nel always calls the landline. I hate talking on those contraptions! She knows that! *She would call the landline...*" Prue reached a hand across and gripped the large, corded telephone on the table near the photos, and Earle had a feeling she'd been staring at that phone for twenty of the past twenty-three and a half hours.

"No worries," said Verity, pulling out her own mobile device and tapping her way to Google Maps. "If you could show me the route, we'll take a look ourselves."

"I did do that, you know! I did walk the route!" Again, Prue's tone was defensive. "I walked it twice yesterday, scoured the place. I'm not a complete idiot. She's not lying on the pathway with a broken ankle."

The woman's anxiety was making her testier by the minute, and Verity offered her a patient smile, just like the smiles she offered Sir George. Then nodded at her device. "Still, worth a fresh look, hey?"

Prue dropped her eyes and her voice. "Of course. Sorry. I'm just so worried. It's just... all this..." She waved a hand at the group. "It feels like a waste of time. I... I need you to find my baby!"

Then she dropped her head into her hands and sobbed like she was the child.

CHAPTER 5 ~
KICKING THINGS OFF

As Verity comforted Prue, Earle gathered the team on the apartment balcony to talk privately and institute a plan. If only he could keep their attention.

The view from the front deck was breathtaking. You could see straight down onto the street below and across that to the sun-drenched esplanade that laced the sandy bay. He gave them a moment to ooh and aah, but all he could think was how windy it would get and how often you'd have to replace your electronic gear with all the salt spray flying about.

"Bet you could write a killer novel, looking out at this, hey Martin?" said Merry.

The author glanced back from the vista and shrugged. "I don't need a view. It's all up here." He tapped his head.

Kila scoffed and Frankie eye-rolled, and Earle thought about how quickly they all slid back into their respective roles. But there was no time to waste, so he popped his Chief Investigator hat on and said:

"Come on, folks, let's focus. There are lots of preliminary jobs to tick off before we head to the oval at nine. So I suggest we split up."

"And I may need to run away at any moment," added Frankie, one eye on her phone.

Earle ignored her and produced a forefinger. "First job is to thoroughly search this apartment, upstairs and down. I didn't want to build false hope, but Merry's quite correct. Chanel may have left a note or something that explains where she's at. These things are easy to overlook when you're in a flap."

"And she's definitely in a flap," said Martin.

"Who can blame her?" said Kila. "Bloody hope we don't find a suicide note."

No one responded to that, and Earle produced a second finger.

"We also need to talk to the other tenants in this building, see who's normally here at this time of the day and what, if anything, they noticed. Perhaps they overheard something or saw her interacting with someone when she left the building."

"There's three other apartments here, I noticed," said Frankie. "Shall we split up?"

"In urgent cases, it's best to do interviews in pairs," said Earle. "What one person misses, the other might catch. Frankie, how about you and Kila focus on that—interviewing is your skill set, yes? And Martin and Merry, you're the evidence and crime scene experts. Maybe Martin can explore this top level while Merry checks out downstairs. I want to put a call through to the Missing Persons Unit, see if I can wake someone from their slumber. Hopefully we'll be done by nine and can meet out the front and retrace Chanel's steps together."

"Nel," said Merry. "She wants to be called Nel."

He nodded, tried not to look impatient but thought monikers were the last thing they should be worrying about.

While they peeled off in various directions—Frankie and Kila to interview the other tenants, Earle to make a phone call and Merry down the inner stairwell of the two-storey apartment—Martin glanced around the main level and wondered where to start. Where would he leave a note if he was thinking of bailing on his mother?

It didn't take him long.

Turning swiftly, he headed straight for the adjoining kitchen. It was relatively large, had all the mod cons, including a massive twin-door fridge, which he was now inspecting. There was the usual array of paraphernalia, including ageing photos, birthday cards and old bills, all stuck there with a variety of magnets, some advertising local restaurants and businesses.

But there was no Dear Mum letter attached to the front.

He hummed and looked around.

The kitchen bench was black-and-white granite and had recently been wiped—probably by Verity he realised, noticing the warm kettle that stood beside a fruit basket. The basket badly needed sorting; bananas and lemons sat alongside paperclips, pens and a long white envelope. He snatched it up.

After glancing back towards the living room, he pulled the letter out, wondering if it was a suicide note but finding instead an official letter from Prue's local government council. It was about some neighbouring development application, and he tried to quell his disappointment.

"What have you got there?" asked Prue, who'd padded in behind him. Noticing the letter, she sighed. "That's just boring council business about some hideous renovations next door, but we've managed to halt proceedings." Then her face clouded over briefly before she pushed her lips into a smile and said, "Can I get you something else? A fresh tea perhaps?"

~

Merry stared into the cupboard under the stairs with a look of utter relief. Shook her head at herself as she glanced at storage boxes, old suitcases, a dusty wine rack and top-of-the-line vacuum cleaner.

"No dead bodies?" said Earle who had followed her downwards.

She whacked him gently across one shoulder. "Don't even say it." Then looked at the phone in his hands. "Did you give the Missing Persons Unit a kick up the proverbial?"

Earle slipped it into his back pocket. "I've left a message; they'll call me soon enough." Although a growing frown suggested otherwise. "Checked her bedroom yet?"

"I'm on my way there," said Merry. "This place is like a TARDIS. It's bigger than you expect."

And she was right. Even though the heart of the house was all upstairs—including Prue's bedroom, the living area and kitchen—the lower level was surprisingly spacious, with another two bedrooms, a strikingly large bathroom between them, an internal laundry and the storage closet she'd just been inspecting.

When they turned their attention to the bedrooms, it wasn't immediately obvious which one Nel had been using. Both beds were neatly made up, although the smaller room featured a single bed while the larger one had a double. Both had built-in closets, both with doors ajar, but only one, the larger room, appeared to have clothes inside. This also had double glass sliding doors that opened to a sun-drenched balcony.

Earle strode straight into that room and began to look around, but Merry was frowning.

The bedside table was bare, and from what she could see, the clothes in that wardrobe looked wrong. It was now winter, unseasonably warm that was true, but these were all bright and summery, and there was a formal floral suit that looked like something her own mother would wear to a wedding.

Merry stepped back out and into the smaller room on the left with the empty closet.

This one had a book by the bed and an empty water glass beside that, and when she moved closer, she also spotted an open suitcase wedged almost out of sight against one wall.

"It's this one," she called out as she stepped towards it.

Earle followed her in and smiled. "*This* is why I like you on this team, Merry."

She beamed at the compliment and then pulled the suitcase out for a closer inspection. It looked like a bomb had exploded inside.

"Didn't they say she'd moved back a month ago? Long time to live out of a suitcase."

"Not if you think it's temporary," said Earle.

"You agree she might've killed herself?"

"I have no thoughts on that at this stage, and neither should you. The key to a good investigation—any investigation—is keeping an open mind, Merry. Perhaps Nel was looking for her own rental or hoped to reconcile with her boyfriend."

"Oh, of course!" said Merry. "Right, yes."

And she felt another pang of sympathy for Prue, who must've loved having her daughter at home again, albeit temporarily.

As Earle used a pencil to pluck his way through the contents of the suitcase, Merry stood back and scoped the room.

He noticed and said, "Tell me what you see. First impressions, Merry."

"Okay, well, apart from the temporary nature of all this, I'm confused why she chose this room and not the other. I mean, I know her mum's summer clothes are in that closet, but it's not like Nel bothered unpacking anyway. That's the better room. Has the better bed."

"Good point," he said, glancing up and about. "The other room has the balcony too. Gets more light. It's far superior. This one just has a small window that looks straight onto a lattice wall. Perhaps this room has sentimental value, or perhaps it has something to do with that single bed."

"Like what?" said Merry. "Everybody prefers a double, surely? My kids have been lobbying for doubles since they turned thirteen."

"We could always ask Prue, but maybe we're overthinking it. What else?"

Merry glanced around again. She was really loving this! The high expectations he had of her. She didn't want to disappoint. "I don't see any signs of a fight, no obvious note…"

"Check the book," he said, now on his knees, looking under the bed. "Maybe it's in there somewhere."

She stepped towards the bedside table and picked up the book, wobbling it, but nothing fell out. Then she turned it up properly and looked at the title before smiling down at Earle.

It was an old edition of a familiar book. One Merry had read herself.

She turned it around so Earle could see:

Men Are from Mars, Women Are from Venus by author John Gray.

Earle gave her two thumbs up. "Great work, Merry. That could very well be our first clue."

"First cliché," muttered Martin, who'd been watching silently from the doorway, his search of the upper level complete.

"You don't think it shows how troubled her relationship was?" said Merry.

"Don't know about that, but it does show how troubled she was for a decent read." Martin smirked. "And by that argument, Merry, there'd be no couples left in this world. That book's a massive bestseller." Then he added under his breath, "God knows why."

After glancing around for just a moment, Martin frowned, then stepped out of the room and back towards the second bedroom, the larger one, the one with the sun-drenched deck. Before he could say anything, Merry was beside him, grinning.

"I know what you're thinking," she said. "We were thinking it too. Why didn't she choose this room? It's *so* much better!"

"Actually that's not what I was thinking at all," he murmured.

Then he opened the screen doors and stepped out onto the small balcony, staring across at a neighbouring building where several windows looked down upon them, one of them sans curtains.

In fact, Martin was thinking of their last case and of a peeping Tom who caused so much chaos.

~

The tenant in apartment three was not answering.

After knocking several times on the door of the unit straight across the corridor, Kila and Frankie were just turning away when Prue popped her head out.

"That's a Japanese fellow," she explained. "Lovely chap. But he'd be at work now." Then she added, "Sorry, I probably should have mentioned that."

Would've helped, thought Frankie, keeping that to herself. "Any idea when he gets back?"

She shook her head. "Late, I know that. Sometimes I hear his door click after midnight. They work him hard, that company of his. Name's Takahashi. Mr Takahashi." She scrunched her face. "I'm embarrassed to say I don't know his first name. Isn't that terrible! Have lived across from him for two years. I couldn't even tell you where he works, now I think of it. Although I *do* know he turned forty last year, because he went home to celebrate it with his mother who was turning sixty, which is like a big deal or something over there. Oh, and I know he adores English literature. His place is full of books by very old and very dead English authors. Oddly."

Frankie wasn't sure that was very helpful either but said, "Okay, well, we should leave him a note. Ask him to call us when he gets back."

As she reached into her tailored jacket pocket, Kila snorted. "A note from a journalist? Don't want to put him off completely."

"Hey!" she said, but he made a good point, and she handed him her pen and waited as he located his own business card from a dented, shabby wallet and jotted something on the back.

Then he slipped it under the door, thanked Prue, and they continued down the communal staircase to the lower level. Just like upstairs, there were two apartments here, each also two storeys. They were just heading to apartment two, directly below Prue, when the door to apartment one opened and a man in his fifties with a mop of greyish-brown hair and red, scaly skin looked out.

"You with the police?"

"Why would you think that?" asked Kila.

He rubbed at his cheek, some skin flaking off. "Prue told me about Nel. I'm still waiting for the coppers to take it seriously."

"You think she's come to some harm?" he asked.

"What else?" The man looked at Kila like he was a fool.

Frankie stepped forward. "We're here to assist Mrs Chambers. I'm—"

"Frankie Jo? The reporter?" His eyebrows were high.

Frankie nodded. "Would you mind if we had a quick word?"

"Oh, I read all your stuff! You doing a story on this?"

The eyebrows had dropped slightly.

"No, no," she assured him, even though she probably would. "Just helping out a friend."

"Right, well, sure, sure, come in, come in."

He had a little jig in his step as he swept his front door wide, and Frankie glanced back at Kila with a smarmy, knowing look.

So much for her being off-putting.

They were barely through the door when the man began clicking his fingers. "Somlak! Somlak! Where are you? We're going to need drinks!" He turned back to Frankie. "You want a coffee? Tea? Something stronger." He gave a theatrical wink. "I know what you journalists are like."

"No, no," she said. "We won't take much of your time."

"Take as long as you need." His gaze turned leery then, just as a short, shapely woman appeared, a tentative smile on her perfectly round face. She looked Southeast Asian and wore a light orange blouse with a decorative sarong.

Before the sleuths could introduce themselves, the man was saying, "Just fetch fizzy waters, Somlak. Then leave us to it."

"Actually," said Kila, "we'd like to speak to both of you, if you're free, er, Somlak is it?"

The woman nodded but said nothing as she dashed off to the kitchen while the man waved them into seats.

This apartment was directly below Mr Takahashi's, the layout a mirror copy of Prue's place, with everything in the reverse direction. But his taste was far gaudier—lots of dark golds and heavy greens and cluttered tizzy furnishings.

"So, I see you know Frankie," said Kila. "I'm a private detective. Name is Kila Morea. We didn't catch yours."

"It's Les. Les Polanski. Been on this block as long as Prue and John have. Well, just Prue now, of course."

Les directed all his words to Frankie, so she sat forward and said, "How long is that, Les?"

"Fifteen years I believe. But I don't want to age myself."

Then he gave her another ridiculous wink, and she laughed like it was the funniest thing she'd ever heard while Kila just frowned beside her.

"So, Les," she said, tapping his knee lightly, "you obviously know Nel. Did you happen to see her yesterday? Before her walk?"

"Or any time for that matter," added Kila.

He smudged his lips downward. "I might've seen her. I mean, she walks every day. So…"

"This is really important," said Frankie, leaning towards him. Locking eyes, batting those lovely black lashes. "If you could try to remember, we'd be so appreciative."

It *was* only yesterday she wanted to add but knew, too, not to irritate the witness. "You didn't see her leaving the building or…?"

He shrugged again, folding his arms, just as Somlak appeared with three glasses of sparkling mineral water, a slice of lemon in each of them.

"Oh we see her, yes!" she said, her voice thickly accented, handing them to the sleuths. "You remember, honey? You say, 'Keep those thighs tight' and she tell you to piss off. It really funny!"

Les did not look amused by that, but Frankie had to hide her snigger behind the water glass.

Kila watched the man stare pointedly at his partner but was not as amused as Frankie. He wondered if Somlak would pay dearly for that revelation later and why Les felt the need to keep that to himself. It felt like a red flag to the PI.

He also noticed that Somlak had not brought a drink for herself and was already turning away as though dismissed, so he quickly said, "It'd be great if you could join us, Somlak." He waved towards an empty chair, but it took a nod from her husband before she sat down.

"So, you *did* see her?" said Frankie.

Les shrugged again. "I guess I did. Days blur a bit when you're retired."

"How did she appear?" Kila asked. "Apart from pissed off with your comment on the size of her thighs, that is."

Kila's tone was casual, and now the man was staring at him, wondering if he should take offence.

"Didn't look any different to how she always looks," Les said. "Nice-looking lass. Bit superior."

"Superior?" Kila echoed while Frankie now fought back a frown.

"Oh, you know. Bit stuck-up. Not as friendly as her mother." Then, sensing a shift in Frankie, he caught her eye again and said, "I'm not saying she deserved to, you know…? I'm just saying, she could be curt. Rude even. Maybe someone said hello to her on her walk and she snubbed him."

Frankie blinked. "Are you saying that might have led to an altercation? To how she vanished?"

"Course not. I mean, not really. I'm just saying…"

You're just saying she deserves everything she gets because she doesn't play nicely with lechers like you, thought Kila, but he kept that to himself. He turned to Somlak. "What do you think, Somlak?"

She looked surprised to be asked and said very softly, almost apologetically, "I don't know about that. But I hope she okay. She always nice to me."

Kila smiled. He liked Somlak, was liking Nel more by the minute. "So where exactly did you speak to Nel, and did you see where she went after that?"

"We were coming in from the beach," said Les. "I held the door open for her." Another glance at Frankie, like he was expecting a bloody medal. "She didn't even thank me. That's what I'm talking about. Anyway, I guess she was heading towards the oval for her usual walk. I watched her cross the road to the esplanade and continue in that direction."

I bet you did, thought Kila. I bet your eyes stayed firmly on her backside, but again, he kept that to himself. He couldn't let Mad Dog Morea loose today. Getting into a punch-up with a chauvinist wasn't going to help Nel.

"And nothing after that?" Kila asked. "You didn't see her return?"

Les shook his head quickly. "I would've been long gone by then. Had an appointment later that morning. And my wife was busy cleaning."

Kila thought it was strange he was answering for his wife and noticed a small crinkle in Somlak's forehead. Or perhaps he was just projecting.

Les continued, "The first we heard there was a problem was when Prue knocked on the door around one o'clock. She was pretty worried by then. Said Chanel hadn't returned. She was stressed, looked like she might lose it. I went out with her to the oval, see if she was still there." Again, his eyes turned to Frankie like he was expecting a slap on the back for that effort. "We did the full circuit but…" He raised a hand and said, "Poof! She'd vanished."

"Any idea where she might be?" asked Kila.

Les looked taken aback. "Why would I know that? I barely know the lass! What are you insinuating?"

Kila looked amused now, but Frankie had a palm up. "We're just worried, that's all." She stood up, reaching for a business card. "We'd best get on, but if you think of anything else, anything at all, don't hesitate to get in touch."

"Oh, okay, *thanks*," he said, looking delighted to be getting Frankie's card. Then he held the card up and said, "Actually there is one thing."

The sleuths turned back, eyes wide with expectation.

"Could I get your autograph, Frankie?" Then he looked at Somlak and added, "Quick, Somlak! A pen!"

"My God he was a piece of work," Frankie said the moment they'd left the Polanskis' place and made their way across the landing.

"He sure liked you," said Kila.

"Everybody likes me, darling. How have you not worked that out yet?"

She winked as she pressed the buzzer to apartment one.

Once again, the place appeared to be deserted, and after a few minutes of buzzing and knocking, they were just turning away when they heard the door creak open and a very soft voice crackle from within.

"H-hello?"

Frankie peered through the crack to see an elderly woman staring up at her.

"Oh hello. So sorry to disturb you," she said. "We're friends of Prue. Can we have a quick word?"

"Prue?" the woman said warily.

"Yes, your neighbour." Frankie pointed upwards. "You know, Prue Chambers, in apartment four."

"Never heard of her!" the woman barked and shut the door on Frankie's face.

Frankie stared flabbergasted at the closed door while Kila couldn't help chuckling beside her.

"And you didn't even get a chance to give this one your autograph."

CHAPTER 6 ~
SECRETS FROM THE STAIRWELL

Kila's laughter floated up the stairs as the other sleuths descended from Prue's apartment, and Merry felt the urge to shush him. It seemed like such an inappropriate sound, considering the circumstances.

"What's so funny, you two?" Earle asked when they got to that landing, obviously as unimpressed as Merry.

"Nothing's funny," said Frankie, glowering at Kila. "Although it is odd." She explained about the old woman and the slammed door. "There are only four units in this block. How could that woman not know Prue? That seems highly suspicious to me."

"Actually, it's dementia," came an unfamiliar voice, and they all looked around and towards the back of the building where a second internal staircase led down to the basement parking garage.

A man was making his way up. He was in his midtwenties, a little on the bulky side, wearing a heavy chequered shirt and a look of disappointment on his tanned, stubbled face. "Please don't try to sell her something. My nonna's got dementia. It's not right."

Merry gasped and said, "Oh, no, we weren't—"

Frankie interrupted. "I'm Frankie Jo, and this is Kila, Earle and Merry. We're helping Prue Chambers, the woman in apartment—"

"I know Mrs Chambers." He took another step upwards.

"Okay, well, she's very worried about her daughter, who didn't return from her walk yesterday."

The man's dismay slipped away. "Oh, wow. Okay. Sorry." He got to the top step and dropped two green bags full of groceries to the floor, several items spilling out. "I didn't realise. Is everything okay?"

"Not sure yet," said Kila, watching him closely. "Do you live here? With your nan?"

"What? No." He smiled apologetically. "That's more than I could handle, but I do look in on her daily. Bring supplies and stuff." He indicated the bags. "Wow, so Nel's gone AWOL. Mrs Chambers must be frantic. She's a worrywart that one."

Sir George had used the exact same description, and Frankie nodded. "So we hear. Have you seen Nel lately?"

He rubbed the stubble. "Not lately, no. When did she take off?"

"Yesterday morning. Sometime between nine and ten, we think."

"Oh, okay, then I wouldn't have. I'm early today, but I don't usually get here until after midday, especially Wednesdays 'cause that's when the cleaner comes through. So I stay out of her way if I can help it. Always use the carpark entrance anyway. So our paths wouldn't have crossed."

"You have a car spot?" said Martin, like he was enquiring about real estate.

"Not me, exactly. Belongs to Nonna, but she doesn't drive anymore, so… Just as well too." Then he made a smashing sound and smiled. "Lost her licence years ago. But hey, I did hear Nel the day before yesterday. Tuesday I think it was. If that helps. She was yelling at somebody."

They all swapped a look, and Earle stepped forward then. "Any idea who she was yelling at?"

The young man shook his head. "I was out on the balcony." A sudden sheepish look. "Having a cheeky ciggie. Don't tell Mamma; she'll be full cranky." Another chuckle. "Nonna's place is just below Mrs Chambers. I couldn't hear very well. It was a kind of low mumble at first—like maybe she was talking on the phone. I didn't hear any other voices. Then I heard Nel say something like, 'I told you before, get lost!' or 'Leave me alone!' or something like that." He glanced at Frankie. Offered another apologetic smile. "Maybe in stronger language than that too, hey?"

She nodded. "What then? Did you hear a reply?"

He shook his head. "Just went quiet. I assumed she went back inside or maybe the conversation was over."

"When was this, exactly?" asked Earle.

He gave it more thought. "Maybe four-ish? Maybe five, on Tuesday. I usually take Nonna for a walk, then get her evening meal sorted and am out of here by sunset. So before then, for sure. Sorry, I didn't give it much thought at the time."

"And you never saw or heard Nel yesterday, Wednesday?" asked

Earle. "When you were here between, what? Noon and six-ish?"

He shook his head firmly, then glanced towards the opposite door. Rubbed his three-day growth.

"What is it?" said Kila, stepping forward.

"Just… well, I'm wondering if you've spoken with Les yet. Dude in apartment one."

"Why would we need to do that?" Kila asked.

"Oh, no reason. He's… Well, he's always here, that's all. He might know something."

Kila squinted. "You think he has something to do with it?"

The young man took a step backwards. "I never said that. I better get this inside. Some of this stuff needs the freezer."

He reached down and scooped up the groceries.

Merry noticed a microwave meal, several chocolate bars, and a bottle of Coke.

"Your nonna's got a sweet tooth," she said, and he looked up, surprised.

"I sneak them in. Don't tell Mamma that either."

Merry pretended to zip her lips shut, and he laughed. It was a lovely laugh. As rich as the prohibited treats.

Then he said, "Sorry my grandmother is not much help, but if I think of anything else, I'll let Mrs Chambers know, yeah? She's always been kind to me. Or to Nonna at least."

"That'd be great," said Frankie. "Thank you…? What was your name?"

"Oh, it's Tommaso Bianchi. Everyone calls me Tommo."

He attempted to release a hand to shake, but the bags looked ready to topple, so Frankie just waved hers in the air and said:

"Thanks, Tommo. Hopefully we'll have some very good news soon and won't have to disrupt your grandmother any more than we need to."

Then they watched as he clumsily tapped a code into a keypad at the front of her door and vanished inside.

As they continued on towards the front entrance, Merry said, "That bit about the phone call was interesting. I wonder if Nel was arguing with her ex. We should have asked Prue more about him."

She then explained about the self-help book they'd discovered in Nel's bedroom and her strange choice of room.

"Martin thinks Nel was hiding from a pervert looking down from the building next door," she added, causing Martin to bristle. "We might have ourselves another stalker!"

"I never said that. But it's worth checking."

"Lightning doesn't normally strike twice," said Frankie. "This isn't one of your mystery templates, Martin—just swap the name of the creepy stalker here."

"What templates? I don't use templates. My books are wholly original. What did you two uncover then? Anything of any value or did you just spend your time flirting?"

"We don't flirt!" she shot back. "Or at least, I don't." Then she gave Kila a pointed look. "But we did find the man in apartment one a little dubious."

Then she launched into an abridged version of their interview with Les and Somlak Polanski, adding, "That guy's a bit of a bully and a sleaze."

"So was my dad," said Martin. "Doesn't make him a killer."

"We don't even know she's been *killed* yet!" hissed Merry, looking back like Prue might be listening in.

"Okay, settle down, everybody," said Earle, his patience waning. "Listen, Verity's out the front now, waiting for us. Why don't you guys go to the oval with her, doorstop any nearby shops while you're at it. Show them the picture of Nel we all copied onto our phones. See if anyone remembers her."

"What are you going to do?" Frankie asked, watching as he began to make his way back towards the stairwell.

"I want to talk to Prue again. See if she knows anything about this conversation Tommo overheard or whether her daughter did indeed have a stalker."

"So lightning *does* strike twice," said Martin, his tone smarmy.

"Hope not," Earle replied grimly as he continued up the stairs.

It took just seconds for Prue to reopen the door, and she had a look of such hope in her eyes—like she was expecting her beloved daughter to be standing there—that Earle felt his heart break all over again for the poor mother.

"Just me," he said. "I have a quick question. Two in fact."

She sniffed, nodded and ushered him in.

"Can I get you a tea? Anything?" Her tone was flat, the offer like rote, and he shook his head. "Find anything interesting downstairs?"

A half shake this time. "That's my first question. Any reason your daughter chose the room she's been sleeping in?" Prue blinked, not quite understanding, so he added, "It's the smaller of the rooms, no balcony. We just wondered."

She blinked again. "I really can't tell you. She was in the larger one but then she moved. Does it matter?"

"It had nothing to do with the neighbouring building, perhaps? The fact that at least one of the apartments can look straight in on her? She never mentioned it?"

Prue wavered. "Well, she's always thought that room was a fishbowl, that is true. Nagged me about curtains from the moment we moved in, but I didn't think it was that big a deal. What are you saying? You think someone was *watching* her?" She grasped her neck like her head was about to topple, so he shook his own head firmly.

"It's just a routine question." They were probably reading too much into it. Being too clever, perhaps. "My second question, Prue. We hear that Nel was arguing with somebody two afternoons ago, the day before she vanished, between four and five on Tuesday. Out on the balcony by the sounds of it. Any idea who that might have been? Did someone drop in, or did she receive a phone call?"

Prue looked alarmed again. "Nel was arguing with somebody?"

Again, he felt bad for the mother, but there was only so much gentle treading he could do. It was all part of an investigation. Yes, the truth could hurt, but it was the painful questions that often led to the right answers. Sometimes the pain was worth it.

"It might be nothing," he said. "But it is important. Can you remember any calls? Any visitors last Tuesday?"

"Okay, um…" She thought back. "No. I mean, Nel didn't have any guests to the house while she was here. She made a million calls—she sticks to that phone of hers like glue." She shook her head. "I don't remember overhearing any kind of argument."

"Did she have any enemies that you know of? Any issues with drugs, gambling debts—"

"Of course not!"

He gave her a reassuring smile. "I mean no offence, Prue, but I do need to ask." She nodded, looked contrite. "And the neighbours? She got on with all of them?"

Again she wavered. Now there was the flicker of a frown.

"Well, she didn't particularly *like* Les, downstairs, if you must know. Thought he was a bit of a bully. And he can be. I feel rather sorry for Somlak. I don't know why she puts up with it."

"Did he ever bully Nel?"

"Oh goodness no!" The frown had vanished. "No one could bully Nel! She wouldn't stand for it. No, Nel thought he bullied *me*." A sigh now. "They crossed swords from time to time, Nel and Les, usually over very little, but if she had an issue with him, she'd speak to him face-to-face. I'm not even sure she has his phone number."

He nodded. "What about her ex? Does he call her on the phone often? Do you know?"

She lifted a shoulder. "Perhaps. I have no idea. I mean, Nel was—is!—intensely private. Always took her calls outside or downstairs. She knows how I feel about mobiles. And about Colin. Was never the type to chat away with me sitting there. You think it was Colin she was arguing with?"

"Tommo Bianchi, from apartment two, says he overheard Nel tell someone to 'get lost' or leave her alone. Something along those lines. We just wondered."

Prue paled considerably then, hand back at her throat. "Was Colin threatening her, do you think? I... Well, I thought he was fine with the break-up. That's what Nel told me. Do you think he was hassling her?"

Earle had his palm up again. "We don't know that. We don't even know if it was Colin."

But it did make the whole thing feel a lot more urgent, and he cursed his retirement and his old age and his own silent phone. Why hadn't the Missing Persons Unit called him back yet? Once upon a time his colleagues jumped when he beckoned. Now the silence felt like a slight.

"I'd like to speak with this Colin fellow myself," he said even though he knew he shouldn't. Knew he should leave it to the investigating officers. If they ever decided to take it seriously that is. "I know Verity has his details but—"

"I'll give them to you!" Prue strode to a side table to an old-fashioned Rolodex and began scrolling through it. "Ah, here it is. His mobile. Shall I?" She didn't wait for an answer, reached for a notepad and jotted the number down.

After handing it to Earle, she said, "I did speak to him twice yesterday. He was very curt. But then he knows how I feel…"

"Feel?"

Her lips pursed a little. "I've never been his biggest fan, and I'm afraid I've never been very good at hiding it."

"What don't you like about him, Prue?"

"Everything," she said quickly, then exhaled and added, "Oh nothing, really. I guess it's just me. But I always found him very curt and haughty and rather, well, *dull* to be honest. As my mother would say, 'dull as dishwater'. And, I don't know about you, but I always hoped my daughter would end up with someone slightly more interesting than dishwater."

He smiled sadly, thinking of his own daughter and her very complicated girlfriend and said, "Ah, well, interesting can be problematic too, Prue, let me assure you of that."

Then he took her earlier cue and excused himself to step outside and dial the dull ex-boyfriend.

CHAPTER 7 ~

A WALK IN THE PARK

The group had just exited the building on their way to the oval when they crashed into someone on the footpath out front. It was a large woman with a mop of frizzy, fire-engine red hair, pulling two similarly coloured bins towards a storage area at the front of Bellavista.

"Oops, watch out, you'll end up in the garbage!" the woman called out, stepping back and releasing the bins.

Verity didn't recognise her as one of the tenants and said, "Do you live here?"

"Here? No. I'm in the building next door." She indicated a larger, art deco block of apartments, one with a FOR SALE sign in its window. "I often bring this lots' bins in. They tend to forget. Often." There was a sprinkle of reproof in the comment.

Martin looked impressed. "That's very neighbourly of you."

She blew a strand of red hair from her face with her thick lips. "Somebody's got to keep things tidy around here." Then gave them all the once-over. "*You* don't live here either. I do know that."

Verity offered a disarming smile and introduced them as friends of Prue's. "She's worried about her daughter."

"Chanel?" The woman looked alarmed. "Is she okay?"

"We're not sure. She didn't return from her walk yesterday. You know her?"

"Of course I know Chanel. We're very close! Practically BFFs. Are you saying she's taken off again?"

"Again?"

Another fringe blow. "It's not her abode, you know? It's so lovely to have her here, of course, but the apartment *actually* belongs to her mother. Chanel comes and goes when it suits her."

Martin cocked his head to the side. "You know an awful lot for a neighbour," he said.

"It's a connected neighbourhood. We all look out for each other."

"I can see that," said Martin. "So did you see her yesterday?"

"Yes, as it happens. I was checking the mail, about nine-ish, chatting with one of Prue's neighbours. Les Polanski. In case I need some kind of alibi. And I'm Rachelle Easterly. Longtime Balmoral resident. My family have been here for generations."

Kila ignored that and asked, "Why would you need an alibi?"

She ignored *him* and added, "Chanel strutted past, all decked out in her high-priced walking gear. Gave her usual quick wave. Didn't stop to chat and that's absolutely fine by me."

"I thought you liked things neighbourly," said Martin.

"I'm neighbourly," Rachelle replied, giving him the once-over, "but I'm not needy."

"Was she with anyone?" Kila asked. "Did she seem distressed, preoccupied?"

"No, no and no. She seemed like her normal self. Look, does Prue really think her daughter's in trouble?"

Verity said, "She's been missing now for twenty-four hours and hasn't called in. So yes, she is concerned."

Rachelle pondered that. "Hmmm, rightfully so. The world's not what it used to be. But then this is a very safe area. We don't usually have any trouble around these parts." She cocked her head to one side. "I assume Prue's called the police. Shall I get together a search party?"

"That won't be necessary just yet," said Verity. "That's why we're here. But if you do think of anything that might assist, please let Prue know."

Rachelle nodded and looked like she might want to say more but then just continued dragging the bins to the storage area. And so they continued on.

It was only once they'd cleared both buildings and were walking towards a cluster of shops that Merry said, "I know I can be a bit sensitive, but did anybody else get a bad vibe from that woman?"

"Bad, how?" asked Martin.

"She doesn't like Nel, that's for sure," said Frankie.

"I know! I got that too!" said Merry.

"Yep, hates her guts," added Verity, making the two men swap a confused look.

"How'd you figure that?" said Kila. "She told us they were great buds. Wanted to get a search party together for her."

"Mere words, my friend," said Frankie, now swapping an eye roll with the women. "For starters, she called her Chanel. We know from Prue that her friends call her Nel."

"And she was so *judgy*," added Merry. "Had that passive-aggressive thing—you know, where you say one thing but mean another."

"Oh yeah," said Verity. "You could read the disdain in her voice. She was so quick to point out that Chanel doesn't *actually* belong here, that the unit belongs to Prue."

"It's not *her* abode," said Frankie, quoting the woman and adding a smarmy tone to her voice. "*She just comes and goes…When it suits her.*"

"*But we're so close! Practically BFFs!*" added Merry in the same smarmy tone, then the three women chuckled while the two men swapped another look.

Martin said, "You women. You're like an alien species."

"That's because we're from Venus, don't you know!" Merry snapped back, then the women burst into laughter.

Martin watched the girls cackle like demons, then he glanced back towards Rachelle, who was still hovering outside Prue's building, pulling some palm fronds from their front garden.

He stopped walking and held up a finger. "I'm going to go back and talk to her," he said, making the others stop now.

"We're just saying she's a bit of a cow," said Frankie. "Not a killer."

"Still, worth exploring I reckon. You guys keep heading towards the park. If I don't catch you up, I'll see you back at the apartment."

Before they could protest, he'd turned and made his way back to the frizzy redhead. She'd finished pruning Bellavista's fronds and was in front of her own building now, rinsing her hands under an outdoor tap, her hair flopping down in her face.

"Hello again!" Martin called out, and she looked up, startled.

Blowing the hair away, she stared up at him. "You're part of the group trying to track down Chanel."

Martin nodded, and she turned off the tap and dried her hands on her billowing skirt.

"I assume you haven't found her in the past three minutes," she added. "So, more questions, yes?"

"Yes," he replied. "But not about Chanel." Then he tried for his most charming smile. "I noticed a FOR SALE on one of the apartments in your building, the one up on the right. Just wondering if you know anything about that? Could you put me in touch with the owner?"

The woman stared at him, surprised, then up to the window he was now pointing towards.

"That's one of mine, actually. I own half the building, but, um, well, that one's not for sale."

"Really? There is a FOR SALE sign in the window."

"Yes, silly me. I should remove it. I've already got an interested buyer; we just swapped contracts... so, sorry."

"What if that falls through? Could I call you—"

"It won't fall through. Now, if you don't mind. I better get in."

Then she swept away and back towards her building, giving him a final furtive glance before vanishing inside.

Martin's spider senses were on alert. Home sales often fell through. Since when did a seller not want to take the details of a backup buyer? Did she not like the look of him? Was she not in a hurry to sell? Or was there something else going on entirely?

Crossing the road to the beach side, he pulled out his phone, searched for the now familiar number and tapped the green dial button. When it picked up, there was a surprised voice on the other end.

"Can I ask you a favour?" Martin said. "I need you to call someone about an apartment for sale."

Then his eyes swept back to the building across the road and the large FOR SALE sign, which included the name, number and photo of a real estate agent, who looked a good deal friendlier than Rachelle had just now.

~

As the others strode the pavement between Bellavista and the oval, they passed four residential buildings and just three shops—a café, a bookstore and a bottle shop—but only the café, Ballo's, was open at that hour. A young woman with a nose piercing and a black apron around her waist was wiping down an outdoor table as they passed, and they stopped to explain their mission and show her the photo of Chanel they had all copied onto their phones.

The waitress studied it closely and shrugged. "She looks kind of familiar, but then she also looks like every second woman who comes in here. Not sure I ever spoke to her, sorry."

"So you might've seen her yesterday?" Frankie asked.

She twiddled with her nose ring and said, "Couldn't say, sorry."

"And you were on duty yesterday?" Kila asked now. "Around this time?" She nodded. "Was there anyone else working then that we could talk to?"

"There's Bronnie, the cook, and our dishie Amoud. I can ask them if you like?"

"I do like," said Kila, handing her his phone.

She headed inside and was gone just a few minutes before returning with another head shake. "No one remembers her, sorry." A waving patron caught her eye then, and she handed the phone back to Kila and said, "I better get on. Hope you find your friend."

They watched her go, then Merry said, "Should we ask the customer? Maybe he's a regular."

"Needle in a haystack," said Frankie. "Let's keep going."

The oval just down from Prue's building was certainly a beautiful place to exercise, with its fitness circuit, cricket pitch and small skate park. Laced with lush green foliage, Merry could see why Nel made the effort every morning. From the oval you had a clear view across the road to the grassy esplanade with its massive Moreton Bay fig trees and kids' playground and down to a small wharf and bay. There were various groups picnicking on the promenade, as well as swimmers braving the winter cold, and sailboarders and boats of all shapes and sizes, bobbing about in the cerulean sea.

It was just Merry's tempo.

She was no fan of the rough waves and raucous crowds of more famous Sydney beaches and wondered why she'd never spent any time here, made a mental note to bring the kids one day. Then she felt her heart flag. As if the kids would want to spend a day at the beach with their mother! Those days were sadly drawing to a close.

Lola, now seventeen, wouldn't be caught dead in the daylight with Merry! And even Archie, now an awkward fourteen, was beginning to dawdle a few steps behind her in public. Like he didn't want anyone to know they were related. She knew not to be offended; it was all part of growing up. But it didn't make it any easier to bear.

And then her mind flitted to Otis, and she felt her heart lurch even further.

"Merry?" said Verity, perhaps for the second time.

They had reached the start of the exercise track, a paved pathway that ran right around the outer perimeter of the oval, starting at a public parking area, passing a sandy basketball court, and ending up back at the car park.

Verity had her phone out in front of her and a curious look in her eyes. "Everything okay?"

Merry nodded. "Yes, sorry, what were you saying?"

"I logged Nel's usual route into my GPS, and according to its calculations, at a steady pace, the journey between the apartment and a circuit of this oval would've taken Nel approximately twenty minutes, no more than that. But Prue says Nel was usually out for about an hour, so I can only assume she circled it a few times."

"Or she could've stopped for a swim at the beach or a coffee?" suggested Kila.

"Not according to Prue," Verity replied. "Says Nel wasn't much of a swimmer and usually had her coffee when she got back. Rarely deviated from the routine."

"Except yesterday," said Merry, a small shiver stretching down her spine.

Frankie glanced at her watch, then stepped onto the path. "Shall we get going?"

Verity nodded and also checked her watch as they began to circle the oval. There were several groups using the space, including a man kicking a soft ball to his young son and two women in spandex frantically trying to keep up with a nuggety personal trainer who was barking orders at them like they were marines.

As they passed each group, the sleuths stopped to ask the same questions they'd asked the waitress, but no one remembered seeing Nel yesterday, or any day for that matter.

"This place is a mecca for walking women," said the young father. "My wife loves it, but we don't usually come down till later. Harry here was impatient today, weren't you, buddy?" He nodded towards the toddler, who'd thrown himself on top of the ball, giggling.

"It's certainly a lovely place to exercise," said Merry. "I'd probably be half the size if I lived in this neighbourhood."

The man smiled like he knew better than to comment on that, then turned his eyes towards the bushland at the furthest end of the oval, which backed onto a rugged hill face and nature reserve. "Except that part," he said. "Wife reckons that's a bit creepy. She cuts across the oval when she gets to it. Especially if there's no one else about."

"Have there been incidents in the past?" Frankie asked, eyebrows high. "Stalkers? Perverts?"

"Oh, no, nothing like that. Leanne just gets spooked easily." He grabbed the ball from his son and lobbed it across the grass. "Good luck with your search," he said before running after the child.

"Come on," said Frankie. "Let's go see just how creepy it is."

As they approached the other side of the oval, they all agreed it was eerily isolated. Far from the main road, the surrounding foliage was thicker, the canopy making it darker and more foreboding. Here a separate pathway broke off from the main track, turning into a rambling walkway through dense bushland and up a steep, craggy hill covered in plateaued steps, long grass, ferns and native trees.

Merry felt a small shiver run down her spine again. Someone could easily be lurking behind a tree and spring out, grab you. And yet...

Something didn't quite fit.

"Prue already did a quick search yesterday," Verity was telling them, "but she probably wasn't seeing straight. I think we need to take a good hard look now." She glanced back towards the start of the track, all the way across the oval. "I just wish Earle was here as I'm slightly concerned about disturbing a potential crime scene."

"You really think this is the crime scene?" asked Merry, still not seeing it.

And not sure why.

"Has to be!" said Frankie. "Seems the obvious place to bump somebody off. It's the furthest from the road, the quietest, the most privacy."

"I agree," said Kila, already stepping off the main path and towards the bush track. "And I'm not waiting for Earle. If Nel is in here, we need to find her. Every minute counts."

That put a rocket under their feet, and they were soon wading through the scrub...

CHAPTER 8 ~
THE DISHWATER BOYFRIEND

As Earle pressed the buzzer on the front door of the mission-brown cottage, he looked around and thought, Colin Boyder's house is as dull as he is. It was part brick, part weatherboard, with a neatly mowed patch of lawn at the front and nothing to indicate that anyone was home. Or if they were home, had a heartbeat of any kind.

Earle's own front stoop had Tessa's old bicycle and his wife's bright potted plants and a motley collection of gardening tools and gumshoes and Gruff's ratty leashes and... Well, the list went on. This stoop was bare.

He frowned and buzzed again and then checked his watch.

"I thought you'd phoned ahead," said Martin, who'd returned to Prue's apartment just as Earle was heading off.

The old copper didn't ask why Martin wasn't walking the route with the others, simply recruited him for the interview. As far as Earle was concerned, Colin Boyder was the prime suspect in Nel's disappearance, and he was glad to have the company. Now he wondered if he'd wasted both their time.

"He said he'd be here," Earle replied. "This is disappointing."

He looked around. There was a side gate, but it was locked.

"I could scale it," said Martin.

"Not on my watch," Earle replied.

The crime writer rolled his eyes. "Did you never break the rules when you were a cop?"

"Waste of energy, mate. I know your Flynn Bold character has a flagrant disregard for the law, like the rest of them, but in the real world, it's poor policing. If you find something while you break the law, you might as well not have found anything. More often than not it's deemed inadmissible in court. And that is even more disappointing."

59

"But if there's a woman locked up in there, under duress…"

"Then of course you do what needs to be done. But I'm not hearing any muffled screams, are you?"

He tried Colin's mobile number again, but it did not pick up.

Now Martin was glaring. "Why agree to meet and then not be here?"

Why indeed? Earle thought.

They were just turning away when the door clicked open and the sleuths turned back, surprised, to see a man standing there. He was tall, dark and handsome, or would have been except there was something oddly lopsided about his face. Like everything was slanting ever so slightly to the right. He was wearing a yellow-and-white-striped men's shirt over dark pleated trousers and made no apology for the delayed response, simply said, "You're Prue's friends?"

They introduced themselves, and he showed them in and straight to his living room. This had a few spots of colour, but for the most part was functional, not flashy. The furniture looked better suited to an office, and you wouldn't know a woman had ever lived here.

Oh the fun Beryl could have, prettying up the place! thought Earle.

"I already told Prudence I have no idea where Nel is, and I really don't know why she's being so fretful," he was saying, his tone flat. "Wasting everybody's time with this. It has only been a day after all."

"Well, mothers can be worried at the best of times, so let's humour her, shall we?" Earle replied as he took a seat beside Martin on a stiff blue sofa.

Colin pulled a high-backed chair from a dining table and sat across from them. "So, what do you need from me?" He made a show of checking his watch and added, "I do have a lot of work on at the moment."

"Oh? What do you do?" asked Earle.

"Administrator. For the State's transport department."

"Nel's in admin too, isn't she?" said Martin.

"Was. That's how we met." Colin glanced at his watch again.

Earle sat back in the sofa, refusing to be hurried. "You work from home, Mr Boyder?"

It was the middle of a weekday after all.

"COVID-19," he said. "It's changed everything."

"Did it change your relationship?" Martin asked.

Colin looked at him blankly. "I'm not following."

"We understand you and Nel have broken up. I wonder whether COVID was—"

"Who told you we'd broken up? Did Prue say that? It's simply not true. In fact, we're getting married next September."

The sleuths swapped a surprised look. Earle said, "Prue never mentioned an engagement."

"Well, she wouldn't, would she? Loathes the air I breathe. But I can assure you, Nel and I are still together. Very much so."

"And yet she's vanished and you haven't heard from her?" said Martin.

"Our relationship wasn't like that. We didn't feel the need to call each other every second. But we are very much together, I can assure you."

"So why has Nel moved back in with her mother?" asked Martin.

"She hasn't. At least not permanently. Nel's simply helping Prue get over John's death. It's hit her badly, God knows why. They were always nagging each other, from what I recall. Still… That's all there is to it."

Earle ignored his snide comment and said, "Prue believes her daughter is saving up to go travelling."

Colin scoffed. "Saving *what*? Nel doesn't have a job. That's one of the many reasons she'll be back. I look after her. I provide all her needs. Just give it a day or two… she'll be back. I can assure you."

Earle and Martin swapped another look, and he bristled.

"Prudence is under the delusion she knows her daughter," Colin said. "She does not. There's another side to my fiancée, and that is why I'm not concerned. She probably had words with her mother and did what she does when we have words—she's off somewhere licking her wounds. Having a little sulk. She'll be back. Always is."

Earle was not sure if he meant to the mother's house or to his, but he was more interested in where she might be doing this sulking. Did Colin have any ideas?

"Not a one. Sorry." Although he didn't sound at all apologetic.

"She take off a lot then?" asked Earle.

"Twice in two years. You tell me. Is that a lot?" His eyes were an icy blue, boring into Earle's.

No wonder Verity had flagged him, he thought. The guy was far too cool. Far too dismissive.

"Tell me about this other side," said Martin.

"I beg your pardon?"

"Of your fiancée. You said she had another side that Prue doesn't see. What did you mean by that?"

He exhaled. Reached for an ear and scratched it. "Look, I call a spade a spade, so does Nel. It's what we like about each other. No fuss. We live a simple life. Don't go in for grand gestures or romance or false niceties. Some people think we're rude. Not everybody likes honesty."

"Did you phone Nel on Tuesday?" asked Earle. "In the afternoon?"

This change of subject threw Colin off-balance, and he said, "What? No, I don't believe so. I told you before, we weren't that kind of couple."

"The kind that cares if the other one has gone missing?" asked Earle.

Colin just glared at that.

As Martin listened to this, something clicked into place. From what Frankie and Kila had reported, it echoed what Les in apartment two had said about Nel. It was also the impression the next-door neighbour, Rachelle, had given of the woman, albeit more passive-aggressively, and he was starting to build a better understanding of her character.

Despite what Prue had suggested, Nel had a prickly side, that was clear. Had that got her into trouble? Nel was no Merry, that's for sure. She wasn't warm and cuddly, as her mother had implied. If her fiancé was to be believed, she was abrupt. Curt. Brutally honest. Had that led to her disappearance?

He knew from his own writing that characterisation was pivotal, and you couldn't always trust your narrator. They weren't going to learn Nel's real character from her mother because a mother rarely saw her child through honest eyes. And even when she did, she forgave them their flaws, played them down. Pretended otherwise.

Or at least, his did.

He thought now of Olivia and how thrilled she had been when he finally reached out and agreed to reunite. The woman had been begging to do so for years. For years he'd ignored her pleas. It took just one phone call from him for all that to be forgiven.

The fact was, if they wanted to solve this crime, the team needed to stop listening to Prue and start asking the people who really knew her or were at least prepared to describe her properly, warts and all, because it's those warts that might have caused her disappearance.

Had her brutal honesty led, in turn, to some brutality?

Could someone like Colin have reached their final straw? Or was it less complex than that? Did a random bystander wolf whistle as she walked around the oval? Did she stop and rebuke him, and he simply snapped?

"If she has, as you say, taken off," said Earle, oblivious to Martin's thinking, "where might she be? And why would she not be answering her phone?"

Colin tugged his ear now, shrugged. "She has friends. Maybe she's with one of them."

"Which friend might that be?" asked Martin, eager to talk to someone else, to continue building up the woman's profile.

But Colin just shrugged again. "I'm simply making suggestions. I don't know where my fiancée is, and frankly, I'm a little tired of all these questions. First from some bossy Irish secretary, then from you two. Prue needs to remember that her daughter is a grown-up and she should mind her own damn business."

This outburst surprised them, and Earle said, "You're not at all concerned for her safety?"

He sighed and made a show of checking his watch. "I haven't got time for this. I have work to get on with."

Earle sighed too but let it go, giving Martin the nod.

They were just heading back down the hallway when Earle turned back to Colin with a bashful look on his face.

"Hate to be a nuisance, Mr Boyder, but would you mind if I used your facilities? Prostate's not what it used to be."

Colin wrinkled his nose and waved a hand back down the corridor.

"I'll find my own way," Earle said. "Martin, could you provide Mr Boyder with our contact details—so he knows where to call should Nel show up here? I'll see you outside."

Martin continued to the front with Colin while Earle headed back into the house.

~

It didn't take long to deduce that there were no dead or wounded women lying in the forest at the secluded end of Balmoral Oval. The foliage appeared thicker than it was. In fact, it was a well-maintained council reserve with strategically planted native grasses, tree ferns and waratah. And so they switched from searching for a body to searching for evidence of an attack—broken branches, ripped clothing. Blood.

"Anything?" asked Verity as Kila and Frankie appeared at the bottom of the wooden walkway.

"Nope," said Kila. "Stairway leads all the way to the road above. But we didn't see anything."

"Still," said Frankie. "He could've had a car up there and whisked her away. I think the police need to comb this place thoroughly. Bring in sniffer dogs while they're at it."

Merry nodded but was still not convinced. Logically, Frankie was right. This *was* the perfect place to launch an attack. But the very fact that Nel's body wasn't here meant her assailant must have dragged her away, and there were only two exits—back across the wide, open oval, which mid-morning would be too obvious, or along the remote bush track and up those steep stairs.

And that would not have been easy.

"I wonder whether we're looking in the wrong place," she ventured. "Could she have been abducted closer to the main road where there's a faster getaway?"

Frankie followed her eyes and frowned. She wasn't used to being contradicted. "I've seen a lot of crime scenes, Merry. Real ones, I mean, not on a Cluedo board. And I've met more than my share of real criminals. Unless they're strung out on ice, they don't generally act in broad daylight on main roads—and that's a pretty busy esplanade, lots of people coming and going, using the beach and shops and cafés. You just wouldn't do it. Or if you did, you'd wait till after dark. No witnesses that way."

"Yes, I get that," said Merry, trying not to be offended by her Cluedo comment (talk about passive-aggressive!), "and I know I'm not the fittest in this group." She giggled now to lighten the mood. "But this area is so difficult to traverse. If someone did attack her here, where's the body? They would have had to carry her up those steep steps—and she wasn't small. Or they would have had to drag her across the oval to their vehicle near the road. Too risky."

"So, what are you suggesting?" asked Verity, who looked much more receptive.

"Not sure yet…"

Merry stepped back onto the main pathway around the oval, heading towards the esplanade again. Frankie made a "Hmf!" sound that Merry chose to ignore, and the others all promptly followed, stopping to check behind a locked storage container and around the basketball court.

It was only as they reached the front of the oval again where the carpark was located that Merry felt things click into place. She stopped at the first parking bay, which was empty, and glanced about. Between each parking spot were clumps of foliage, and between the parking area and the main road was a row of midsize trees.

Just enough protection if you played your cards right.

Merry held out her hands and said, "Here. This is where you would do it."

Frankie's frown had returned, but the others were glancing around, curiously, so Merry forged on, tapping her watch. "It's mid-morning now, and it's really quiet."

The man and his son had left the park, and they could just see the exhausted women trailing their trainer towards the beach. A fresh couple had arrived, but they were preoccupied doing stretches right in the middle of the oval, looking in the opposite direction.

Merry pointed at the parking area. About a third of the bays were filled, but there was no one in their vehicles. The place was deserted.

"Sure, there are cars here," she told them, "but where are all the people? They're obviously exercising or sailing or at the café. Makes more sense to me that if you wanted to kidnap Nel, you'd do it here. In this car park. It butts right up to the oval. You'd wait until she'd done a lap or two, then, as she was striding past, oblivious— probably with buds in her ears, listening to a talking book or something—you'd grab her from behind and wrestle her straight into the boot of your car without anyone noticing. It could all be done in less than a minute. Not nearly as risky as dragging them up a set of steps or across a public oval."

They all stared at Merry like she'd spoken a foreign language, then Verity's face lit up.

"You know, I think you're onto something."

"Good work, Festive," said Kila, before glancing upwards. "Pity there're no cameras in this car park."

Frankie just continued frowning. "I'm still not buying it, sorry. It just feels far too risky."

"Still, it's worth checking," said Kila. "Come on, let's see if we can find us some evidence."

And so the group spread out across the car park, searching through and around the low shrubs that separated each bay.

It took just five minutes for Merry to be vindicated.

"I think I have something!" called Frankie, pointing into a thick clump of native grass.

And Merry could have sworn the journalist did not sound happy about it.

She rushed over just as Verity yelled out, "Don't touch it, whatever it is! Not without gloves!"

Merry gave Verity the thumbs-up and then glanced down to where Frankie was pointing, and towards what looked like a blue cap with a grey Nike swish on the front.

Exactly as Prue had described it.

CHAPTER 9 ~
CALLING IN THE TROOPS

As Earle pulled his car into the curb outside Prue's building, he said, "Looks like the cavalry have arrived."

Martin glanced from him to the street and back, not understanding.

"That's an undercover police vehicle if ever I saw one," Earle said, pointing to the nondescript white sedan in front of them. Apart from dark tinted windows and a suspicious cluster of radio antennas on the roof, you would never know it.

"I thought Prue had to attend a police station to make the missing person report," said Martin.

"That is the usual procedure," Earle said. "Perhaps there's been a development."

Prue's apartment was abuzz when the two men got inside. The other sleuths were seated around the dining table, Merry gesticulating wildly as a uniformed officer furiously took notes while Prue was on the couch, deep in conversation with a plain-clothed officer Earle did not recognise, Verity hovering nearby.

The latter waved them over and echoed Earle's earlier statement. "There's been a development." Then she turned her eyes to the stranger on the couch who was now staring up at them, her face creasing with delight.

"This is Detective Soderbergh from the Missing Persons Unit," said Verity.

"*Odetta* please!" the woman said, already on her feet, one hand thrust out. She had very short, Nordic-white hair and an intense look in her enormous green eyes. "It's such an honour to meet you. I'm your biggest fan!"

Martin smiled and stepped forward, used to this kind of attention, but it wasn't Martin she was referring to, and she brushed straight past him towards Earle, vigorously pumping his hand.

"You're a bit of a legend down at HQ, DI Fitzgerald," Odetta said, and Earle glanced back at Martin with surprise.

"Oh, it's not DI anymore, Detective, but that's nice to hear, I think," said Earle.

"Your reputation precedes you, that's for certain." The detective chuckled, like there was some inside joke, then glanced at the author and said, "And you are?"

Earle had to stop *himself* from chuckling as Martin looked offended by the question while Verity rushed in to answer.

"This is Martin Chase. The author."

Odetta stared at him blankly. "Oh yeah? What do you write?"

"Crime," he said coolly, one hand now stroking his nose.

"Right, well..." She turned back to Earle. "I'm informed that you and your team are here to assist Mrs Chambers in the search for her missing daughter, is that correct?" There was a nod towards Prue, who sat on the couch, clinging onto her pearls again.

"Yes, we are," agreed Earle. "We've been asked to help out, but we appreciate it's the early stages, and I can assure you, we won't get in your way."

"What way?" said Martin. "You guys haven't shown any interest thus far."

"It has only been one day, Martin," said Earle, but already the detective was shaking her head.

"Oh, we no longer sit on our hands in missing persons cases, sir. We do take them very seriously. In fact, I was just going through the report when we got the call about the cap."

"Cap?" said Earle and Martin together.

"Of course you wouldn't have heard." Odetta produced her smartphone and began to scroll through it. "One of your team located an item of clothing in the parking area in front of Balmoral Oval. Near where Ms Chambers was last... Aha, here it is!"

She held her screen up so they could see the image that had been forwarded to the detective. Earle had to wipe his glasses before he could make out what he was looking at—a blue cap wedged deep inside some thick green grass.

"We believe this item belongs to the missing woman," said Odetta, her eyes darting back to Prue, whose own eyes had that haunted look once more. That was confirmation enough. "We will of course have it tested for DNA. My team are bagging it now, and I've got a local unit roping the area off. We'll start door-knocking nearby residents and businesses this morning. Fortunately, your, er, associates had the good sense not to touch the item when they located it."

"We're not novices, you know," said Martin.

"Oh I *know*," she replied, her doe eyes twinkling at Earle. "Now I'm about to do a thorough search of this premises, so I'll need you lot to wait on the balcony until that's completed."

"I don't see why—" began Martin, but Earle was already grabbing him by the elbow and steering him out.

"Learn to pick your battles, mate," Earle told him once they'd closed the sliding glass doors behind them. "We need to stay on that detective's good side if we want the inside track."

"You're already on her good side," he replied. "She was practically salivating at the sight of you."

"I'm not sure that's a fair assessment...," he began just as Verity stepped out to join them. "Ah, Ms Vine. Tell me, what else did Detective Soderbergh have to say?"

Verity pulled out a deck chair and sat down. She looked almost as weary as Prue. "Not a lot. While it is up to Prue at this stage, apparently, the detectives are not keen to go public until they cross their *T*s, so to speak. Going missing is not a crime after all, and chances are Nel will turn up within the week, like you said. But there is some concern around her being a young woman and this being so out of character. Anyway, they're currently phoning friends, old work mates, anyone Prue might have forgotten to call. They're also accessing Nel's bank accounts, mobile phone records, social media pages, hoping they provide some clues."

He nodded. "That can all take time."

"Which is exactly why we need you to stay on the case." She glanced through the large glass doors to where Odetta and her officer were now pulling on plastic gloves. "I didn't hear Detective Soderbergh warn you off just now, Earle. Or did I miss that bit?"

Earle rubbed his white beard. "No, she didn't, did she? Now that's interesting..."

As Earle mulled that over, the others joined them on the balcony.

"Not a bad place to be banished," said Merry, leaning on the railing as she stared out towards the shimmering bay.

"I haven't got time to sit around, enjoying the view," said Frankie. She looked at Verity. "Is Odetta going to release this to the media? Do a public call-out, do you know?"

Verity shook her head and repeated what she'd said to Earle. "Don't worry. I'll let you know when and if it breaks."

"Good, do that," Frankie replied. "Meantime, I've got an actual breaking story to get on with."

"And I've got an apartment to check out," said Martin. "I'm looking for a new abode."

"Didn't you already do that?" said Kila, his dark brown eyes narrowing.

That caused Martin to flush a little, and Earle didn't know what that meant but held a palm out.

"Before we all scatter again, can we quickly catch up on where things are at and work out our next moves?"

"Hang on," said Merry. "Are we even allowed to keep investigating? I mean, now that the police are here…"

"Oh for goodness' sake, Merry!" snapped Frankie. "Did you learn *nothing* from last time? *Of course* we keep investigating. The police can't stop us from helping a client. Besides, they're a pack of morons; they'll probably stuff it up. I'll start because I need to dash soon."

Frankie launched into an account of their circumnavigation of the oval and of the people they had spoken to along the way. "I couldn't believe it when I found that cap!" she said, ending with a victorious smile.

Merry blanched at that, and Kila was about to say something when his phone began to ring. He looked at it, frowned, then looked away.

"You need to get that?" asked Earle.

Kila shook his head, so Earle took the opportunity to outline what they'd learned from the fiancé, Colin Boyder.

"Fiancé?" echoed Frankie. "Since when? I'm sure Prue said they'd broken up."

"Yes, but then we only have his word for that."

"And Prue's," said Martin.

"You don't trust Prue?" said Verity.

He lowered his voice. "It's not that. I'm just wondering whether she knows her daughter as well as she thinks she does. I mean, how could she not know about the engagement? Was Nel keeping that from her? And she didn't seem to know her daughter had switched rooms downstairs, didn't you say, Earle? Even though there could very well have been some creep staring in at her. I think Prue may be what we authors like to call an unreliable narrator."

Frankie snorted. "*Unreliable narrator.* Seriously, Martin, get back to the real world! *Nobody* tells their parents everything! Nel probably knew Prue didn't dig on Colin—that's pretty obvious—so didn't know how to break the news about the engagement. As for switching between bedrooms? I can't believe you're still on that. You've got your author's hat back on again, Martin. We can't possibly have another creepy stalker watching through darkened windows!"

"Hey," he shot back. "I thought I was on this team *because* of my author's hat, so you can cut the attitude, Frankie."

He almost told her how he'd tried to inspect the apartment with the "darkened windows" and been quickly rebuffed. The fact that he also happened to be interested in purchasing the place was neither here nor there. But there was no way he was going to mention Rachelle's behaviour now, not after that sledging.

Martin glanced at the PI, expecting a matching sneer, but Kila's sneer was focused on his mobile phone. He looked like he wanted to throttle it.

Earle noticed too and said, "Look, I know you're all busy, and that makes some of you testy"—a pointed glance at Frankie—"but can we try to keep this civil? We were each hired for our unique skill set, and Martin has every right to express his opinion and explore leads he thinks are viable."

"I'm just—" began Frankie, but he cut her off.

"Let's just take a break for now, okay? Those of you who are busy should take this time to get on with your to-do lists. We can only hope the *morons*"—Frankie earned another glare for that comment—"will do us all a favour and soon find Nel safe and sound."

"Oh, I do hope so!" said Merry, more gently. "But that cap... well, it doesn't bode well does it? I almost wish we hadn't found it. You should have seen the look on Prue's face when we showed her the picture of it, Earle. She was so gutted! Like we'd just told her poor Nel was... was..."

Merry couldn't finish that sentence, and Earle gave her shoulder a quick squeeze.

"She may still show up, Merry. Everything might still be okay."

But none of them truly believed that. Or at least Earle didn't.

He tried to add a note of calm to his voice as he added, "If Nel is going to be found, and more importantly found *alive*, we need to work together and keep things rolling. How about we meet back here at, say, two this arvo? How does that sound? Detective Soderbergh didn't exactly warn us off, and as I've got nothing on my schedule—nothing at all—I'm happy to hang around and see what else I can uncover. Besides, I should fill the detective in on what we learned from Mr Boyder."

And so they all nodded and adjourned for now, Merry feeling anxious, Martin still seething, Frankie looking vaguely contrite, and Kila glaring daggers again at his phone.

~

Earle remained seated out on the balcony, staring blindly at the view for some time, his own feelings shifting between concern for Nel and consternation towards his own daughter. It was a lie to suggest he had nothing else on his plate. He had Beryl's ham-and-pickle sandwich for a start—hadn't he promised her he'd be home for lunch?—not to mention a daughter whose own plate was now overflowing...

"Penny for your thoughts?" came a voice from the doorway, and he looked around to find the detective standing there, peeling her gloves off. "This place is squeaky clean, nothing of any interest. But of course you already learned that for yourself."

"Listen, Detective Soderbergh—"

"Odetta please!"

He nodded. Couldn't get used to using first names with colleagues or those who were as good as. "I apologise if we've overstepped or infringed your investigation in any way—"

She waved him off. "Most missing people are actually located by family and friends. So I appreciate the help." Then she gave him a sly look and added, "Not like some." Taking a seat beside him, she asked, "So, what else have you uncovered?"

He smiled. He liked this one. Would have enjoyed working with her in his heyday. So he filled Odetta in on everything he could think of, from the conversations Frankie and Kila had with the neighbours, through to his recent chat with Colin Boyder.

"Ah, the elusive ex-boyfriend," she replied. "He's not returning my calls. Any idea why?"

"He did say something about a packed work schedule."

"But?"

"But he seemed evasive to me. Acted like Nel was just off on a tantrum and would be back in time for dinner. His disinterest, it seems…" Odetta leaned in, waiting. He said, "Disingenuous maybe. At least I hope it is, or the poor girl's marrying the wrong man. Because, according to him, they are still together and engaged. Just don't tell the mother-in-law. You think there's cause for suspicion here? Indications of foul play?"

She nodded. "Nel didn't just wander off into the sunset and forget to phone home, at least that's what I'm hearing from contacts and friends, despite what this alleged fiancé told you. They all say it's completely out of character. Nel was not an erratic person. Devoted to her family. Would never leave her mother to worry. So why would Mr Boyder suggest that? It's interesting, yes?"

As she spoke, the detective's phone rang, and Earle went to get up, to give her some privacy, but she waved him back down as she took the call. She spoke for just a moment, listened for a few moments more, then hung up with a smile on her face.

"That was HQ. They've just traced Nel's mobile phone records."

"That was fast."

"I'm telling you, we're not the sloths we used to be. Turns out Nel made just one call yesterday, between nine and ten in the morning. Nothing after that."

Earle's eyes widened. "That's when she went missing. Do you know who that was to?"

"I do. It's registered to a man called Crispin Regatta. Even better, I know where Mr Regatta lives. It's just up the road from here."

Then she surprised Earle further by adding, "Fancy coming along for the ride, Detective Inspector?"

CHAPTER 10 ~
PHONING A FRIEND

Frankie was dumping her spanking-new oversized Prada tote bag under her office desk when she got the call, and she could not have been more relieved. If it had come through five minutes earlier, she would have missed it entirely. Because this was one call she could not take on her mobile. It had to come through the *Herald* landline.

Frankie was fearless, but she wasn't a fool.

As the automated voice announced that she had an incoming call from Silverwater Correctional Centre and that call would be both monitored and recorded, she muttered, "Yeah, yeah, heard it all before," then smiled to herself as a deep, croaky voice took over.

"Hey, Frankie Jo! Good to get ya message, babe. How's life out there in the free world?"

It was her old pal Shane Moneghetti, outlaw motorcycle gang member, convicted murderer and fodder for past articles. "Same old, same old, Shane. Seriously, you're not missing much."

"Ah bullshit, Frankie, but it helps to hear that and to hear ya sexy voice. What're ya wearin'?"

She laughed. "Now, now, let's not get cut off like last time."

He laughed back. "Hey, I liked that last article you wrote. Made me King of the Kids in here for a bit."

"Glad I could be of service. I thought you sounded a little scary myself."

He sniggered. "You don't know the half of it. Anyway, what can I do for ya? You sniffin' for another story? Runnin' out of tough nuts to interview for that piece of shit you write for?"

"Nah, not this time, although I might hold you to that, Shane. No, I do want to ask you a question about someone else. A fellow alumni."

"A fellow *what now?*"

She tried not to snigger, reminded herself to keep it simple. "Phillip Weaver. I'm investigating his murder. He was an inmate there, I'm told."

"Weaver? Nah, don't know any… Oh, you mean *Weevil*. Yeah, right. Heard he got shanked the other day. Surprised the crap out of me that did."

"Really? Why?"

"Dunno. Maybe 'cause he wasn't the violent kind, y'know?"

"He was in there for armed robbery, Shane."

"Yeah, but armed with a pocketknife? Pft! He was pissin' about; that's not his game. Bit of a wheeler-dealer, sure—hence the nickname. He could weevil your last ciggie from you with just a few slippery words. A conman, not a killer."

"Any idea how he ended up *shanked* in Kings Cross then?"

"Not a clue." There was a muffled murmur, and he said, "Piss off, mate, I only just got on!" Then, "All right, Spider, keep your hair on. Gotta go, Frankie Jo. The animals are gettin' restless."

"Okay then," she said, feeling deflated. She'd learned nothing of any value. "Well, don't hesitate to call if you think of anything that might help."

"Always happy to chat with my favourite reporter." There was a pause, and she wondered if he'd hung up before he said, "You know, you should talk to Weevil's cell mate. He'd know more than me. Guy by the name of Dragon Malone."

She sat forward. *Now why did that name sound so familiar?*

"Strange little nerd," he continued. "Went too far on a Tinder date once." He chuckled like that was hilarious and added, "Okay, gotta go. Think of me next time you're in the shower."

As the phone went dead, Frankie's mind was buzzing, but it had nothing to do with Shane or his lewd comments.

She was thinking of Kila Morea's sister. And a blind date that ended in murder.

~

Merry tried to think positive thoughts as she opened the door to her ex-husband, Darren.

He was leaning against the doorframe, a large carton of her favourite chocolate-covered nuts in hand, wonky smile on his face.

"Thanks for seeing me," he said as he thrust the gift out like it was a diamond ring, and she smiled like she still ate the nuts (she didn't, but how was he to know that?) and waved him in, her own smile a little wonky.

Merry was glad the kids weren't there to witness this. They'd be so disappointed in her. Especially Otis. The mere thought of him made her eyes well with tears, and she blinked them back as she led the way to the kitchen.

"You look good, Mustard," he said, using the nickname he'd given her soon after they'd met. Darren had found her maiden name, Kean, hilarious. It reminded him of the Keen's Mustard brand and so he'd started calling her "Mustard" soon after. Merry hadn't liked it (both the product and the nickname), but somehow it had stuck. "Lost a few kilos too, I can see."

That was thanks to giving up treats like chocolate nuts, but she didn't tell him that either, was just chuffed someone had noticed. She could walk in with her head lopped off and Lola and Archie would just ask what's for dinner.

"Thanks so much for agreeing to this," he said again as he followed.

"No worries. But I haven't got long. I've got to be somewhere soon."

"Another of your little investigations?" Darren snickered ever so slightly, and she frowned.

"How did you know? Ah, the kids told you."

"Just that you'd done great. They were so proud of you, Mustard. Although why you helped some rich folk for nothing I'll never understand."

She smiled, relieved the kids hadn't told him about *that*. Darren hadn't paid a cent of maintenance since he'd moved out, so he certainly wasn't getting access to her million.

"I heard you're also doing more Cluedo championships," he continued. "Sounds like you've got your life back on track."

She nodded but wondered why it didn't feel that way. As she set about making tea—reaching for the kettle, filling it at the sink— he opened the fridge like he owned the place, pulling out the milk.

And that's when it hit Merry. Oh my God! He did own the place! At least, he owned half of it. Was that why he wanted to see her? To break the news that he wanted to sell the house?

Darren took a seat at the kitchen bench, oblivious to her thoughts.

"Kids tell me you've learned to drive. I couldn't bloody believe it!"

"Why not?" She swivelled to face him, unsure whether to be offended.

"Because I'd been wanting to teach you for years, remember? You never let me. Insisted you never wanted to drive."

"Oh right." Except that's not quite how she remembered it. "Well, Otis did the honours, before... Well, before..."

"You miss him badly, don't you?"

"Of course, don't you?"

Something crossed his face then, and he said, "Yes, Meredith. But I'm used to it. You should be too. By now."

She flinched. Was sick of people saying that.

"He's not *dead*, you know!" Lola had screamed at her just last night when she'd caught Merry back in the foetal position on Otis's bed. "Why do you keep acting like he's carked it? I heard you talking to Mrs B the other day. The way you discuss Otis, like you're never going to see him again, Mum, when we all know he's living in Melbourne and we'll see him at Christmas!"

And Lola was right. Despite how she'd been behaving, despite her wrenching grief, all Otis had done was move to another city. Merry *was* overreacting. But she couldn't seem to stop. No one had prepared her for empty-nest syndrome, for the utter immeasurable loss of a child. And even though he wasn't dead and she still had two others at home, his departure felt like a death.

And in some ways it was.

It was the death of the tight little unit she and kids had become after Darren had moved out. And the death of her role as a mother to her eldest, who would never need her in quite the same way again. He had his new job and his fun flatmates and his own life to lead. And she was happy for him, really she was. But it didn't assuage her loss. And that's why she didn't want to move houses or upgrade to somewhere nicer. Because she had lost enough this year, and it was her only link to her eldest child.

And she sure as hell wasn't going to sell his childhood home!

"I won't do it!" she burst out.

"Sorry?"

"I won't sell this house. You can't make me. I love it too much. It reminds me of Otis and all the good times! I won't do it!"

He looked bemused. "I'm not here to make you sell the house."

"Oh… Okay. Sorry." Then her face crumpled. "I just miss him. I miss him so, so much!"

Darren got up and drew her into a hug. She resisted at first and then melted, enjoying the human contact. It felt like months since she'd hugged another human being so tightly. Lola hadn't hugged her willingly in years, and Archie's hugs were like clinging onto the ironing board.

"Aw babe, I do get it," he said. "How do you think I felt when you first kicked me out, hey? It was really tough." Then, as *her* body turned into an ironing board, he quickly added, "Not that I blame you! I know why it happened. But I still miss the kids. Miss you too, Mustard."

Merry felt a deep blush fill her cheeks and broke the hug off. Stepped into the pantry now, hiding herself inside. "Let's see if I can find something sweet to dunk in our tea."

"Good luck!" he called back before glancing around. "I'm surprised you want to keep this old dump. But we did have some good times, hey?"

She kept scrounging. "Yes, yes we did. Ah, here are some digestives." She half laughed. "Typical Archie. He's left me the driest, most boring treats."

"I'm not with Penny anymore. The kids tell you?"

That comment came out of left field, and Merry's back went stiff again. Penny, the taxi driver. The woman who'd destroyed her life, not to mention her patio. "No, they didn't tell me."

"She…," he began. Stopped. "She wasn't right."

Merry held her breath.

"She wasn't *you*," he added. "I want to come home, Mustard. I want us to be a family again."

Merry exhaled and didn't know what to say. She just stood inside the pantry, her throat as dry as the biscuits she was clutching.

CHAPTER 11 ~

THE BLOND KAYAKER

As Earle pulled his Holden sedan in between Soderbergh's unmarked vehicle and an obscenely sized black four-wheel drive, he felt a twinge of anticipation. He didn't know who this suspect was or what if anything he had to do with Nel's disappearance, but he did know how to investigate a case and that each tiny clue took them a giant step closer.

And he couldn't believe he was right here beside the investigating officer, albeit a few steps back.

Odetta had suggested Earle drive himself to the Mosman address, just up the hill from Balmoral Beach, and stay firmly in the background, and that was fine by him. Preferable, in fact. He'd learned the hard way what happened when you meddled in an investigating officer's case. Despite several attempts at a peace offering after the Burlington murders, his old buddy Detective Inspector Morgan had wanted nothing more to do with him.

Cut him off entirely.

"You good?" asked Odetta, now out of her car, her sidekick, a stiff-looking constable by the name of Jeremy Logan, close behind her.

"It's number twenty-three," Odetta said, glancing from her phone to a row of beautifully restored semidetached bungalows that hugged the leafy avenue.

As she knocked loudly on the pretty blue door, she turned back to Earle and said, "Good thing about COVID, everybody's always at home."

And she was right. Within seconds, steps could be heard coming towards the door, which was promptly opened by a tiny brunette in tight yoga gear, her long hair up in a tussled topknot, her skin porcelain, her eyebrows arched high.

"Yes?" she said, eyebrows reaching higher.

"Mrs Regatta?" asked Soderbergh, and the woman glanced behind her to the younger officer and then to Earle before nodding, mutely. "I'm Detective Odetta Soderbergh." She produced her ID card and held it up. "My colleagues and I would like a word with your husband, Crispin. Is he in?"

The woman's brows drew together. "Is everything okay? Has something happened?"

"We'd just like to speak with your husband thanks, Mrs Regatta. Shouldn't take too long."

For just a brief moment the woman looked like she might object, but then she held the door open and began striding down the sunlit hallway.

"Cris!" she called out as they followed her through. "Cris, honey! You have visitors!"

The house was largely open-plan, the sun streaming in from all sides and from large skylights on the ceiling. The timber floors had been painted white, matching the crisp white of the walls and the furniture, making the room feel cold, almost chilly. At least that's how Earle felt. His Beryl would've added some thick rugs and bright knickknacks, a much-needed splash of colour. The only colour came from a bright pink yoga mat stretched out on the floor in front of a wide-screen television, which was now paused on a woman doing a complicated one-legged pose. There were several Bratz dolls in a tangle nearby, and Mrs Regatta quickly scooped them up, dumping them in a wicker basket, then reached for the mat.

"You have kids, Mrs Regatta?" asked Odetta.

She looked up with a start. "Yes, Isla and Zoe. They're both at childcare." Then she began rolling the mat up as she called out again for her husband.

A door creaked somewhere, and a handsome, sunburned face peered out.

"What is it, babe? I'm on a conference call, yeah?"

The wife offered the police a stiff smile and turned to her husband, her voice equally as stiff. "The police are here." Then she nudged her head at Soderbergh.

The man's eyebrows shot up, he gaped at them for a moment, then held up a hand. "Let me just sign off." He vanished behind the closed door again.

For a moment, Earle wondered whether he was about to do a runner. Hoped not, he was too old to chase the bloke down and Soderbergh and Logan were already settling into the snowy white lounge.

"Can I get you a drink?" said the wife. "A water? Anything?"

All three shook their heads, and she glanced back at the closed door like she, too, wondered if her husband was about to bolt. But then the door creaked open again and Crispin reappeared, striding confidently towards them, pulling off a jacket he was wearing over a T-shirt and board shorts.

"Bloody Zoom," he said. "Loathe videoconferencing."

When he reached the living room, he glanced at his wife and said, "So, Emma, what's this about?"

Like she had brought the police to his door.

Soderbergh returned to her feet and reintroduced herself, using the word *colleague* again for Earle. "I have some questions regarding a missing person enquiry. Would you like to step outside, or can we talk here?"

The man looked confused for a moment, glanced at his wife again and then said, "Here is fine."

He waved them back onto the lounge, then sat on the edge of a lone armchair, hovering over them, while Emma Regatta lingered at the doorway, like she wasn't sure exactly where she fit in.

Odetta said, "Your name is Crispin Henry Regatta, is that correct?" He nodded. Warily. "Your mobile number is…," and she read out the number.

He frowned, then nodded again. Another quick glance at the wife.

"Are you currently in possession of that phone?" Odetta asked, and he balked, then patted his pocket and nodded.

"It's on me now. Why?"

"Where were you yesterday morning, Mr Regatta, around 9:40?"

The change of subject surprised him. He rubbed a hand through his thick head of hair, as snowy white as the sofa, and said, "Um… I guess I was kayaking then, why?"

"Alone?"

He smiled disarmingly. "It *is* a one-man kayak."

"Do you know a woman called Chanel Chambers?"

Another change of subject, another glance at the wife. She was still at the doorway, her expression blank. "Chanel? No I do not."

"You don't know her at all? She also goes by the name of Nel."

"No. I thought I just said that. Listen..." He sat forward, applied a stern look to his handsome features. "Are you going to explain what you're doing here or—"

"Chanel Chambers is a local woman, from Balmoral Beach," said Odetta. "She went missing yesterday morning, and we hold grave concerns for her well-being."

"Oh." He sat back. "Okay. Well, I'm very sorry about that, but..." He let out a small, soft chuckle that was more relief than joy. "It has nothing to do with me. I don't know her. Have never heard of her."

His eyes were back on his wife, but she didn't look so amused.

Soderbergh smiled disarmingly and said, "Yeah, see that's where we have a problem, Mr Regatta, because we have records to show Chanel Chambers called your mobile phone number yesterday morning at exactly 9:40, right around the time she vanished. Would you care to explain that?"

Crispin blinked a few times. So did his wife. Rapidly. "Hang on, what?" he said, sitting forward again.

The detective repeated the comment, and he looked perplexed.

"You must have that wrong. I mean, I *was* at Balmoral, sure. I kayak most mornings—or if the surf's good I head to Manly—but I'm telling you I never met the woman. In fact, I don't know any woman by the name of—" Then he stopped. Put two hands at his cheeks, Macaulay Culkin-style. "Hang on, what time did you say again?"

"Nine-forty a.m."

"Ohhhh..." Crispin visibly relaxed, exhaling as he threw a relieved smile at his wife. "That must be the woman. Oh, I get it now."

"What woman?" said Emma, beating Odetta to the question.

"Yesterday, after my paddle, I was at the car, and I couldn't find my mobile. Thought I'd lost it down the front seat somewhere. So this random chick comes along, from the oval. She's got her phone out, right? So I just asked if she could call my number so I could see where my phone had fallen. I figured if it rang I'd know where it was." He glanced at his wife again. "We do that all the time, don't we, Em? Usually when you lose yours down the back of the sofa."

Emma stared at him for a moment, not answering. Then she said, "You never told me about her."

He shrugged. "Because she was nobody."

Earle and Odetta shared a look during this, and Earle could see that Odetta was excited, but when she spoke, she was as cool as the furnishings.

"So let me get this straight, Mr Regatta. You were down at Balmoral Beach yesterday morning. You had a paddle, then you returned to your vehicle, which was parked at Balmoral Oval, is that correct?" He nodded. "You couldn't find your phone, so you asked a woman walking past to call your number for you. A complete stranger. And she happily did that. No questions asked. Is that what you're saying happened?"

"That *is* what happened." His tone was starting to sound surly.

Odetta smiled benignly. "Just a *random chick* as you say? You'd never met her before?"

"No, I told you that. She just did me a favour."

"Okay, then what? I gather you found this mysterious lost phone of yours?"

He tapped his pocket again. "Yes, as it happens, I was right. It was inside the car, down the back, actually. Under some crap." His jaw tightened then, and Earle spotted it, but Odetta didn't seem to notice.

She said, "Then what?"

"What do you mean?"

"What happened to the woman? After you found your phone?"

"Nothing!" A light blush began to appear below the man's tan. "Nothing happened. She called it, I found the phone, I thanked her and… and she headed off."

"Headed off? Where?"

"I don't know! Why would I? I told you, I don't know the woman. She just did me a favour and—"

There was a sound from the doorway, and they all looked around to see Emma striding away while Crispin just blinked maniacally in her direction.

"What car do you drive, Mr Regatta?" Odetta asked, and he looked back.

"What? Um, a Jeep Wrangler, the new four-door Night Eagle. Why?"

"The black one with the tinted windows that's parked out the front?"

He scowled. "Yeah, why?"

"Any other vehicles?"

"No, we're a one-car family. Again, *why*?" Then it must have clicked, and he said, "Good idea! Look for the cameras near the beach. You'll see. I had nothing to do with her disappearance."

"Oh, we will be checking all available cameras, let me assure you of that," Odetta said cheerfully before nodding at Constable Logan and standing up. "In the meantime, we're going to need to continue this conversation down at the station."

Now Crispin looked confused again. "But... but nothing happened, I promise. She just... she walked away. She was *fine*!"

"Still, if you don't mind." Odetta waved towards his front door, and he stood up, eyes darting about.

"But... But how long will this take? I have a lot on this afternoon."

"All goes well, we'll have you back in time for dinner," she replied. "Although I wouldn't schedule anymore Zoom conferences for a while."

She swapped a smile with Earle while Crispin's colour now matched the floorboards.

CHAPTER 12 ~
A TRIP TO THE ZOO

Out on the sun-dappled Mosman avenue, Earle watched Constable Logan escort Crispin Regatta to the police sedan, then pulled Odetta aside and congratulated her on the breakthrough.

"*Walked away*, my arse," she replied. "Even the wife didn't believe that porky. I'll get him down to HQ, see if we can get more out of him. Definitely get a search warrant to check this place over and his fancy wheels."

She stepped towards the Jeep Wrangler and glanced through the tinted glass windows at the back, seeing nothing but a few towels and a wetsuit.

"You know about Jeep Wranglers, right?" she said, and he lifted his eyebrows in response. "Have plugs in the floor so you can remove the carpet and hose the whole thing out. Pretty damn convenient, don't you think?" Then she wiggled her own eyebrows mischievously before adding, "This is where I leave you, good sir. I hope I haven't rained too much on your parade."

"Hey, if he's got the answers, I'm not complaining. Let's just hope they're answers Prue Chambers can live with."

She agreed and then held out a hand to shake. "It's been such an honour to meet you. It really has."

"Really?" said Earle, still quite confused. He'd been a decent detective in his day, but he wasn't sure he'd earned such reverence.

"Oh, you have no idea." She winked as she got into the driver's seat of the car where Crispin Regatta sat, still pale-faced in the back with Logan.

Earle watched them drive off, then got into his own car, feeling both hopeful and dispirited—and not just for Prue Chambers. Like Odetta, he had a feeling Crispin Regatta held the key to her missing daughter, and it was game over once again for the amateur detectives.

Another case aborted prematurely.

He sat there for a moment thinking about Crispin. It was clearly not the first time the guy had approached a stray lady, if his wife's reaction was anything to go by. But perhaps it was the first time he'd taken it further. The first time he'd taken it too far.

Earle reached for his phone and began scrolling for Verity's number, wanting to fill her in and then the others, when he noticed the front door to number 23 open slowly and Emma Regatta appear on the doorstep, oversized sunglasses on, handbag slung across one shoulder. She looked left and right, then closed the door behind her and headed straight for the Jeep.

Without appearing to notice Earle in his car, she zapped it open, jumped in and brought the engine to life.

He frowned. Where did she think she was going? That vehicle could hold crucial evidence in a missing person enquiry. He couldn't just let the suspect's wife drive off with it willy nilly. Especially if it could be hosed out so easily!

Earle opened his car door and jumped out to stop her, but it was too late. Emma had already steered the vehicle onto the street and was driving away in the opposite direction. So he returned to his car, buckled himself in, and did the only thing he could do.

He followed.

~

Kila only had one pressing item on his to-do list, and he didn't have the stomach for it. Not today. So he switched off his phone and got busy at his desk in the small office he ran from the back of an inner-city warehouse. There were invoices to be sent out, distressed clients to be called back, including the case of a missing lorikeet that he blamed Ace Ventura for. Kila had just finished telling the worried owner he wasn't a pet detective, that he should try animal shelters and the RSPCA, when he heard a gentle knock on his office door.

It was his lovely lawyer, Sheila Bonneray.

"You got a minute?" she asked, before heading straight for his spare chair.

"For you, I got hours," he told her, smiling as she dropped into it.

He adored his lawyer, and he knew that was unusual, but she'd got him out of hot water more times than a pensioner's tea bag, and she always did it with such good humour and patience.

"What's with the artwork down the sides of your lovely new car?" she asked, grappling now in the handbag she'd brought along. "You haven't been harassing clients' husbands again have you, Kil'?"

"Not this week. Not sure what that's about. Somebody doesn't like me. But then, nothing new there."

"Listen." She pulled a lipstick from the bag and wiped a smudge of red across both lips. Made a pucking sound. "My old mate from Legal Aid phoned. You ignoring his calls, Kila, or just head down, arse up?"

He looked at her nonchalantly through his floppy fringe, and she sighed.

"He just wants a quick word. Says it won't take long."

"Not interested," Kila replied.

"His client has something very important to tell you. Says it will only take five minutes."

"That bastard took *all* my sister's minutes, Sheila. He doesn't get any more from me. Not one."

"Fair enough. I get that. But..." She dumped the lippie back into her bag. "What if he has vital information? On Chili."

Hearing his younger sister's name spoken aloud still made Kila's heart wrench. "What more information do I need? That cretin tricked an innocent young girl into going on a date and..." He stopped. He'd never been able to fully describe what had happened to his sister that night. Like uttering *those* words aloud was a pain he could not endure. "He just wants to relieve his conscience, and I'm not going to give him the satisfaction."

She rubbed her lips together and leaned back in the chair. She looked around his messy office and back. "I thought you were going to use some of that lovely cash you earned to get a nicer space. Maybe move out of that crummy bedsit you call a home."

"It *is* a home, thanks, Sheila. Good enough for me."

"Yeah, well, it's not *you* I'm worried about." She offered him a pointed look. "Still hanging in bars, Kila? Trying to save young girls from themselves?"

He looked away. Said nothing.

"Oh, Kila, I feel your pain, I really do, but it's no way to live, constantly worrying about other people dying. You can't save every—"

"I know." He interrupted because he had heard this so many

times, mostly from Trevor, the barman at Taboo Bar, where he did most of his saving.

"Well, it's your decision, your call." She grabbed her bag, stood up and made her way to the door, then hesitated. "But if it were me, I'd take *the cretin's* call, because I think you might be surprised what he has to say. Might finally get some closure. And your life back."

And she left the gumshoe sitting stiffly in his chair, thinking, *I don't want my life back. I just want my sister.*

~

Crispin's wife pulled the Jeep into a parking spot just outside Sydney's iconic Taronga Zoo, then jumped out and headed straight for the decorative arched entrance before vanishing inside. Earle frowned.

What was the woman playing at? Her husband had just been taken in for questioning regarding a missing woman, and she was off to feed the lions?

He parked his own car and quickly followed.

"That'll be forty-four dollars, thanks, sir. Or thirty-five concession."

"Hang on, what?"

The attendant went to repeat that, but he held a hand up and reached for some cash, grumbling to himself about daylight robbery as he threw it down, grabbed his ticket and continued inside.

It took just five minutes to realise he'd been a fool. How on earth was he going to locate Emma Regatta in here? Paths led in all directions, and there were people everywhere—families, tour groups, hordes of excitable school kids. He was just considering whether to cut his losses when he glanced towards a café that was nestled under a huge gum tree and spotted her.

Emma was deep in conversation with a bald-headed man, their heads together, staring down at something on the table between them.

"Good afternoon, sir. Table for one?" said the maître d' at the café entrance. Earle nodded and the man handed him a menu. "There's plenty of space. Help yourself."

Earle looked down and headed for a table on the other side of the tree, then hid his face behind the menu while sneaking glances in Emma's direction.

She now had her back to him, but he got a good look at her companion. The man was older, dressed in a crumpled shirt, ear-ring in one ear, wrap-around sunglasses covering his eyes.

Earle wondered about him.

A relative of Emma's? A confidante, perhaps? There was no obvious contact between them, and he looked about twice her age.

And what were they staring at? Was that a small iPad on the table?

"What are you after?" came a woman's voice beside Earle, and he glanced around with a start. She didn't seem to notice. "Coffee? Smoothie? Bite to eat?"

"Oh…" He looked back at the menu. The prices took his breath away again. "Just a tea with milk, thanks."

"English Breakfast? Green—"

"Just black tea, any tea will do."

She shrugged and jotted it on her pad, then went to snatch the menu, but he held it fast.

"In case I get hungry," he told her, and she shrugged again and walked away.

Earle glanced back at Emma, but she was already making moves to leave, pulling her handbag onto her shoulder as she stood up, while the man remained seated, staring up at her, the tablet still before him. Earle studied him closely, trying to imprint him in his brain, but his vision wasn't what it used to be nor was his memory for that matter, so he took a leaf from the younger generation and reached for his mobile phone. Careful not to bring attention to himself, he opened the camera function, then held it up clumsily to one side of the menu, clicking a few pictures off.

A woman at a nearby table glanced across at Earle then, so he steered the camera towards a fenced enclosure and snapped a few shots of some tree kangaroos before glancing back towards Emma. She was now shaking the man's hand and hitching her bag tighter. Then she turned swiftly and walked directly towards Earle.

He whipped the menu up and hid his face behind it, hoping, if she'd noticed him at all, she would have seen an old guy who needed better reading glasses, not a nosey amateur sleuth who'd just sprung you meeting another man less than twenty minutes after your husband was taken into custody.

It was strange, very strange indeed.

Earle was just considering whether to approach the man when the waitress appeared with his tea. And by the time she'd fussed over whether Earle needed her to pour the milk and Earle had assured her he could manage, Emma's mysterious friend had also vanished.

And all that was left was an empty table and a flock of disappointed pigeons.

CHAPTER 13 ~

MEANWHILE, BACK AT BALMORAL

Prue Chambers was nowhere to be seen when the sleuths returned to her Bellavista apartment right on two p.m. as planned. Verity informed them she was resting, then drew them back out to the balcony where she had placed a range of snacks, including sandwiches, sushi boxes and muffins.

"I'll leave you to it," she said. "I need to head back to Seagrave. Check on George."

"How is Sir George?" asked Merry, helping herself to the sushi. "He didn't look so good yesterday."

Verity grimaced slightly. "His health has taken a bit of a nosedive since you saw him last. I think the loss of his children, the stress of it all, is finally catching up on him. My assistant is with him now but... well, I'd better get over there."

"You have an assistant?" asked Martin.

"The PA has a PA?" added Frankie.

"And not an especially good one," said Verity. "Hence the reason I'd better make tracks."

"Where's young Charlie? Why isn't she with him?" asked Merry.

"He sent his granddaughter overseas before the court case started. Wanted to get her away from all the drama. She's staying with some relatives in London. Fresh start and all that." She looked sad though. "He's very much on his own now, George. So I'm dropping in a beef stew I cooked for him. Cheer him up a bit."

"You *cook*?" said Frankie, glancing at the food, which was in takeaway containers, much like all the meals they'd been furnished with during the Burlington case.

Verity smiled at that comment. "I'm more of a feeder than a cook, Frankie, that is true. But I do what I have to. I always find a good meal makes things so much better, and he *really* loves my Irish stew."

Then she laughed lightly and left them to it.

"So, what happens now?" asked Merry as all eyes swept to Earle.

That's when he filled them in on the police interview with Regatta.

"It's not good news," he agreed as he watched several of their faces deflate. "But it looks like this fellow could very well be responsible for Nel's abduction. First he claims not to know Nel. Then he gives some cock-and-bull story about her helping him to find his phone. Then he insists she simply walked off after that, never to be seen again."

"Highly suspect," said Frankie. "I don't believe a word of it."

"I do," said Merry. "I mean, about the phone. I lose mine all the time. Lola is so exhausted by me! Just last weekend she had to call it over and over while I scrambled around the house, trying to find it. Turns out I'd left it on the top of the washing machine."

"Yes, we've all called our phones to try to find them," said Frankie. "That's not in dispute. What I'm saying is I bet he used that as an excuse to get her near his car, close enough to abduct her."

Merry nodded. "Right. Yes. I see."

Frankie drew her eyes back to Earle. "Will Detective Soderbergh call you? Let you know what she learns?"

"I can't see why she should. Although I have cause to ring her..." Earle produced his phone and found his way to the images he had snapped at the café, explaining how he'd followed Emma Regatta to the zoo and her strange rendezvous.

"Okay, that's an interesting twist," said Martin, squinting at the image. "Who do we think he is?"

"Could be a lover," said Merry.

Earle was not convinced. "There was no intimacy between them, and he didn't seem her sort. Unless she's into crumpled older men of course."

"Nothing wrong with crumpled older men," said Kila, smiling at Frankie, who just rolled her eyes in reply.

"He still harassing you?" said Martin before scowling at Kila. "You ever give up, mate?"

Kila shrugged. "The squeaky wheel gets the oil."

Merry giggled at that while Earle held the phone up.

"Mind if we get back to this, folks?"

They settled down and began to pass the images around.

"My guess," said Earle, "is that he's an older friend or relative.

Perhaps an uncle? A confidant of some sort."

"Could be a lawyer?" said Frankie, handing the phone to Kila.

"Or a private investigator," said Kila, quickly zeroing in on the image with two fingers. "Yep, definitely a gumshoe."

"You know him?" asked Earle.

Kila nodded. "He's lost all his hair and aged considerably, but it looks like Bob Taylor to me. Didn't know he was still in the game. Last I heard he'd cut his losses and headed for the Gold Coast."

Earle reclaimed his phone and studied the man again. Okay, that made sense. *Sort of.*

"Why would the wife go straight to a private investigator after her husband is detained?" asked Frankie.

"Maybe she's going to put a tail on the hubby?" suggested Kila. "Maybe she's worried what the cops will discover."

"Oh, she's worried all right," said Earle, "but it's not the police she's worried about. I'd say she's already had this PI tailing her husband. The way she behaved when we arrived, she seemed more like a jealous wife than a concerned one. I got the feeling she thought Crispin was having an affair with Nel. And that it wouldn't be the first time."

Merry's eyes widened behind her cat's-eye spectacles. "Maybe she's right! Maybe Nel was sleeping with Crispin but had had enough and met with him to break it off." She began to click her fingers. "Remember the lad downstairs, Tommo was it? The grandson of the woman in apartment two? He said he overheard Nel talking to someone, telling them to back off. Maybe it was *Crispin* she was yelling at, and he wasn't prepared to take no for an answer. Maybe he met with her at the oval to try to win her back and things got out of control?"

"That's certainly one theory," said Earle, now used to Merry's galloping imagination.

"Did you tell Odetta about that phone call, Earle?" asked Frankie. "See who she was telling to back off the day before she vanished?"

Earle shook his head. "Didn't get a chance to." Held up his phone. "Another reason to give Odetta a call. While I'm doing that, she might share what more she's learned from the suspect."

"And if she doesn't?" said Frankie. "What if she does a DI Morgan and tells you to back off?"

Kila tossed a sandwich crust into a pot plant and said, "Then I'll get the inside story from my old mate Bob Taylor. You saw him near Taronga Zoo, Earle?" The older man nodded. "Then I think I know where I might find him at this hour."

Kila glanced at Frankie. "Fancy a stiff one?"

Then he waggled his dark eyebrows while Martin said, "There he goes again. Hashtag me too, Kila. You are such a dinosaur."

As Merry watched them banter, she felt a stab of disappointment, half wishing that Kila had invited her along too. She didn't want to return home. Darren was still there, doing some odd jobs about the place, or so he said. Waiting for her answer more likely. And she didn't know what to say to him. Because she didn't know how she felt.

"What about me?" she said to Earle. "There must be something I can do."

"There is," he replied, "and Martin can help you. We need to reinterview the shopkeepers again."

Martin groaned. "Wasn't that already ticked off?"

"Nope," said Kila. "Only the café was open when we walked past earlier. There were two other shops we didn't get to."

Earle checked his watch. "They'd have to be open by now. And you'll need to talk to the café again anyway. This time don't just ask about Nel, ask about Regatta. Last time there was an assumption that Nel was on her own. Go back and ask if anyone saw her with a man fitting Regatta's description or near a black Jeep Wrangler four-wheel drive. It's a monster of a vehicle. Might jog someone's memory."

"Here," said Frankie, tapping into her iPhone. "I googled Crispin Regatta. He runs some swanky software company. Found a picture of him on their website. I'll text you all the link so you can show that picture around."

"Good work," said Earle. "It'd be good to know if anyone saw Nel with Mr Regatta that morning or, more importantly, if they saw her walking away from a large black Jeep."

"If indeed she did walk away," said Merry, softly, because it was such an ugly thought she could barely vocalise it.

~

The Gherkin's Head Sports Bar was located just up the road from

Taronga Zoo and made Kila's favourite haunt, the Taboo Bar, look exotic, Frankie decided as they strolled in ten minutes later. It wasn't a dive so much as dull. Too well lit. Too lacking in style. It was right next door to a betting shop and packed mostly with men of a certain age, clutching betting slips, eyes glued to one of several television screens positioned around the bar.

"This is a bit sad, isn't it?" she said as she soaked up the sporting memorabilia and smelled the desperation in the air. "How'd you know he'd be here?"

Kila pointed to one screen that was showing the races. "Gambling addiction. I thought loan sharks had scared him north years ago. Besides, there's nothing wrong with this joint. At least the grog's cheap. Better than the kind of bars you frequent with their thirty-dollar kale lemongrass cocktails."

"When have you ever seen me order a cocktail, let alone a kale lemongrass one?" She slapped him playfully across one arm. "Is that even a *thing*?"

"Martin would know. Sounds right up his alley. Let me just get some real drinks."

As he ordered three lagers and a lemon squash, Kila's phone rang, and he didn't even look at it this time, let alone bother answering.

"Avoiding a lover?" said Frankie, almond eyes twinkling.

He stared at her flatly. "No, Frankie. That's your schtick, not mine."

She blinked back at him, face crumpling a little, so he quickly added, "It's just Dragon Malone, the cretin that hurt my sister. Or his lawyer, at least. Dragon wants to talk, but he can shove that where the sun don't shine. Thanks, mate," he said to the barman, then paid for the drinks and glanced around.

They soon found Bob at a weatherproof resin table out in the beer garden. He was hunched over a beer glass, smoke in one hand, pen in the other, a form guide below that.

When he spotted Kila, he looked up and away, then back again as recognition registered on his heavily wrinkled face. Frankie noticed he quickly pocketed the guide before standing up, transferring the smoke to his left hand and reaching out to shake Kila's.

"Mad Dog Morea! Long time no horn butt. How are you, mate?"

Kila smiled and dropped the drinks on the table beside him and then returned the handshake before introducing Frankie.

Bob glanced between the two of them and said, "You're not here by coincidence I gather?"

Frankie smiled. "How do you figure that?"

"Three factors, actually." He sat back down and produced a finger. "Kila's so far below your league, babe, there's no way he'd be dragging you anywhere just for a drink." He produced a second finger. "But especially not this dump. Has to be for me." Then he produced a third finger and pointed it at the beer Kila was now pushing towards him. "Beer bribe did the rest."

"All right, stop showing off, Sherlock," said Kila, before pointing to the matching plastic chairs across from him. "Mind if we?"

Bob waved them down and then drained his own glass before reaching for the bribe. He took a good gulp of that, then dragged on his cigarette, squinting through the smoke down to the lemon squash that had remained untouched.

"You still wasting good drinks, mate?" he said, shooting Frankie a quick worried glance and back.

"Not a waste to me," Kila replied, his tone flat.

The soda was his sister Chili's favourite. The fact that she couldn't touch it was irrelevant to Kila.

Bob shrugged, turned his eyes back to Frankie. "You're the journo, yeah?"

"Guilty as charged."

"This about an old case? One of mine?" The questions were directed at Kila now.

"One of yours, yes, but it's new. Or at least it is for us." He leaned forward. "What can you tell us about Emma Regatta?"

Bob sat back with a stunned look. "Emma? Wow, okay, that I did not guess." He smiled at Frankie. "Got me there, babe. Why do you want to know about Mrs Regatta?"

Kila took a gulp of his own beer. "We've been hired to look into the disappearance of a young woman from Balmoral Beach."

"Upmarket end of town for you, Mad Dog." His eyes drifted back to Frankie. "Must be your influence."

She smiled but let Kila explain.

"The woman's name is Chanel Chambers—Nel. Been missing since yesterday."

"Yesterday?"

"I know it's fresh, but they're the best kind, right? The mother,

Prue, might be getting ahead of herself, or she might be on the money. Any case, the cops have linked Nel to Crispin Regatta."

"Oh yeah?" Bob reached for a fresh cigarette.

"Yeah. Turns out, Crispin was one of the last to see Nel alive— around 9:40 or so yesterday morning. He says it was a random meet and that was that."

"Random meet? What does that mean?"

Kila explained about the lost mobile phone.

The other PI gave it some thought. "You don't believe him." It was not a question.

Kila shrugged. "Cops don't. Me? I keep an open mind."

"Good tactic," said Bob. "But what's this sad, sorry story got to do with me?"

Frankie spoke up now. "It's to do with your client. Emma Regatta. Crispin's wife."

Bob leaned back and studied them both for a moment as he drank his beer. "Client?" Then he looked at Frankie and said, "How you figure that?" repeating the question she'd thrown at him earlier.

Now it was Frankie's turn to dazzle, and she held a finger up, mirroring him. "One of our associates tailed Mrs Regatta to Taronga Zoo not long ago and saw you both at the café there together." She produced a second finger. "That associate took a few happy snaps." Then she pointed a third finger at Kila and said, "Mad Dog joined the dots."

Kila grinned like he'd just caught a snapper. "Want to fill us in?"

Bob just looked disappointed. "Come on, mate, you know how this works. We're not priests, but we're as good as. Client confidentiality," he explained to Frankie. "I never break it. It's the reason I've survived this long. And the reason I don't have my licence whipped off me every two months like Mad Dog here." He chuckled as Kila rallied.

"Hey, I'm licensed. Nothing's ever stuck." Then he leaned forward again. "Look, I'm not expecting you to tell all, just a bit of intel to help us find this poor girl. Her mother's desperate, and if Crispin really is responsible—"

"He didn't do it."

That surprised them both. Now Kila was asking, "How you figure that?"

Bob didn't bother with the fingers this time. "Not his usual MO.

Let me see how I can word this without breaching my client's confidentiality…" He gulped his beer and then nodded. "The guy liked to… er, *shop around*, if you get my drift, but that's all he does. Bit of window shopping. Sometimes he samples the goods. Never more than that. And never with any kind of coercion; it wasn't his style. He's a shit husband, but I'm not convinced he's violent."

"So, was he *shopping* with our missing woman, can you tell us that?" asked Frankie.

He lifted a shoulder. "I'll tell you what I told my client. I've never heard of any Chanel or Nel Chambers." He dragged on his cigarette as the sleuths shared a disappointed glance. Then he said, "What's she look like? This Chanel?"

Frankie produced her phone and the image of Nel.

He took one look and shook his head. "Wasn't amongst the images I took, mate. Nor does she look like his usual type of, er, shop, I can tell you that for nothing, although a fresh beer wouldn't go astray."

Bob looked pointedly at his empty glass, and Kila smiled and jumped up. "Same again?" he said to Frankie, but she shook her head.

While Kila returned to the bar, Bob said, "How long have you two been going out?"

Frankie scoffed. "We're not going out. I thought you'd already deduced that."

"No, I said he was out of your league, but I didn't say you weren't playing down."

"Well, I'm not. We're not." She reached for her own glass, took a small sip.

He leaned back and dragged on his smoke again. "If you say so."

"We are not going out!" Frankie was feeling irked suddenly.

"Okay sure…" Then, as Kila returned with two beers, Bob returned to the subject of Crispin. "The guy's not just a disloyal shopper," he told them, warming to the metaphor. "He likes to shop downtown, if you get my drift."

Now both Kila and Frankie were frowning at him.

"Think about it like this," he said. "Emma is a lot like Frankie here. Classy. Upmarket. Let's call her Gucci. Crispin's other shops were more your two-dollar kind."

"You saying they were prostitutes?" asked Kila.

"Nah, just cheap and nasty."

"So what's Chanel then?" Frankie said, holding the image up once again.

He smiled. "She's, well, *Chanel.* Obviously."

Then he laughed like he was the funniest man in the beer garden, and Frankie sighed loudly. All this shop talk was annoying her. She wasn't big on metaphor, especially one as poorly drawn as this. She liked to say it how it is.

"Let's cut to the chase," she said now. "So, Crispin's wife's a babe, and he liked to sleep around with bogans. Was that because they moved in different circles? Less chance of getting caught...?"

"I think it had more to do with shopping for a different, slightly saucy flavour. Something he'd never normally get at home. Bit like what you're doing, I'd suggest."

Then her scowl returned full throttle along with his laugh.

"What was that all about?" Kila asked as they headed to her car. His had remained back down at Balmoral.

"No idea," Frankie snapped. "The guy's slightly unhinged. Okay, so, what now? Shall we pay the wife a visit?"

"The less-saucy shop you mean?" said Kila, chuckling. "Yeah, he is a bit eccentric. I'd forgotten that about Bob. Sure. While you drive, I'll call Earle, get Emma's address. See if Ms Gucci can tell it to us straight this time."

As she made the short trip to Regatta's residence, Frankie's mind began to wander to something Kila had said earlier, about Chili's murderer, Dragon Malone.

Unlike Kila, Frankie was desperate to talk to the guy. He once shared a cell with her dead Spice Boy, Phillip Weaver, and might know more about his murder. Problem was, her official interview request with the governor of Silverwater prison had gone unanswered. She'd checked her emails before they headed off, and there was nothing but a bit of spam and a grumpy one from her editor. If only she could find another way in...

Glancing across at Kila, her brain began to crunch into overdrive.

Kila noticed her gaze and held it. "You all right, Frankie? What's going on?"

"Oh nothing." She quickly glanced back to the road.

"You're up to something. I can just smell it on you."

"Hey, all you can smell is my very expensive Chanel No. 5! Speaking of Chanel, what's your vibe?"

He shrugged. "I'm certainly not buying Bob's theory that Crispin only had one type."

"You think they really could've been in a relationship?"

He caught her eye and smiled. "I've seen stranger couplings."

CHAPTER 14 ~
MEETING BOOKSHOP MAN

Merry and Martin made an odd couple as they strode along Balmoral Esplanade, Merry chatting incessantly about her kids, Martin barely feigning interest as he fiercely stroked the bridge of his nose. Of the five sleuths, Mumsy Merry was the one he felt the least affinity with. He might lock horns with Kila and Frankie, but it was Merry who left him wanting. Sure, she was sweet and smarter than he'd expected, but apart from their age, they had nothing in common. Merry had no real career to speak of (because playing board games certainly didn't count), and her complete devotion to her kids had him baffled.

Martin had grown up without his mum, his angry father distant at best, and so he couldn't fathom what that kind of devotion felt like—to give or to receive. He'd never been devoted to anyone or anything his entire life. Not a pet dog, not a best mate, certainly never a partner. And, sadly, not even the protagonist of his best-selling Flynn Bold crime series.

Hell, he'd bumped the guy off in book twenty without so much as a second glance—despite the fact that Flynn had made him a small fortune, and even more fans. His agent, Lizzie, had wept like a baby when he'd handed in the final draft, and he'd received thousands of similarly weepy fan letters demanding he resurrect the detective, pronto!

Martin sighed as Merry prattled on—something about Archie and his extraordinary soccer prowess—and he wished, suddenly, that he had just a smidgen of her enthusiasm.

For anything.

"Okay, here we are!" Merry announced as they reached the first shop, the café she had been to earlier with Frankie and Kila.

They had just entered Ballo's when the waitress appeared, and Merry explained why they were back and asked if she'd seen a man fitting Crispin Regatta's description—coiffed blond hair, suntanned, athletic. Drives a fancy four-wheel drive.

The waitress laughed at that. "Every man in this suburb fits that description. And every vehicle, just look outside!"

Then she pointed to the curb where a Land Rover Discovery sat between a Mercedes GLE and a shiny Porsche Cayenne.

Merry laughed. "Okay, fair enough. But we were wondering if you saw this fellow with the woman we were asking about earlier? The one in the yellow sweatshirt and the blue cap? Maybe they were talking? Kissing? Fighting?"

Her tone was hopeful, but the waitress was now shaking her head. "Like I said last time—and to the police when they dropped in earlier—she doesn't ring a bell. Sorry."

"No, no, don't worry. It's not your fault," Merry gushed, but Martin was feeling grumpy.

"This is a waste of time," he muttered as they returned to the sidewalk.

"Not necessarily," said Merry, pointing with glee at the bookshop next door. "It's open; let's give them a whirl."

First Chapters bookstore was a cosy, cluttered little space, with a brightly painted red front door and warmly lit interior. There were books piled high in floor-to-ceiling shelves and out on the street in several rustic wooden carts. A man in his fifties with soft golden curls, a dimpled smile and a bright yellow jumper stood just outside the open door, assembling greeting cards in a mobile rack.

He smiled as they approached and said, "Go on in, folks, and let me know if I can help with anything."

"There is something you can help us with," said Martin, taking the lead this time. He produced his phone and the image of Nel and held it up. "Do you know this woman?"

The shopkeeper barely glanced at the photo before continuing slotting the cards into place. "Don't think so, sorry."

He didn't seem to recognise Martin either, which seemed strange to Merry. Most bookshops would kill to have the famous author in their midst, be locking him in for an appearance, pronto. Martin took it in his stride, stepping away, but Merry was not yet done.

She grabbed his phone and held it within eyesight of the man and said, "If you could take a really good look, we'd be so grateful. She's gone missing. Her mother is extremely worried."

That got his attention. "Oh dear. Yes, of course." Then he pulled out a pair of round Harry Potter-style glasses from a top pocket and inspected the image again.

After a few moments, he shook his head. "I'm so sorry. The police were in here earlier, and I must tell you what I told them. I'm not very good with faces, and she looks a little like a lot of women who come in here. What's her name?"

"Chanel Chambers. Nel." That didn't ring a bell either, so Merry added, "Prue Chambers' daughter. Prue lives just down the esplanade in the red-brick block of four. Bellavista?"

Another vague look, a sorry shrug. Prue clearly hadn't bought any books from First Chapters lately.

Martin began to move away, stopping to inspect a discount bin on the pavement—wondering if his were in there, perhaps?—so Merry tried a different angle.

"You might not remember her, but we think she was with a man called Crispin Regatta. A kayaker with blond hair, athletic build. Drives a large black Jeep."

Merry waited for the inevitable scoff about athletic locals and oversized vehicles, but the shopkeeper was now cleaning his glasses with the end of his shirt, giving it some thought, so she said, "Here, I have a picture of him!"

Then she reached for her own phone and tapped on the link that Frankie had sent them. Held up a finger as it slowly began to load. "Sorry, it'll just take a moment."

"Not at all," he replied. "It's not like I'm overwhelmed with customers."

Then he gave a sweet little chuckle, and Merry couldn't help chuckling along.

"Things been quiet today?" she asked.

"Quiet all year, I'm afraid. COVID."

"I read so much during lockdown! I thought book sales were up. Nothing much else to do."

"Maybe for most books, certainly genre fiction, but I sell first editions. Collector's items. That kind of thing. My sales always dip when belts need to be tightened."

So *that's* why he didn't recognise the popular crime writer!

"Oh, I'm sorry," Merry said, and he looked heartened by that.

"Thank you. I appreciate that. What was your name?"

She smiled. "Merry. Meredith Kean. This is——" She went to introduce Martin, but he was already heading towards the bottle shop next door.

"Well, nice to meet you, Meredith Kean. I'm Dougie. Douglas Dollarway. Although there's not been too many dollars my way lately."

Then they both chuckled at that.

"Oh, here it is," Merry said, when the image appeared. She held the phone out so he could see the website picture of Crispin.

Dougie studied it for some time but eventually had to concede he didn't recall the man either.

"Okay, well, thanks anyway," said Merry. "And nice to meet you, Dougie!"

"Likewise, Merry," he replied, a second dimple appearing in his cheek as his smile widened.

Merry was just walking away when the man called out to her:

"When did they vanish? These friends of yours? You never said."

She turned back. "Oh, it's just the woman who's gone missing. Yesterday sometime between nine and ten, we think."

He looked disappointed. "Well, I wasn't working then, see, was out pretending to catch dinner." His dimples deepened. "I'm no Ernest Hemingway when it comes to fishing, but boy do I give it my best shot. My daughter opened for me yesterday."

"Is she around?" Merry asked and he shook his head.

"I can ask her for you, if you like. I'll see her later. If she graces me with her presence." He raised his eyes to the sky and added, "Teenage girls!"

Merry giggled. "I know! I'm lucky to get a glance from mine these days. Well, see how you go. Thanks so much, Dougie."

Merry felt a little skip in her step as she headed off to find Martin.

He was just striding out of the bottle shop, a purchase in hand, when she approached and he said, "They had a cheeky little shiraz for a very good price."

"In this posh neighbourhood? I'm surprised. So, how'd you go? They see anything?"

"No. They don't remember her either." Then he glanced around and said, "Actually, I might just fetch a second bottle..."

It was good to see where his priorities lay, she thought as he headed back in.

~

Emma Regatta did not play with words like the PI she'd hired.

"My partner has been an unfaithful prat since before we were married," she announced. "Stupid me thought I could change him." She offered Frankie a pointed look. "You can't. Don't even try." Then she glanced between Frankie and Kila, and again Frankie felt her shackles rise.

Why did everybody keep assuming they were a couple?

They had presented themselves at the Regatta home soon after interviewing Bob Taylor, explaining who they were—friends of the missing woman's mother—and what they were after, expecting to find the door slammed firmly in their face. Instead, Emma welcomed them in, not at all perturbed to be interrogated about her husband's cheating ways. In fact, she seemed as determined as Bob to prove that Crispin had nothing to do with "some woman's disappearance". Like Bob, she insisted Crispin was a lover, not a killer.

"I'm the one who takes that karma on," she said, quickly adding, "Cockroaches, spiders, mice... Never humans, certainly not women. At least not yet. But give me time."

Frankie looked affronted by that, but Kila smiled. He liked Emma Regatta. Wondered why the good ones always found their way to the tossers. Probably had a lot to do with those fancy wheels out the front and the luxury home they were now seated in because she looked like a lady of leisure in her yoga gear. He also knew the pigs would be here soon with a warrant to inspect the aforementioned car and house, and they did not have long, so he forged on.

"You've never heard the name Chanel before?"

"Not outside of a fashion label, no. When the detective mentioned her, I just thought, okay, here we go again. Another one. All Cris's slags have those kinds of names. Exotic. Aspirational. They're usually the complete opposite. Skanky."

"Why do you stay with him?" Kila asked. The eternal question.

Again, the wife did not mince her words. "Like I said, thought I could change him. But not anymore. One more skank and he's out for good. And he knows it."

Frankie and Kila swapped a look. If that wasn't a motive for murder, they didn't know what was. Perhaps it wasn't Nel who tried to break things off. Perhaps it was the *unfaithful prat* trying to save his marriage.

How far would Crispin go to shut up a chatty lover?

~

When Earle phoned Detective Soderbergh, he was secretly chuffed she took his call, expecting to be palmed off to a subordinate. Odetta was busy with her suspect after all. He was even more chuffed when she suggested he "pop into HQ around four" and fill her in on what he'd discovered. Face-to-face.

It left the old cop swelling with pride and self-satisfaction and all the things he hadn't felt a lot of since retirement. But it took just two steps into his old stomping ground for that to come crashing back down.

"Oh, look what the cat dragged in!" came a booming voice from one side, and he looked around to find Detective Inspector Morgan staring across at him.

His old friend and nemesis.

"You've got a nerve!" Morgan said as he marched across. "You're bloody lucky I never had you and your pals up on charges over the Burlington-Brown case."

Earle stood his ground and cocked his head to one side. "What exactly were you going to charge us with, Morgs? Doing your job for you? Repairing incompetent policing?"

There was a muffled titter from several young constables near reception, and that had Morgan fuming, as Earle knew it would, and the DI let out a stream of obscenities, followed by an ungallant threat to punch Earle's lights out if he ever saw him anywhere near one of his cases again.

"Good thing I'm not here for you then," said Earle, nodding in the direction of Odetta, who was seated at a far desk, grinning like the player she was. Because, yes, Earle and Morgan had both just been played by the young detective, and the look of delight on her face proved that.

Morgan was Odetta's nemesis too, as it turns out.

"Sorry to do that to you," she said after he shook the angry DI off and approached her desk, "but that was *so* worth it!"

"Glad I could entertain you," he replied, silently kicking himself for his hubris.

How else did he think Morgan was going to react to his arrival? With a tickertape parade? He'd shown up the senior detective in the last case, made him look sloppy in front of his bosses, his colleagues, underlings like Odetta. Only a saint would let that slide.

"You knew he'd have a fit," Earle said, and she made an apologetic grimace.

"I did. That is true." Then she lowered her voice and whispered, "I just wanted to see someone put the obnoxious pig in his place for a change, and I knew you'd be the one to do it. We all heard how you worked the Burlington case, didn't take any of his crap. Found the real culprit. You've become a bit of a legend round these parts, especially with the younger ones."

Earle felt a little hot under the collar then. He was both shocked and flattered, and she laughed at his discomfort.

"Sorry, Earle. I didn't mean to embarrass you."

"Yes, you did." But he didn't mind one bit. He dropped into the seat beside her desk and cleared his throat. "So, how'd you go with Regatta?"

Odetta smiled slyly. "Nice subject change, Earle. Okay, this can be your reward for that priceless bit of entertainment." She reached across the desk to grab a file and began riffling through it. "I'm not real sure what to think of our preppy kayaker. He's stuck to his story like cement: Chanel Chambers was just some random chick who helped him find his phone. She called it, he found it, thanked her and she walked away. Still breathing, apparently. And, as far as he recalls, in the direction of her apartment block. But that's a bit hazy. Other than that, he saw no one and nothing. Insists it was just an innocent interaction."

"And you believe him?"

"No, I do not. Or, at least, there's definitely more to it. I just know he's hiding something, but when I pressed him on it, he threw the *L* word at me and that was that. We're waiting for his *lawyer* to saddle up now." She leaned back in her chair. "Problem is, Regatta's story does line up. If he's not surfing, the guy kayaks most mornings at that hour, and he's usually alone—fellow kayakers attest to that." She rubbed a hand across her prickly white hair. "Tough life, hey? Starting each morning with a paddle. My days usually start with a puddle of something from one of my six French bulldogs."

"You have *six* French bulldogs?"

"For my sins, yes. Back to Regatta. He has no priors. Logan's called his boss, his colleagues… no one has a bad word to say about the guy."

"Maybe you need to speak to an ex-lover," said Earle, and her eyes widened.

"You got that vibe from the wife too? I did put that to him, but he was outraged that I would suggest such a thing. I didn't buy it. Pretty sure the wife doesn't either."

"She doesn't."

"Oh? Is this your juicy news?"

He outlined again how he'd followed Emma to the zoo and seen her talking with a man who turned out to be private investigator Bob Taylor.

"At risk of sounding like Morgan," said Odetta, "what exactly were you doing, tailing Mrs Regatta in the first place?"

"I had good cause. Immediately after you left, she appeared from the house and then drove off in the Jeep. You'd just told me how it could be hosed out, so I was concerned she was taking the car to be cleaned."

"Oh, so you were doing us a *favour*?" Odetta shook her head, then reached for a pad and pen. "Bob Taylor, you say?"

"He's an old associate of Kila's. Probably specialises in surveilling unfaithful partners if he's anything like his mate."

She tapped the pen on her desk like a metronome. "Okay, so Regatta lied to us about that. Makes me wonder what else he's lying about. I better have a word with this Taylor fellow. Mrs Regatta was no doubt enquiring if he'd seen Chanel in his surveillance. And it's a good question. I'll follow up."

"Just one thing you should know," said Earle, preparing himself for some splash back. "Kila is 'having a word' with Taylor now— one gumshoe to another."

Odetta stopped tapping the pen. "Okay, now I'm starting to have some sympathy for Morgan."

Earle's face creased into a smile. "One other thing," he said. "The relative of a tenant in Prue's building thinks he overheard Nel having an argument with someone the day before she vanished. Thinks it was over the phone around four, maybe five p.m. on Tuesday. You might want to check her mobile records again, see who that was. Could be important."

She nodded, jotting something into her notepad when the desk phone began to ring. After checking the incoming number, she said, "I've got to take this."

Earle went to get up, but she held a finger to stall him as she said into the receiver, "Hey Jackie, can you hold for a sec?" Then she placed her hand over it and said to Earle, "I am going to have to pull a Morgan on you and ask you guys to step back a bit, okay? Not saying you can't keep searching for Nel—the more eyes on the ground the better—just steer clear of the potential crime scenes: the oval and the apartment. Got it? And maybe no more chatting to the other tenants. We haven't even got to them yet, but I have a strong feeling Crispin's our man. Any case, wide berth, yes?"

He nodded, thinking how annoyed this would make his fellow sleuths as she mouthed the words "Thank you" before returning to her call.

CHAPTER 15 ~
A CAUTIONARY CALL #1

Frankie was striding into the *Herald* office when she got Earle's "back off" text. Had just stopped to tap an indignant response when the newspaper's editor appeared, his expression matching hers.

"Oh, here she is at last, the great Frankie Jo!" he announced, causing several of her colleagues to look up with a mixture of concern, sympathy and delight. "Nice of you to grace us with your presence, O esteemed one."

Frankie looked at Ruffus Jones unfazed. The *Herald* editor was aptly named—a tiny man with a yapping voice and a bark that was notoriously bigger than his bite.

"Sorry, Ruffus, I was—"

"Just because you've now won *three* Walkley awards, Frankie, doesn't make you any better than the rest of us who turn up every single day and do our bloody jobs."

"I know that. I have been doing my—"

"Where's the Kings Cross laneway murder at? D'ya get my email?" Then, seeing her look of confusion: "God's sake, Frankie. You're not off on another tangent, are you? Trying to score more gongs?"

"What? No!"

Nel's disappearance had not yet been made public, and that suited Frankie just fine. The moment it broke, she suspected Ruffus would pull her from it and hand it to someone else. He'd become oddly combative since she'd won the last two awards for the Burlington murders—one for Investigative Journalism, one for Scoop of the Year—and she was sure he'd tear the story from her, and she couldn't have that.

She wanted the Nel Chambers case. She was greedy like that.

And now *Earle* thought he was going to apply the brakes? No way. She wouldn't allow it.

"Check your email," Ruffus snapped. "And get that follow-up copy to subs pronto!"

Before Frankie could attempt another aborted reply, he had swept away to the sports desk where she was heartened to hear him blasting them now.

"Circ' figures are in," whispered the junior reporter at the next desk, a cadet journalist who mostly did the council rounds but had grand ambitions of taking over the world one day, starting with Frankie's job. Frankie didn't hold it against her. Her name was Katie Speers, she was just nineteen, and she reminded Frankie of herself at that age.

Katie was pointing two thumbs downwards to indicate the slide in the circulation figures, but Frankie wasn't surprised. Sales had been heading south since some fool invented the internet and with it, free access to news and information.

"Still, doesn't give him the right to abuse me," said Frankie as she slipped behind her desk. "Ruffus is just lucky I don't call the union on him. Someone ought to teach that man a lesson in politeness."

"I wouldn't say that too loudly," said Katie, glancing around. "D'ya hear what happened to his car?"

Frankie brought her own screen to life, typed in her password as she murmured, "His vintage Valiant? What about it?"

"It was vandalised last night."

"Well, I'm not surprised," said Frankie. "Was probably one of his kids."

She laughed at her own joke and then trawled through her emails to find the one Ruffus had sent earlier. It was forwarded from the police and contained a link, which she greedily clicked on. Within seconds she was watching more CCTV footage of their dead ex-con, Phillip Weaver, this time striding down a more dimly lit city street.

The monitor read 12:28 a.m. Later than the last one. This must be fresh footage, she realised. A new "last known sighting" perhaps?

"See the clip?" came a voice behind her, and she didn't look up. It was the photographer, Yang. She nodded, about to click out.

"Wait! He comes back." Then, "Actually don't wait, this bit takes about twenty minutes. Nothing really happens. Fast forward and you see him come back in the opposite direction, head down before he vanishes up the street."

"What street is that?" she asked.

"Victoria Street, the Potts Point end, just down from where he was found. Cops say it's the likely last movement before he was stabbed. They think he rendezvoused with someone in that twenty minutes, but it's a dead zone, so..."

"Dead zone?"

"No CCTV on that strip, or none that they can find, so for that missing twenty minutes, they can't say who he met up with."

"Okay," said Frankie, sitting forward and pausing the video, "but maybe we might be able to say where he *went*." She opened Google Chrome and brought up Google Maps. "Victoria Street, Potts Point... Now what's along Victoria Street?"

"Still a busy part of town, Frankie, could be any number of shops, restaurants. Maybe he didn't go anywhere. Maybe he was just standing out of sight, making a call, having a smoke..."

"Or a drink perhaps." Frankie grinned and tapped at a bright orange icon with a martini glass in the middle of the screen. "Maybe he went into a venue for twenty minutes, and *that's* where he met his killer."

She grabbed her bag and headed back to the elevator.

"Now where are you going?" Yang called out.

"To see a bar man called Trevor!" she replied as the elevator snapped shut behind her.

~

Merry got Earle's "back off" message just as she was arriving home after a trip to the supermarket—a twice-weekly ritual, even with Otis now gone.

Odetta thinks Regatta's our man, Earle had written, a long text for him. *Been ordered to stay away from P's place and oval. Let's give it a break tonight and meet @ 9 tomorrow, in front of building. Reassess then.*

She responded with a thumbs-up emoji before opening her boot to haul out the groceries. Merry had gone a little mad this time, bought the kids' favourites—chocolate iceblocks for Archie, so-called superfoods for Lola who was on some newfangled diet—and then thrown in some rump steaks and a cheesecake, just in case Darren was still lurking. Maybe they'd have a lovely sit-down family dinner for a change!

Yet as she unlocked the front door, it was immediately obvious the place was deserted.

"*Hello!* Anybody home? Can you help me with the groceries?" she called out despite knowing the answer.

This old house was in Merry's bones. She knew every creak and groan, every flickering light bulb and humming TV. And there were no such noises now. Then she remembered: Archie was at soccer training (she hoped he'd taken his shin pads this time), and Lola was studying at a friend's place (a likely story but she let that one slide).

And so the place echoed nothing but loneliness.

As Merry dragged the grocery bags in herself, she resisted the urge to leave them unpacked on the kitchen benches and return to Otis's empty room to phone him. It had become an evening ritual. She'd coil up on his bed, phone at one ear, and he'd tell her all the exciting things he'd done that day. Reminding her why it was so important that he live his own life.

Of course he had to live his own life! She did not begrudge him that. She just missed him, terribly. Ached for him, in fact. Pretended to be happy for her eldest child as the tears slid down her face...

Instead, Merry went into autopilot, putting all the groceries away in their requisite places, then stuffing the steaks and the cheesecake deep into the freezer. There would be no happy family dinner tonight.

Then she grabbed her car keys and headed back out.

~

Earle's daughter, Teresa, was standing at the fridge, one arm at her back, the other rubbing her belly, a dreamy look in her eyes, when he walked into the kitchen. Before he had a chance to neutralise his expression, she'd looked up and caught Earle frowning.

Her dreamy look evaporated.

"It's not the end of the world, Dad," she said, slamming the fridge door and folding her arms across her pregnant stomach. "You don't have to catastrophise it."

"You going to tell me who the father is yet, Tess?"

"It's irrelevant."

"I don't see how it's irrelevant! Now Fiona's kicked you out, who else is going to look after you and your child?"

"We will, of course," came a firm voice from the kitchen door, and they both swung around to see Beryl standing there in a snug tracksuit, scruffy slippers on her feet.

Earle had begged her to use some of the Burlington money to buy some nice things for herself, but she just couldn't do it, like she was proud of her old gear. Like she'd be throwing away more than old slippers.

He was quietly grateful she'd been frugal, now they had a mother and child to pay for.

"Thanks *Mum*," said Tess, flashing her father a scowl. "But I don't need you to look after me. I'm not sixteen. And I don't need a man to save me either, Dad. Women can step up and save themselves these days, didn't you get the memo? And we can save anyone else who comes along." She rubbed her belly again and waddled out of the kitchen, leaving Earle to the wrath of Beryl. Which was always so much worse.

"Why do you do this, Earle?" she said, her voice thick with disappointment. "What are you so afraid of?"

"I'm not afraid of anything, Beryl. It's just that we haven't had a chance to book another lovely cruise yet—"

"Who wants to go on another cruise? Pandemic's put me right off."

"It's not just that. We were finally in control of our lives again, Beryl. Thanks to the last case, we could afford to do what we really wanted for once."

"I am doing what I really wanted," she said, sounding confused.

"Well, I'm not! I haven't even had a chance to get my private investigation consultancy up and running yet, and now it's all been smashed to pieces."

"Why is it smashed?" She followed his glance towards the living room where the television was now blaring, and she shook her head at him. "No one's asking you to give up your new business, Earle. Did you really think we would expect you to sit in a rocking chair and mind a baby all day? You didn't do it for *your* child; why would you do it for Tess's?"

Before he could respond to that, Beryl had shuffled out and Earle was left with yet more regrets. Because he *did* know he'd been a dud dad, had always told himself he'd be a better grandfather. But now he was being asked to be a father again, or as good as. He didn't want the responsibility. He just wanted what his old golfing buddies had— the chance to enjoy the little one for a bit, then hand the kid back.

He wanted to be the good cop for a change. The favourite one.

It had nothing to do with laziness or sitting about in rocking chairs. Even less to do with his PI business if he was being honest— because that had gone exactly nowhere since he'd conjured it up six months ago. And it had everything to do with fear. Grandfathers didn't stuff up kids. Only *fathers* did, and he didn't want to be this child's primary male role model.

He'd seen how that had turned out.

CHAPTER 16 ~

A BARMAN CALLED TREVOR

The Taboo Wine Bar on Victoria Street was quiet when Frankie strode in, and it took just a glance towards the leather bar stools to see that Kila was not at his usual perch, a half-drunk schooner of lager in front of him, an untouched glass of lemon squash beside that.

"Too early," Trevor called out as she strode up. "Come back after nine."

"Oh, I'm not looking for Kila, thanks, Trev. It's you I wanted to have a word with."

Trevor's ginger eyebrows shot up. "Okay, that's got me intrigued. No one ever comes in to talk to me. Talk *at* me, sure, but *to* me? Very intriguing. This about Kila? We gonna do an intervention?"

She dropped her bag below a stool and sat on top. "I didn't think he drank *that* much."

"I'm talking about his vigilantism."

"Oh." She smiled sadly. "I'm not sure I want to intervene there. I mean, it is a very depressing way to spend your evenings, but I kind of get it."

He nodded. "Yeah. I know what you mean. He's a good man, our Kila. Okay, this must be about one of your cases then? Do you need a drink for this?"

"Why not? The usual, thanks."

He winked and went to fetch her a large gin and tonic. As he did that, Frankie glanced around. She didn't mind the look of this bar—lots of rustic wood and flattering lighting, soft lounges mixed with leather stools—but would never have thought to stop in here if it weren't for Kila. Located in the hip, inner-city suburb of Potts Point, just down from bustling Kings Cross, it was a popular hang for young people, a bit of a meat market at certain hours, and that was far too predatory for Frankie Jo.

She was above all that.

Of course that's the very reason Kila frequented the place. Not for the picking up, at least not lately, she hoped. He was here to keep any eye on the prey.

Ever since his sister's murder, he'd made it his life calling to protect young girls from predators like Dragon Malone. He couldn't save Chili, but maybe he could save someone just like her.

Frankie sighed and glanced around. She wasn't one for lounging in bars in the best of times, much to her editor's chagrin. While the rest of the team behaved like proper journalists and boozed up after they put the paper to bed, Frankie always headed straight home where her old friend Jan would meet her, bottle of champagne in one hand, bags of fresh food in the other, ready to cook up a feast and hear all about it. In all its glorious detail.

Not lately, of course. Not anymore.

Frankie shoved the thought of Jan away and wondered if Ruffus was right. Maybe she needed to celebrate her stories like a regular team member, not like an idol.

"One gin and tonic, easy on the ice," said Trevor, dropping the tall glass in front of her. "This one's on the house."

"Oh, there's no need."

He waved her off. "Happy to help a member of the Fourth Estate."

She launched in, telling him of the case of the murdered ex-crim. Then produced her phone to show him an image of Phillip Weaver. "His last known movement was in this general area around twelve thirty last Tuesday night. He vanished somewhere for twenty minutes, and I can't help wondering if he came in here for a drink."

Trevor nudged his lips downwards. "Show me the bloke again."

She handed the phone over. "I know it's a long shot, but from what I could see, Taboo is just down from his last known sighting and would be about the only place open at that hour. I mean, I know there are terrace houses and apartments along this strip, so he could have gone into one of those to meet with someone, but…"

He shook his head as he returned the phone. "I don't think so, sorry." Then he noticed a growing queue of customers and said, "Let me just clear these orders."

As he stepped away, Frankie glanced around again. There was a group of young women seated at a nearby booth. They looked comfortable, familiar. Probably regulars she decided and headed over, smartphone in hand.

"Hey there," she said, tone light and conversational. "I'm wondering if I can have a quick word. I'm a reporter for the *Herald* newspaper. My name's Frankie Jo."

They all looked up at her like it meant diddly squat, and she wasn't exactly surprised. They were young. Got their news via Instagram, no doubt. Hence the reason her newspaper job was in peril. She produced the image again.

"Have any of you seen this guy recently? I think he might have come in here for a drink around twelve thirtyish last Tuesday night."

The prettiest in the group took one look at the image, then screwed up her perfect little face and said, "Oh my God. Kill it before it lays eggs!"

Frankie blinked at her. Huh? "Actually, he's already dead. Was stabbed just down the road, two nights ago."

"Oops. Sorry."

Frankie waved her off. "I'm trying to work out what happened. Did any of you see him? *Smell* him, maybe? He was wearing a really full-on aftershave."

"I saw him," said a redhead who had just returned to the table, fresh drink in hand. "He was here about a week or two ago. With some other guy, don't you remember, Sophie? That guy was creepy."

This was exciting news to Frankie, or at least most of it was. "Are you sure it was so long ago? Could it have been Tuesday just past?"

The woman shook her head firmly and then nodded at one of the girls. "You *have* to remember them, Soph!" The woman just shrugged, but she persisted. "They were hassling those Islander girls over by the pool table. Trevor was raging. He pulled them aside. Must've kicked them out because I didn't see them again after that."

"Trevor spoke to them?" Frankie was surprised.

"Pretty sure it was Trev. Why? What happened to them?"

"They were murdered!" squealed the pretty girl, and Frankie shook her head.

"Just this one, actually." She tapped the image of Weaver again. "Can you describe the other guy he was with?"

The redhead slurped what looked like a Tequila Sunrise.

"Tall, skinny, stacks of tatts, like right up the neck and all over his face." She poked out her tongue and said, "Urgh! I mean, I like ink, right?" Then she flashed an elaborate dreamcatcher tattooed on one thigh. "But you leave your face and neck alone. What guy thinks a girl wants to go home with *that*?"

They all eye-rolled vigorously in reply.

"You think that's what they were doing?" Frankie asked. "Trying to pick up?"

The woman looked at Frankie like she was clueless, then turned to the others and said, "Hey, did you catch the babe who just walked in? Oh. My. God."

"I call dibs!" said the pretty girl.

"Nah, he looked at me!" said the redhead.

And with that, Frankie was dismissed.

Returning to her stool, she quickly tapped the information into her Notes app on her smartphone, lest she forget, then glanced around, wondering who else to interview when Trevor returned to her side.

"Okay, that's the wolves at bay for now. Show me this dude again."

Frankie did, adding, "The girls over there reckon he was definitely in here about a week or two ago."

"Really? He doesn't look familiar."

"They said he was with some skinny guy with full neck and face tattoos. Said you spoke to them and kicked them out. Might've been hassling some girls."

"Ah, okay, that makes sense. If they were hassling chicks, I would've evicted them for sure. Kila's been rubbing off on me. But I honestly can't remember this one's face. Sorry. Not everyone's as memorable as you, Frankie." He gave her another wink. "Doesn't mean he wasn't here, just means I was busy that night. In fact, now I think of it, last Tuesday was a shocker. They're usually pretty quiet, but we had a hen's party in, they were wild, and then a bunch of blokes came in after some Rugby match." He looked up from the image. "Is this the case you're working on with Kila?"

Her almond eyes narrowed. "He told you about that one?"

"Nah, but I can tell when he's working a case. Very distracted. Less of the vigilantism." He glanced over at two young blondes giggling in the corner, a trio of men lingering nearby, eyeing them off over their craft lagers. "I might have to step in for him, make sure those two get home safely tonight."

"You're a good man too, Trevor," she said, then asked, "Was he here that night? Kila. Do you know?"

Trevor went to answer, then stopped and frowned. "Would it matter if he was? You don't think *Kila* had something to do with it, do you?"

"What? No!" Frankie was surprised by the suggestion and even more surprised by the way her mind was beginning to gallop in that very direction.

Kila had spent the past few years, trying to protect young women from lechers. It wasn't such a stretch to think he might take it too far one day.

Had Kila been here when this man came in? Had he watched as the ex-crim got sleazy with one of the girls from the hen's party? Weaver was fresh from prison, wasn't such a stretch he'd be looking to hook up. And it wouldn't be so unusual if Kila had followed him out and taught him some manners.

Or was it more specific than that? Had Kila somehow connected Weaver with Dragon? Learned they were prison mates? And had he enacted his own kind of revenge? After all, if he couldn't get to Dragon, maybe his old cell buddy was as good as...

Trevor was watching Frankie closely now, looking almost worried, and she went to say something when her phone beeped with a message. She glanced down at the text and felt her heart lighten.

"Was there anything else?" Trevor asked, eyes still a little squinty.

"Maybe another G&T?" she replied, sending him away lest her lips caught up with her thoughts and she asked Kila's best friend a question she could not take back.

~

It was almost seven on a school night, and Merry wasn't quite sure what she was doing back down at Balmoral Beach. All she knew was that she didn't want to sit in her empty house, waiting for her life to return. And by life, she meant the kids because what other life did she have?

There was no Cluedo championship scheduled for many months, and it was too early to pack her bags and visit Otis in Melbourne. He'd be horrified! He'd only been gone a month!

She could already picture the evening ahead, like it was written in stone.

The kids would return home and instantly vacuum up their dinner, grunting at every question she asked, then fleeing to their bedrooms like she was the Spanish Inquisition. Oh how she missed adult conversation and someone to accompany her in life—to movies, to restaurants, to the nearest couch to watch a romcom. Neither of them were leaving home anytime soon, but she already felt like they were slipping away. And she was all alone.

That wasn't the only reason Merry was here though. She was quietly terrified she'd find herself phoning Darren, inviting him back, and with him all the issues she'd left behind. Like the way he called her Mustard even though he knew she didn't like it and the way he never encouraged her to get a job and always mentioned her weight, like it's the first thing he noticed. And what did he mean she'd shown no interest in driving? She recalled now an early attempt to use a gear stick and how much he'd laughed and told her some people just shouldn't be drivers. And yet she'd discovered she was actually quite a good driver, thanks very much! And she was a bloody good sleuth too, and so she would stalk the Balmoral Esplanade and see if she could come up with any fresh leads on the case.

She'd just parked her car near Prue's block and was glancing around, her confidence suddenly failing, when she spotted a familiar figure standing under a streetlight, glaring at his mobile phone like he wanted to punch it.

Merry smiled and made a beeline to Kila.

The PI's snarl turned into a smile when he saw her approach, and he pocketed the phone and pulled her into a hug like he needed comfort as much as she did.

"What are you still doing here, Festive?"

"I could ask you the same question," she shot back, grinning at Kila's nickname for her, one she simply adored! At least it sounded positive.

"I'm avoiding my house," he said.

She laughed. "That makes two of us!"

"Does yours have a sleazy lawyer parked out the front?"

"What? No just skateboards and stuff. Who's the lawyer?"

He waved that question off. "Truth is, I didn't get very far. I've been catching up with my old mate Bob Taylor, up at the

Gherkin's Head. I'm just back to grab my car, but me thinks I'd better grab some tucker first, soak up all the alcohol." He pointed towards the oval. "I noticed Ballo's serves food at night. Do you want to grab something with me?"

Merry was thrilled by the invitation but automatically went to say no—the kids would be home soon, wondering about their dinner—then she remembered all the grunting and said, "Why the hell not?"

As they strolled along the esplanade towards the beachside café, Merry launched into an account of her children's latest antics—something about soccer and studying and the Spanish Inquisition—and Kila couldn't help smiling. She was a chatty Cathy that was for sure. He loved that about Festive. Wondered why he hadn't stayed in touch with her this past year, like he promised he would. Probably had something to do with all those kids, all that chatter. She had such a full life, no time for ratbags like Kila!

They were just passing a small bookshop when the door burst open and a rotund, redheaded man who looked a little like Ronald McDonald jumped out like he'd been lying in wait for them.

"Hello! Meredith isn't it? Merry Kean? Have I got that right?"

Kila looked at the man and then across to Merry and saw a warm smile ignite her face. It was the first genuine smile he'd seen on her since they'd reunited.

"Yes, hello, Dougie! How are you?"

"I'm great!" He looked proud of himself for some reason. "How are you going with your search? Found that poor young woman yet?" Then his eyes darted across to Kila and back again.

"Oh, not so good," Merry replied. "She's still missing, and it's very distressing. The longer it takes, well, you know?" Then, noticing the man continue to flick glances at Kila, she added, "This is my friend Kila. He's helping us find Nel."

"Oh, okay, great!" And Kila swore the guy had a hint of relief in his voice.

Merry didn't seem to notice. "Hey, how'd you go with your daughter? Any luck?"

He held up a finger. "Can you wait a sec? I can grab her for you!"

Then before they knew it, he was scuttling down the side of his shop, leaving the front door wide open. It was only when he'd reached the end of the narrow lane that he seemed to remember, and he turned back and called out, "Do you mind watching the shop? Won't be a tick!"

Then he vanished behind the building and out of sight.

The sleuths shared a look, and then Kila glanced inside. There was no one about. "He's very trusting."

"I've never worked in a shop before," said Merry. "What if somebody needs us to look up a book or use the cash register or something?"

Kila waved at the street. The bottle shop next door had a few patrons scouring the shelves, and the café next to that had morphed into a rather pretty restaurant complete with twinkling fairy lights and a lively crowd.

"I don't see a rush of book nerds anytime soon. We'll be right. Who is this joker?"

"Oh that's Dougie! Martin and I didn't get a chance to fill you all in yet. Douglas Dollarway is his name. We spoke to him and the other shopkeepers earlier this arvo. Lovely fellow but we didn't have much luck."

"I think your luck might be changing."

He nodded back down the lane, and they saw the man re-emerge with a grumbly looking girl behind him. She was a younger, female version of Dougie, with blue tips added to her hair and minus the dimpled smile.

"My daughter Pip," the shopkeeper explained when he got back to the front, then for Kila's benefit, he added, "Pip opened for me yesterday. I was out fishing until noon. Have you got that picture you showed me, Merry? The one of the missing woman?"

Merry produced her phone, scrolling through it to retrieve the image of Nel while Pip yawned and made no effort to hide it.

"Here she is," said Merry, holding the phone up.

"Take a look, honey," Dougie said, "see for yourself."

The daughter offered them a smile that barely moved her lips and then glanced at the phone Merry was now holding out. She squinted and then said, "May I?"

Merry nodded and handed it over. Pip zeroed in with her fingers.

"Mmm, I've seen her before. Why?"

Merry gasped, delighted, while Dougie looked cross.

"I told you this, Pip! She's missing. Help the people out!"

"I am, Jesus! Chill out!" Then to Merry, "Don't know her name or anything, but I've seen her walk past a few times. Came in the other day. Bought something, don't you remember, Dad?"

Now Dougie looked taken aback. Was that a blush Kila saw creeping up his neck? "No. I think you have that wrong, sweetie."

"I'm eighteen, Dad. *My* memory still works, unlike some." Then she offered him a pointed look in case he didn't know who she was referring to.

Dougie's eyes narrowed behind his Harry Potter glasses. "What book did she buy?"

Pip shrugged like it was inconsequential and stared at Merry with defiance. "She *definitely* came in."

"Okay, that's good to know," she replied, now bouncing on her feet. "So, what day did she come in? Wasn't yesterday was it?"

Kila could swear Merry's fingers were metaphorically crossed.

"Yesterday? Nah. It was Monday... yeah, Monday."

Merry's bouncing stopped. "You're sure it was Monday?" she asked, risking a spray from the snappy teenager.

"Well, I work Mondays and Wednesdays and she didn't come in yesterday, so it had to be Monday." Then, almost flippantly, she added, "But she walked past yesterday, does that help?"

"Yes!" Merry was bouncing again. "What time was this?"

Pip half shrugged. "Not really sure, soz."

Merry wasn't taking that for an answer. "I know you've got a good memory, Pip, so it'd really help if you could try to think." Flattery always worked a treat with kids. "Was it around nine? Nine thirty?"

"Um, okay..." The girl darted glances at her dad. "I know it was when I was opening up, so..."

"We officially open at ten," Dougie chimed in. "But we always fling the doors open ten minutes earlier, just to get the setup ready outside. Pip knows that. So it would've been around 9:50. Five to ten at the latest."

The girl stared at her father. "Nice mansplaining, Dad. But yeah, something like that."

Merry and Kila swapped a triumphant look. Then the PI stepped forward. "Listen, this next question is really important. Did you see this woman with anyone? Anyone at all?"

A quick flip of the hair. "Maybe," Pip replied. "I mean, there was a guy near her, but I can't be sure they were together."

Now Kila was bouncing. Metaphorically, at least.

"Tell us about this man."

"Was he in his thirties?" Merry rushed in. "Blond hair? Kind of preppy-looking?"

Kila frowned. She was leading the witness—it was a classic rookie error—but the girl would not be led anywhere. She was already shaking her head.

"His hair was dark. I know that. But he could've been in his thirties, I guess. I mean, he was a lot older than me. I don't know what you mean by 'preppy,' but he was just ordinary-looking. Might've been wearing yellow?"

Merry's jiggle had stopped. "He had *dark* hair? Are you sure?"

"Maybe it was wet," said the father, clearly keen to help out. "That makes hair look dark. He could've just had a swim!"

The girl frowned at her father like he really was demented, but her certainty didn't waver.

"Nope, it was darker than that. Bit like his." Then she nodded at Kila's chocolate-brown curls.

"Could he have been Indigenous? Or an Islander, like me?" said Kila. His father was from Papua New Guinea, but now she just looked uncertain.

"Hmm, not so sure about that. I think maybe his hair was straighter."

"Okay, forget the hair," said Kila. "Can you remember anything specific about him? Was he carrying a kayak or a paddle? Was he wearing board shorts? Did he have a hat on?" Now *he* was leading the witness, but he couldn't help it. He really wanted to know if that man was Crispin.

The girl was more interested in the woman. "*She* wasn't wearing a hat, I know that. Because I could see her pigtail and it was all kind of, like, messed up and stuff. She looked really sad. I remember that."

"Sad?" Merry and Dougie said together.

"Yeah, she was, like, holding her head and crying and stuff, and the guy was kind of hovering. He looked worried; that's why I thought they were together. I thought maybe they'd had a fight or she'd got some bad news or something. That's why I remember her."

"So, let me just clarify," said Kila. "You saw this woman"—he pointed at Merry's screen again—"walking along the esplanade with a man yesterday morning at around 9:50?"

The girl glanced uncertainly at her father, who was staring at her expectantly, then said, "Yeah, I guess. I mean, that sounds about right."

Merry was bouncing about again, but Kila wasn't quite so excited. As far as he was concerned, Pip's account just confused everything.

After thanking Pip and her father, they excused themselves and continued into the café, although Kila could swear Dougie was lingering longer than he needed to. Hoping for an invitation, perhaps?

They both ordered pasta, then Merry texted her children, telling them to help themselves to leftovers, and Kila gave Pip's statement more consideration.

If Pip's memory was as astute as she boasted, then this cracked the case wide open. They had assumed, from the start, that Nel had been abducted from Balmoral Oval sometime around 9:40 a.m. when, according to Earle's intel, she had called Crispin's mobile. But this bookshop was a good five minutes' walk from the oval and Pip had spotted her ten minutes after that phone call.

He wished he'd thought to ask which direction Nel was walking, but the fact she was with a brown-haired man, not a blond, just seemed to muddy things further.

Merry wouldn't hear of it. "I should've shown her the photo of Crispin—duh! But it has to be him. The timing is perfect! Nel must have *called* him at 9:40, but that doesn't mean that's when they met! They obviously rendezvoused at the café ten minutes later, had a fight—hence the tears—then walked back to the oval, and *that's* when he bopped her over the head, dragged her into his car, and... well you know the rest."

Because it had now been a day and a half since Nel had vanished and Merry's positivity was starting to waver.

"You might be right," he said, but for some reason he felt like Pip had it all wrong or was deflecting, maybe even lying. She had that shifty look in her eyes, the same look he'd seen on too many guilty husbands.

But why would young Pip need to lie about such a thing?

He glanced back at First Chapters and saw Dougie Dollarway still standing just outside his bookshop, watching them closely.

CHAPTER 17 ~
DAY TWO BEGINS...

Martin swallowed a mouthful of fried, free-range eggs and tried not to grimace. The eggs were fine—quite tasty in fact—that was not what was making him grumpy. It was now Thursday morning, and he was due to meet the others at Balmoral soon but for some reason had found himself driving to Olivia's house.

"Another latté?" his mother asked, hovering by her small espresso machine like a bored barista.

"I'm good, thanks, Olivia." She seemed disappointed, so he quickly added, "I'm meeting some people for a coffee soon. More than two coffees and my head is spinning like a Yo-Yo."

"Fair enough." Now there was relief on her face, and he was surprised all over again how quickly he could disappoint her.

Yet it was himself he was disappointed with.

Martin had told himself to stop doing this, stop dropping in on her at all hours. It was cruel and unnecessary punishment, especially in the light of the future plans he had that did not involve cosy breakfasts with his so-called mother.

"Thanks again for the wine," she said, now leaning against the bench, clutching her own mug to her chest, her eyes on the unopened bottle of shiraz he'd presented earlier. "But I didn't really do much. It was just a phone call."

Yet it wasn't just any phone call.

Olivia had done him a massive favour, calling the estate agent listed on the apartment for sale in Rachelle Easterly's building, the one that looked in on Nel's bedroom. Rachelle had insisted it was off the market, but he didn't believe that for a moment. And sure enough, the agent had been delighted to hear from Olivia and assured her the unit was still "very much available". She was welcome to inspect it any time.

"How did you know the owner was lying to you?" Olivia asked him now.

"It's just a vibe I got," he said, not adding that he was an expert at lying, knew all the signs. "In my experience, sellers always hedge their bets. Even if there was another interested buyer, most try to hook you in just in case that deal falls over. Rachelle couldn't get rid of me fast enough. I suspected she just didn't want *me* to see it. The real question is—why?"

"The agent said I could inspect whenever I was ready," said Olivia. "I just have to tee it up with Rachelle directly. Do you want me to do that? Dig around a bit for you?"

He shook his head. Felt a little foolish suddenly. "Doesn't matter now anyway, Olivia. Turns out they've got some totally unrelated suspect in custody, a guy they think Nel might have been having an affair with. I think the case is coming to a close."

"Oh well, that's good, I guess. Better to have some answers, yeah? And now you can get back to your new book. I can't wait to read your next Flynn Bold adventure!"

"Actually, I'm trying something new. Something more literary."

"Oh... well, I'm sure it'll be just as great. What's this one about?"

He shrugged. "Still formulating it at this stage." Then, keen to change the subject, "I've been offered a good price on my apartment, did I tell you? So I'll have to find a new house soon if I want to accept. Otherwise I'll be homeless."

"You know you can always move in here," Olivia told him, her voice suddenly very soft. "You know that, Brax... I mean Martin. You've always got a home with me."

He pushed his plate aside and stood up, noticed that she flinched. She did that when he made a sudden movement. Like he was his father and was about to produce a fist. It made him sad to see it— and scared too. Almost as scared as she was. He didn't like the idea of coming from violent descendancy.

"I've got to run," he said gently. "Thanks for the breaky. Again."

"Oh, always welcome, you know that, honey."

Then he got out of there before she started moving him in.

~

Frankie licked her lips and felt how dry they were, reached for the glass of water she kept by her bedside, then remembered where she was. Shit! She sat up with a start, grappled for her phone—8:18 a.m. —and then glanced down to the bulky figure in the bedsheets.

Shit, shit, shit! This should not have happened. She should have learned her lesson last time. *So much for being above all that.*

Carefully she plucked her way off the bed, terrified of waking him. The reporter knew first-hand what the consequences were and wouldn't suffer that fate again.

She should have left last night. Should never have come in the first place.

As she softly scooped up her things—lacy underwear, designer suit, stilettoes—Frankie made a quick pit stop to the bathroom, then threw her gear on, snatched up her handbag and scuttled for the door.

Clicking it open quietly, she held her breath, waited a beat, then looked outside, one way, then another, before stepping out quickly and closing the door gently behind her. Inhaling deeply now, she glanced up and down the street one more time, then put her head down and raced towards her car, falling into it as though into a rescuer's embrace.

Only when she had driven three blocks, did Frankie take time to calm her breathing. Inhaling. Exhaling. Inhaling. Exhaling.

Remember what the mindfulness teacher told you: Breath is the elixir of life. Breath will save you. Breath will get you through.

At the first set of lights, Frankie was feeling more centred. She scraped fingers through her tussled locks, then flipped open the mirror above her head and groaned at her reflection before swiping a finger under both eyes. Then she reached for her make-up bag in the glove compartment.

Three sets of lights later, the renovations were done—fresh mascara on her lashes, touch of foundation on the cheeks, a daub of subtle lip gloss. By the time she got across the bridge, Frankie's breathing was back to normal and she looked as fresh as a daisy. Just two more steps to go. She reached across to the back seat and tugged a clean blouse from a hanger she kept there, then waited until the next lights before whipping the old one off and pulling the new one on—delighting a group of boys in a school bus close by—then she plucked an extra strong mint from a container by the gearstick, chewing on it madly as she smiled to herself.

Another successful escape.

~

As the waves gently lapped the shores of Balmoral Beach, the team sat at a nearby wooden table and sipped takeaway coffees and reconsidered the evidence. It was just after nine a.m. Nel had been missing for forty-eight hours and everyone agreed things were heating up, and fast.

Yesterday afternoon, they had all dispersed to track down different leads and had so much to report—Kila and Frankie hadn't yet divulged their interview with Bob Taylor nor had Merry had a chance to tell the others what young Pip Dollarway had said last night.

But it all felt like background noise in the light of the evidence against Crispin Regatta.

They had to agree, he was the most logical suspect. He knew Nel—either as a fleeting encounter, if you believed his mobile phone story, or as a lover, if his wife's suspicions were correct—and had admitted to interacting with her the morning she vanished.

What that interaction really entailed was still open to conjecture.

"Odetta's working the Regatta angle hard, should have more on him this morning," said Earle. "It took a while to get a search warrant for the vehicle, but they've seized it now and are going through it this morning, also accessing his phone records, looking at any street cameras in the vicinity, interviewing potential witnesses, including the residents of Bellavista. Which is why she needs us to keep away."

Then, before the usual suspects started moaning, he added, "Of course we're here on the invitation of Prue Chambers and have been officially hired for three days, so there's no reason we can't keep the momentum going—as long as we give the building a wide berth. Maybe Regatta is guilty; maybe he's not. Doesn't change the fact we still haven't located young Nel. I want to keep at it. We just have to do it at arm's length so we don't inadvertently contaminate any evidence."

"Oh, he's guilty all right," said Kila, eyeing off the large cappuccino in Earle's hand.

Kila was late this morning, hadn't had a chance yet to grab one. He filled them in now on what his old gumshoe pal Bob Taylor had told them—or tried to tell them via a clumsy metaphor—as well as the conversation they'd had with Emma Regatta.

"Frankie and I wonder if Crispin was having an affair with Nel and she threatened to reveal all to his wife, so she had to be silenced. According to Emma, there would be no more second chances. Or twenty-second chances by the sound of him." He rubbed his stubble. "I do not get why women stay with cheating men."

Merry flinched at that, and Kila noticed.

He reached out a hand. "But you *didn't* stay with your cheating husband, Merry. I'm not talking about you. You're better than that."

She swallowed hard. Offered a bright nod.

Despite their lovely meal last night, Merry hadn't told Kila just how close she'd come to calling Darren. Even when she'd got home late, buzzing after her dinner out, the kids hadn't asked where she'd been. Like she'd just come in from the clothesline! Instead, Lola launched into hysterics about her upcoming exam, and Archie barely looked up from the video game he was playing. She'd calmed Lola down—"Just do your best. That's all I ever ask!"—then confiscated Archie's PlayStation—"No games on school nights! You know that!"—before heading to her own room and its large empty bed and the landline beside it.

It took all her energy not to phone Darren. Or Otis for that matter.

"Anyhoo," she said, shaking off her melancholy, "I hear what you're saying, Kila. But what if we're looking at this the wrong way? What if *Emma Regatta* is the one responsible? Maybe the long-suffering wife just ran out of tolerance. Maybe she caught him with yet another woman and overreacted. Maybe he helped her after the fact; maybe he didn't. Maybe Nel really did walk away after her rendezvous with Crispin that morning, and Emma followed Nel and…"

"Smacked her over the head? Overpowered her? Sorry, Festive, but I'm just not buying it," said Kila. "I've seen Emma for myself. She looks like she eats lettuce leaves for dinner. According to Prue, Nel was almost six foot, athletic, strong."

"Yes, but if she surprised her from behind," said Merry.

"Never underestimate the power of a woman scorned," said Frankie, surprising Merry by agreeing with her for a change. Then she surprised them all by happily handing over her half-drunk coffee to Kila.

He thanked her and took it without a second glance, and this, too, surprised Merry, who was about to comment when Earle began pointing towards Prue's building where a familiar white sedan was just pulling in.

"Odetta's here," he said. "I hope this doesn't mean there's bad news."

"Oh no," said Merry at the exact time Frankie said, "Great!"

Then the reporter smiled apologetically and added, "I just mean, it's good to get some movement, right?"

"Sure, if you're a ruthless reporter itching for a story," said Martin, clearly still grumpy with the way she'd dismissed his ideas yesterday.

"Honey, I'm sorry I was so abrupt yesterday," she said. "But you don't need to be rude either. I was just trying to say that crime fiction is very far removed from the real world. It's light entertainment. Not to be taken seriously."

"*Never underestimate the power* of a story well told," he replied, slapping her quote back at her. "My light entertainment happens to be taken seriously by a lot of my readers, including my mum."

"You're in touch with your mum?" Merry asked, and he looked at her like he'd been sprung.

"I'm heading over," said Earle, clambering to his feet. Tired of their spats. "I'll see what's going on."

"Hang on," said Merry. "I haven't told you what Pip Dollarway said yet!"

Earle turned back. "Pip who?" Then, "We'll talk later. I don't want to miss Odetta."

"Okay then, good luck!" Merry sang out.

Kila stood up and stretched. "I'm grabbing a cuppa. Anyone need anything? Tea? Latté? Goat's milk macchiato with a twist of lemon for you, Martin?"

Martin's frown deepened, but before he could respond, Merry was scrambling to her feet.

"I'll come with you!" she said. "I could do with another caffeine hit."

But it wasn't coffee Merry was after. It was company. And friendly company at that.

~

Odetta had her mobile phone at one ear when Earle caught up with her at the entrance to Prue's apartment block. He took one look at her face and knew the score.

"I'm on hold," she told him, but her expression spoke volumes.

"Grim news?" he said, watching as Constable Logan did an about-turn and headed back to the sedan.

"Too grim for this stunning day." Odetta looked past him to the cloudless sky, then back. "We found blood. In the back of Regatta's Jeep."

Earle's shoulders slumped as she added, "There wasn't a lot but enough to know it's the same blood type as Nel's."

CHAPTER 18 ~
THE GRIMMEST OF NEWS

Earle waited patiently on the pavement in front of Bellavista as the detective finished her call, his eyes drifting across to the sleuths. Kila and Merry had gone walkabout, but Martin and Frankie were still at the table, and whatever Martin was saying, Frankie was not agreeing. She had her hands raised in a dramatic gesture, and he was shaking his head over and over.

Earle smiled sadly suddenly. And not just for the Chambers.

They were certainly a motley crew, these supersleuths that Sir George and Verity had first brought together, as different from each other as five personalities could be. Yet somehow, together, they got results. They worked.

Except now it seemed there was no more work to do...

"Sorry about that," said Odetta, ending the call. She looked more flummoxed now than grim. "Um, what was I saying? Oh yeah, we impounded Regatta's vehicle, found blood in the back. Of course we'll get it matched for Nel's DNA, but it doesn't look good."

She glanced up towards Prue's apartment, exhaled again.

Earle agreed. There could be no good reason Nel's blood should be in Regatta's vehicle. Especially if you believed his story that he'd never met the woman before that fateful morning. "At least you're giving the mother some answers, Odetta. That counts for something. And even better, at least you've got one more killer off the streets."

"If indeed he is a killer," she said, surprising him.

"You think Regatta could be innocent?"

"I don't, that's for sure. He's a lying bastard, has told porkies from the start..."

"But?"

Her scowl deepened. "That was Morgan." They shared a silent grimace. "Regatta wants to change his story. His lawyer says he can

134

SMART GIRLS DON'T TRUST STRANGERS

explain the blood and it has nothing to do with any abduction."

"I'd like to hear that," Earle scoffed.

"*Apparently*," she said, giving that word all the emphasis she felt it deserved, "Nel dialled Regatta's mobile number, like he said, and they could both hear it ringing at the back of the four-wheel drive. He says the tailgate was open and there was an *accident* when she leaned in to look for the phone. Apparently one of his surfboards was resting up against the back seat and fell down and hit her on the head."

Earle snorted. He'd heard some unlikely stories in his time.

"I know. Absurd. But he insists that's what caused the blood. There was a 'minor cut' to the back of the head, and then she walked away and he drove home. He's sticking to that story. His latest story."

"Why didn't Regatta say all this earlier?"

"Lawyer claims he was afraid of the consequences, that he'd be charged with reckless endangerment over the surfboard or something. But now we're accusing him of abduction and suspected homicide he's happy to take that rap. Decided to come clean on the flying surfboard incident."

"*Alleged* flying surfboard," said Earle. "Surely you don't believe him."

"Course not. More like flying pigs, if you ask me. Did I tell you we clocked his Jeep Wrangler driving past the traffic camera up at the corner of Spit Junction? At 9:52 that morning, twelve minutes after she called his mobile. That's plenty of time to stash her in the back, chuck a few towels over the top, and drive to that junction. The wife has already told us he returned home just in time for his ten-o'clock Zoom meeting, and that meeting has also been confirmed. So what I want to know is, where is Nel? Where's her body? It's not in his house, not in his car. Not down here, from what we can see."

"He must've kept her in the car and moved her later that same day," Earle said, heart sinking again.

Odetta agreed. "We'll have to sift through more CCTV, reinterview witnesses, but for now..." She glanced back towards Prue's apartment and looked suddenly very tired. "Look, I'm not even going to mention Regatta's latest porky. It'll just confuse matters. I'll simply explain that we have someone in custody, evidence of foul play. Keep it general if I can manage it. She doesn't want to know the details."

"She'll want to know where her daughter is, so I wish you luck on that front. I gather from Regatta's latest deflection, you're not going to learn that in a hurry. But it doesn't sound good."

"No, it doesn't. Why can't they ever just roll over and confess? Like in one of Martin's Flynn Bold mysteries."

Earle blinked. "I didn't think you recognised Martin?"

"Of course I recognised the great Martin Chase. Just didn't want to give him the satisfaction."

Then they both smiled at that, and it felt incongruous considering her next mission. She swallowed it back down.

"Listen, where's that Irish woman? It'd be good to have her here. I know Mrs Chambers is alone up there, and she's going to need some support."

Good question, thought Earle. He hadn't seen or heard from Verity Vine since she'd headed off yesterday afternoon. "I can call her, if you like. Ask her to come ASAP."

"Do that please." Then she signalled for Logan, who jumped out of the car where he'd sat, as though offering them privacy.

Or perhaps he was distancing himself, thought Earle. A smart move. He didn't want to get into Morgan's bad books.

"Thanks for everything," Odetta was saying. "And I mean that."

Then they made their way slowly into Prue's building to break the grim news.

Earle had to break the news too, first via a phone call to Verity, who promised to come straight back, then to his fellow sleuths, who were together again at the table by the beach.

"Looks like it's game over," he said as he took his seat and outlined what Odetta had learned.

Unsurprisingly, Frankie wouldn't hear of it. "So, they found blood? It's not a body. I say we keep on it! Like you said before, Earle, we were hired for three days, and it's only been two. Besides, you haven't heard what Merry and Kila discovered from Pip last night."

And with that Merry repeated exactly what the bookshop owner's daughter had told her, almost verbatim. "She saw Nel walking with some bloke around 9:50 that morning."

Earle frowned. "That can't be right, Merry. The timeline doesn't fit.'"

"Yes, it does!"

Then, her voice a little whiney, she asked, "Why? What are you saying?"

"Exactly that. The timeline does not quite work. Odetta has Regatta's Jeep passing the camera up at the corner of Spit Junction at that time. Nine fifty-two to be precise."

"How long's the drive? From here to that camera?" asked Frankie.

"Not two minutes, I can tell you that," he replied.

"Pip probably just got her timing a bit off," said Merry. "She was a little uncertain about that, did you notice Kila?"

"And the hair colour and the man's age," he said. "She thought he *might* be wearing yellow, couldn't even say if he was Indigenous."

"Young people are terrible witnesses when it comes to details," said Earle.

"That is true." Merry had to concur. "My kids think everybody over the age of twenty-five looks ancient."

"I'll pass that information to Odetta," Earle told Merry, "but as far as I'm concerned, it just confuses things. Perhaps Pip saw Nel earlier than she thought or on a different day? Or perhaps she saw a different woman entirely. Either way, I'm not sure it matters now. The evidence against Regatta is compelling. Nel called his mobile. Directly. He confesses to meeting her that morning. Her blood is present in his vehicle. I don't think anybody believes his flying surfboard story. Odetta thinks he's guilty. So do I."

"So that's it then?" said Martin. "It really is case closed?"

"But we haven't found the poor girl's..." Merry's lips drooped southwards.

Earle knew what she meant, but it wasn't their job to find Nel's body. They had been hired to find Nel Chambers alive. They had been given three days to do it, and by the sounds of things, they had failed.

He said, "I'll wait around and talk to Verity, double-check what George wants us to do. She's on her way down now to be with Prue. It could take a while, so I'd suggest the rest of you head off."

He cleared his throat, hesitated for a few beats.

Then Earle said, "Now they've found what they believe to be Nel's blood in Crispin Regatta's car, Odetta's team will switch gears and start searching for a body, I'm sorry to say. My guess, from past experience, is that Regatta disposed of the young woman late that evening. Waited until his wife was asleep, then drove somewhere remote. If we're lucky, they'll catch his Jeep on CCTV footage at a service station somewhere."

But that didn't sound lucky to any of them.

CHAPTER 19 ~

AND SO THEY SCATTER

Merry was not yet ready to return to her silent house. Again. She knew exactly where that would end up. If she didn't phone Darren—how had he managed to ingratiate himself so quickly?—she'd probably find herself back in Otis's old bedroom, hugging his pillow.

She was depressed enough as it was and not just about how the case had turned out—poor Prue, poor *Nel.* Merry was also disappointed by the way everyone had abandoned ship so willingly, so quickly! There was barely a goodbye, just another empty promise to keep in touch. But why would they? They hadn't last time.

She strode back to the oval where she'd parked her car and noticed the police tape strung up around one parking bay.

That's where they'd found Nel's cap.

That's where Nel had met her fate.

Merry shivered just as voice called out, "Mary!"

She swung around to find Pip Dollarway running towards her, a worried expression on her face.

"Hi, Pip," she said, adding, "But my name's Merry, as in Merry Christmas." Then she went to giggle and stopped. It was an old joke, and she wasn't feeling festive.

"Okay, well, whatever," said the girl, glancing back towards the bookshop her father owned. "Um, so, how's the case going and stuff? Did you tell the police what I said?"

Her face was awash with anxiety, and Merry wasn't quite sure why. She said, "Actually, the police have a suspect now, but we will mention it to them, yes."

"Oh, okay. Right."

The anxiety had not diminished, so Merry said, "Everything okay?"

"Yeah, yeah." Pip thrust her hands into the pockets of her high-cut jeans and glanced back towards First Chapters again.

Yet still she loitered, so Merry announced, "I was just about to do a lap of the oval, if these old legs will let me. Fancy a walk?"

The truth was, Merry didn't really care for exercise; she just had a hunch Pip had something important to tell her, and she knew the best way to get kids talking was to get them, well, *walking*. Eye-balling youngsters never worked. She was reminded of that at the dining table every night.

Pip threw another glance her father's way, then said, "Okay, sure."

~

"Come on, Kila, please!" said Frankie. "I don't ask you for much."

The two sleuths had not moved far from Balmoral either, recamping to the Gherkin's Head Sports Bar, which was not far from Spit Junction and the camera that had snapped Crispin's Jeep passing by that fateful morning.

But Frankie hadn't dragged Kila there to discuss that.

Her mind was on another case, another criminal, one she was desperate to interview—Phillip Weaver's ex-cell buddy, Dragon Malone. Despite her pleas, however, Dragon had refused to talk to her—via phone or in person. Until she had dropped the bait, that is. She was a friend of Kila Morea's. Did that help?

Suddenly Dragon couldn't wait to chat. But it had to be in person, and she had to bring Kila with her.

Those conditions were non-negotiable, so now Frankie needed to convince Kila. And she needed to do it in private, away from their usual haunts. Images of that scratch along his brand-new Toyota kept circling through her brain.

"Please," she said again, sipping a bottle of Corona while he stared up at an overhead television that was broadcasting an American baseball game. She grabbed his face and drew it to her. "I can't do this without you. You're my only way in."

"So *now* you want me?" he said, his voice half teasing. But she could hear the catch in his throat. He shook himself free. "I am not talking to that bastard so you can sell papers, Frankie. I don't give a shit about the *Herald*."

"Then what about me?"

She batted her eyelids ever so slightly, and he smirked.

"You're seriously going to try to win me over with that shit?"

She laughed just as that blasted car scratch flitted in front of her eyes again. "Look." Frankie's voice turned serious. "Dragon shared a cell with the victim. Who knows what else they shared? He could hold the key! Come on, Kila. You're a moral crusader. Don't you want to catch a killer?"

"A killer of a convicted criminal? Yeah, nah, I'm good, thanks. The world's a better place without him."

Frankie frowned now, remembering how she'd suspected Kila of doing the killing.

Did she still?

She dropped the frown. Just couldn't see it. But she could see him getting her access to the victim's cell mate, Dragon Malone. And she could see the exclusive articles that access would deliver.

"You'll do anything for a story, won't you?" he said, reading her mind as he often did.

"That is not true!" she replied, even though she knew damn well it was.

Frankie had a flashback now of a sleazy politician, an even sleazier night out where she managed to wheedle a story of government corruption out of him, then sit back and win her first journalism award for Scoop of the Year while he was unceremoniously dumped from Parliament and then took his own life.

Not her finest hour.

Now *Jan* was flashing through Frankie's thoughts. Her old bestie had not only witnessed her unethical wheedling—yes, Frankie had slept with him to get the story, yes she had also told him everything he said was off the record—but had helped her cover it up for years afterwards. Then used that cover up to cement their friendship. A kind of friendly blackmail if you will.

"Don't stress, Frankie. You'll find another way," said Kila, misreading her thoughts this time, and who could blame him?

She was all over the shop this morning!

Giving her head a good shake, she said, "There is no other way, Kila. I've really tried. I know this is hard for you. I know it's a massive ask, but Dragon won't see me. Not unless you're with me. That's his one condition."

"How does he even know we're mates?" Then, "Oh you *didn't*?"

"It was collateral. He was really frosty. So I got in touch with his lawyer. I might've thrown your name in the mix, and... well, he defrosted suddenly."

Kila shoved a hand through his long curls, like he was taking his anger out on them.

"I'm sorry," she said (another fib), "but I'm desperate. Are you going to help me or not?"

"Not."

She pouted at him. He looked away. She moved into his line of vision. He shook his messy curls at her. "Sorry, Sexy Reporter Girl, but there is absolutely no way I am going to waste my time talking to that dirtbag, let alone take you with me. I'm not letting you anywhere near him. So forget it. Okay? It will never happen."

"I thought you were all about helping damsels in distress." It was her trump card, but it didn't work.

He laughed heartily at that. "Oh Frankie, I'd *never* call you a damsel! I wouldn't dare!"

Then he laughed some more, but Frankie wasn't listening now. She was staring at one of the many television sets, this one above the bar. The baseball game had been interrupted for a breaking news story.

"Is that Nel Chambers?" she said, sitting forward, pointing upwards.

Kila followed her gaze to the TV, where a picture of Nel was, indeed, being plastered across the screen. It was one of the photos Frankie had seen sitting beside Prue's old landline telephone just yesterday morning.

The screen then cut to another familiar face, and Frankie felt her blood run cold. She leapt from her stool, nearly toppling it over, and yelled at the barman to pump up the volume. Then she held her breath as the Channel Seven reporter, Timothy (Bad Tie) Tagger, proceeded to tell *her* all about "a missing twenty-six-year-old woman from Balmoral Beach". Like he was breaking the news—and getting his facts wrong while he was at it.

"How did he—?" began Kila, but she held a finger up.

"Shhh!" Then glared at the screen as an image of Crispin Regatta appeared. It was the same image she had downloaded from his company website.

Tagger's voice could be heard saying, "A businessman from Mosman is currently assisting police with their enquiries," just as footage of the blue front door of Regatta's house was shown, all the blinds drawn. A moment later Tagger was back, smirking this time (Frankie was sure that was a smirk) as he chatted like some kind of expert to the anchorwoman who'd asked some leading question:

"That's exactly right, Jenny," he was saying. "Police tell me they're still hopeful of finding Nel Chambers alive but hold grave fears for her safety and are asking anyone who has any information—anything at all—to come forward or contact Crime Stoppers."

As he rattled off an 1800-number, Frankie grabbed her bag.

"Shit, shit, shit! Why didn't Prue tell me that was breaking? Why didn't *Verity*?"

Kila shrugged. "Maybe they didn't know."

She turned to offer him a withering look. "Tagger didn't get that photo of Nel by *osmosis*!"

Then she fled the bar, leaving him staring up at the baseball game, which had resumed like nothing had happened.

~

Pip and Merry had almost completed a lap of the oval, and Merry was fast running out of small talk. She had learned that Pip was an only child and her parents had divorced when she was "just a bub", so she shared her time equally between both households—although she much preferred Dad's place, just don't tell her mother! She also learned Pip loathed school more than she loathed all her ex-boyfriends combined (apparently there were three and none of them had been particularly nice), and so she had dropped out the minute she turned seventeen and was now working weekends in a café near her mum's place (just a bus ride away) and in her dad's bookshop on Mondays and Wednesdays (but it was the most boring shop, *ever*!).

"That's how you first saw Nel," Merry said, noticing her fall silent again the moment the woman's name was brought up.

Okay, enough with the small talk. "So, what is it you want to tell me, honey?" Merry asked, and the girl looked at her, surprised, so she added, "I'm sure it's not as bad as you think."

Pip's face suddenly contorted, and she looked like she was five years old and had been busted with her hand in the cookie jar.

Pip said, "Okay, well, it's about Nel."

"Oh yeah?" Merry had already figured that out.

"I didn't quite tell you the truth yesterday."

Merry nodded. Yep, she'd figured that too. "You didn't really see her, did you?" Poor Pip. Probably wanted to impress her father so much she'd fabricated the whole thing.

The girl stopped walking. "What? No! I saw her. For sure!"

"*Really?*" said Merry, still not quite believing, because she'd heard all the evidence from Earle, and it was quite clear—from the blood in Crispin's car to the CCTV footage—that Nel Chambers was in the back of Crispin's Jeep at 9:52 a.m. when he passed that camera up the road from here. Pip simply could not have seen Nel strolling past the bookshop alive and well at around the same time.

It didn't add up.

"I did see her! I know I did!" the girl persisted. "It's just... I lied about the time."

Oh. Okay, that also made sense. "So you saw her earlier? Yes? Earlier than 9:50?"

Again the girl looked confused. "No! I saw her later. Much later." Then she glanced around like someone might overhear, face contorted again. "I slept in that morning. I didn't open for Dad like I was supposed to. He goes fishing on Wednesdays, right? And it's my job to get the shop open, but, well... I was late. But I couldn't very well say that, could I? Not with him listening!"

"Okay, so when did you open?"

"More like ten past ten, at the *earliest*. Probably ten fifteen. Yeah, ten fifteen for sure! Does that make a difference?"

Merry blinked. Yes, it jolly well did! "You think you saw Nel after ten on Wednesday morning? Are you sure? Because the police think she was well and truly abducted by then."

Dead, no doubt, thought Merry, but she didn't want to go into the gory details.

"It was definitely well after ten because that's when Dad called me and woke me and said, 'Are you in the shop?' like he's clairvoyant or something. So I said, 'Yah, of course!' Then I dragged on some clothes and bolted down there so it had to be 10:10 at the earliest. That's when I saw her. The missing woman. She was walking past—"

"In which direction?"

"What? Um, that way." Pip pointed away from the oval, back towards the shop.

"Hang on," said Merry. "Are you saying, Nel was heading *away* from the oval, like, back to her apartment?"

She shrugged. "I don't know where she lives, but yeah, I guess."

Merry frowned. This, too, was new.

"Anyway," said Pip, "when I flung the shop door open, she looked really startled, you know? Like I'd given her a shock. That's how I know she was crying because she stared straight at me and she had tears in her eyes. But it was definitely later than I told you. I mean, not by much, but you guys seemed so fixated with the time, so… well, I thought I should fess up."

"Huh." Merry exhaled. Held a hand out to brush Pip's arm. "Listen, I'm glad you did, but I wonder whether you're mistaken. I'm not saying you didn't see a crying woman at that hour, but it can't have been our missing Nel, honey. The police already have a suspect, and he was seen leaving the area half an hour earlier—by a street camera, and they don't lie."

Merry debated herself for a second, then continued. "The police think he had Nel in the back of his car then, most likely dead. It's shocking, I know. But she can't be in two places at once. So you must have that wrong. You must have seen someone else."

"Huh," said Pip now, echoing Merry.

Merry offered her a warm smile. Gave her arm another rub. "It's so lovely you want to help. But I'm sad to say none of us have been able to help Nel. The police have the horrible man in custody, and they will find out what happened."

"Okay, I guess that makes sense." Pip's voice was so much lighter as they continued to walk again. "It must've been somebody else. Sorry about that. Makes more sense now why you didn't mention the tatt."

Merry stopped walking. "Tatt?"

"Yeah." She stopped, too, and pulled her hair into a topknot. "It just seems like something you'd mention if you were searching for someone."

"*Tattoo?*" Merry said again, louder.

She'd forgotten all about Nel's tattoo. Prue had made out that it was insignificant. Not something anyone would notice. That Nel covered it up anyway. "Tell me about the tattoo," she said, trying to keep her voice steady.

Pip pulled her sleeve up to reveal two small lines of black ink running down one shoulder, in some sort of decorative script she could not decipher.

"Mum went *off* when I got this," Pip said, like her mother was the fool, not her. Then added, "It's Sanskrit for Love and Friendship. The woman I saw had the exact same one. We probably went to the same tattooist!"

She smiled, but now Merry's head was spinning and she had to confess, she had *not* been expecting Pip to say that.

CHAPTER 20 ~

INKY MATTERS

Earle looked up from the newspaper he'd just bought to kill some time and was surprised to see Merry waving her hands frantically as she dashed in his direction. What was she still doing at Balmoral? He thought she'd left ages ago.

The others had cleared off, and he should have left too. Should be home, with his family, facing his own reality. But he hadn't had a chance to talk to Verity yet, let alone Odetta, who were both still holed up inside with Prue. He wasn't sure he was even going to mention Pip's witness statement, felt like it just confused matters.

Now, it seemed, things were about to get even more confusing, because Merry was upon him and rambling about Pip again and how she'd changed her story. And everything was wrong, wrong, wrong!

"Crispin didn't hurt her! Or if he *did* hurt her, then she wasn't killed when we thought she was!" Merry announced, her words tumbling into each other. "Or maybe she wasn't killed at all! Pip saw Nel at ten fifteen a.m. *Ten fifteen*! She was walking away from the oval, back towards her mum's apartment! And that's not all she saw!"

"Whoa, hang on, Merry!" said Earle, waving her into the seat beside him. "Take a breath. Say all that again, but slower."

Merry plonked down, inhaled deeply, and then launched into what Pip had just told her while Earle stared at her, perplexed.

"I know!" she said. "It sounds crazy to me too, but I believe her. I really do!"

"Merry. Young Pip might think she's being helpful, but she's a very unreliable witness. First time you spoke to her she didn't know the age of the man with the woman, got the hair colour wrong, and now she admits to lying about the time she saw them. I think we can safely dismiss what she has to—"

"She saw the tattoo!"

"What tattoo?"

"*Nel's* tattoo, the one Prue told us about—with the line about Love and Peace? Except it doesn't say Peace, it says Friendship. In Sanskrit!"

He frowned. Like Merry—like all of them it would seem—he'd completely forgotten about that. Okay, that was a coincidence, and he didn't like coincidences, but he also didn't like loose ends, and this was a mighty great one. "She can't be the only woman in the world with that tattoo."

"She's not! Pip has one too. Look!" Merry produced a photo she'd just taken with her phone of Pip's shoulder. "This is Pip's tattoo. The woman Pip saw had the exact same words scribbled down her back shoulder, just as Prue said she did. But Pip didn't see her at 9:50, she saw her at *ten fifteen*! Over twenty minutes later! And I believe her, by the way, because kids don't confess to a lie, not if they don't have to."

She stopped, drew breath. Launched again: "I say we show this picture to Prue and see what she thinks. See if it really is the same as Nel's tattoo."

Earle balked at that. He did not want to upset the mother any more than he had to.

Reading his mind, Merry said, "It might actually cheer her up. Might give her some hope."

"But false hope?"

"I know… but it's that thing you like—evidence. I don't think we can ignore it."

"Odetta's got the suspect, Merry. He's admitted to meeting Nel. He's admitted to hurting her, to the blood in the car. Of course he has his own explanation for that, but Odetta and I do not believe him."

"But what if it's true? What if it really was an accident and she really did walk away? It fits perfectly with what Pip is saying. Nel hits her head, blood splashes about, and then she heads home, back towards her building. That timeline would fit perfectly. By the time she got to the front of the bookshop—where Pip saw her—"

"Allegedly."

"—it would be closer to ten fifteen. Don't you see? Crispin could be telling the truth and for all we know, Nel could still be out here, somewhere, waiting to be found! Or maybe…" She stopped, swallowed, didn't look happy suddenly. "Maybe she's with somebody else—a man with brown hair—just like Pip said she was!"

~

By the time she got to the *Herald* office, Frankie was fuming. She didn't know who to be angrier with—Odetta for leaking the Nel Chambers story without telling her, Verity for not informing her as she promised she would, Prue for handing over that precious family snap, or Tagger for stealing what should have been her exclusive. *Her story!* A story she'd been working on for days! Just wait until she got her mittens on all of them!

Turns out, it was Frankie who was about to get her comeuppance.

The moment she stepped out of the elevator, Ruffus was upon her. The editor dragged her into his office, slammed the door hard, then pointed to one of several screens on his desk, this one with an image paused on the face of Nel Chambers. Beneath it were the words POLICE CLOSE IN ON MISSING WOMAN.

"You know anything about this story? Some missing person story down in Balmoral? How did we miss this one?"

Frankie took a deep breath. "Actually, I do know about that story. I've... well, I've been working that case for days. I just wasn't allowed to say anything yet. The police said—"

"The *police*? Who cares about the police? Last time I looked you worked for the *Herald*. For me! Not the cops. They don't get to decide whether a story runs or not. Why didn't you tell me about this woman? You know our readers lap this shit up."

"I know, but—"

"Is this where you've been all this time? Working this missing person case?"

"Yes! I've got the inside track."

"It doesn't bloody look like it!" He slapped a hand at the screen. "Channel Seven are all over it, the ABC and the *Tele* are playing catch-up, and we haven't got so much as a blog post about it. Where have you been?" He leaned closer. "Is that beer I can smell on your breath?"

"What? No, I mean, I was trying to lure a lead out of a guy I know."

"A lead on this case?"

"Actually, no, on the Kings Cross murder. Phillip Weaver."

He looked confused for a moment, then held his arms up. "Oh, that's a relief, Frankie, because for a moment there I thought you'd dropped the ball on that story entirely." His voice was laced with sarcasm. "So where's today's follow-up on that one? Subs tell me they haven't seen so much as a sentence from you about it all day. And what is this nonsense I hear that you're hassling the prison, trying to interview someone?"

"Yes! See! I'm trying to get the inside track from the victim's cell mate. He might know more about why Weaver ended up dead. It's a completely fresh angle."

Ruffus made a scoffing sound now. "Let me save you a trip, Frankie. Weaver ended up dead because he hangs out with rats and murderers. Nobody gives a shit about his motivations. He's an ex-con. Be lucky to get our readers to read beyond the headline. It's a simple case of lie down with dogs, get bitten. Move it along."

"Actually, I think it's lie down with dogs, get fleas." She noticed his nostrils flare and quickly said, "But it's a lot more complicated than that, Ruffus. I think there's more to this story."

He sighed now, like he was talking to a child. "Not every case has a triple twist like the Burlington one. You're not a cop. You're a reporter. You report the story; you don't become it. You don't solve it. That's not your job."

This was not the first time he had rattled those lines out to Frankie, and she nodded along, impatiently. "I understand that," she said, her voice equally as tense, "but I am a journalist and it's my job to ask *why*. I want to know why Weaver was stabbed on a public street nine days after he was released from prison, and for no apparent reason."

"There were five thousand reasons," Ruffus spat back. "He was stabbed because he had five thousand dollars cash on him."

Frankie was stunned. "Hang on, what? He had that much money on him?"

Ruffus shook his head, incredulous again. "Another thing you've missed! I sent you an email about it. Cops released that little morsel this morning."

"Okay, well, that's really interesting," she said. "I mean, *why* did Weaver even have five thousand dollars? How? He'd just been released from prison. He'd be lucky to have a fiver."

"Who gives a fuck? I don't. Our diminishing readers don't.

Not everything is a series of articles and an award-winning story, Frankie." He fell into his chair, exhausted by the conversation. "We haven't got the space for that shit anyway. They're cutting my pagination again. Did you see the size of yesterday's edition? Thinner than an anorexic on a diet! Or did I get that saying wrong too?" He glared at her. She didn't dare open her mouth. "I sure as hell am not wasting more ink space on an ex-con who got conned out of his cash. In fact, I don't want *you* wasting any more time on it either. I'm handing it to Katie."

"What? No!"

He had a hand up again. "She can do any follow-ups; you can get back to the missing woman story—see if you can catch up to bloody Tagger!"

"But... but the Weaver story is *mine*!"

"Ah, no, Frankie, you're reporting on it for the *Herald*. For us, the newspaper, yeah? Or did you forget about that too? This is not your own private detective agency."

"But I've done so much groundwork! And I really think there's more to it." She found herself batting her eyelashes, leaning into him, desperate. "Look, Ruffus, please, just give me one more day on it. I've got a contact who's going to get me in to see his old cell buddy—"

Ruffus leaned back. "Forget it, Frankie." He never did fall for her tricks. "You know what your problem is?"

She inhaled, waiting for the avalanche. One she'd been pummelled with before.

"You think *you're* the story, Frankie. You put yourself at the centre of every single one. You're not a team player, you never were, but you do good work, win some gongs, marketing nobheads adore you, so I let it slide." He exhaled angrily. "But I'm over it. I'm done. You can play catch-up with the missing woman piece, and Katie can put the Kings Cross story to bed where it belongs."

Then, before she could object again, he stood up, strode to his office door and flung it open. "And that's my final offer."

Frankie wasn't batting her eyelashes now. She could barely contain her fury.

"Fine," she said, sweeping past him before turning back. "But just for the record, *Ruffus*, I think that's a massive mistake. I know there's more to Weaver's murder than simple robbery, and if somebody else gets the scoop, you are going to be so sorry!"

Then she turned on her heel and headed for the elevator again, not keen to see the smug look on Katie's face when Ruffus handed Frankie's story to the junior reporter on a platter.

CHAPTER 21 ~
A BLAST FROM THE PAST

It was just on eleven a.m. and Merry and Earle were seated on either side of Prue as she frantically flicked through old photo albums, trying to find a picture of her daughter with a bare shoulder. Anything that revealed her tattoo.

Earle and Merry had now spoken with Odetta, waiting until she'd left Prue's building to reveal what Pip Dollarway had said, and Odetta had sounded as sceptical as Earle, but something must have stuck because she promptly marched off towards the bookshop, her constable close behind.

That left Earle and Merry to head up to Prue and ask about the tattoo.

"But we need to tread carefully," said Earle as he waited for Verity to let them in. "This poor woman has just been told they have a suspect in her daughter's abduction, evidence he might have hurt her. We have to be careful about offering false hope."

She nodded. She understood. Yet Merry couldn't help feeling hopeful.

If Pip really had seen Nel at ten fifteen, perhaps the young woman was still alive. Perhaps there was still a chance.

"Let me do the talking," Earle added as Verity buzzed them in.

When the PA opened the apartment door, she looked like she'd had a rough morning. She nodded behind her to where Prue was seated, head in her hands and said, "She's not good."

"Of course," said Earle. "Who would be after that news?"

"But we might have some good news!" said Merry, causing Earle to flash her a scowl, so she pretended to zip her lips shut.

Earle quickly filled Verity in. "I think it's all going to be a giant misunderstanding"— another glance at Merry— "but it is worth asking about the tattoo. Merry took a picture of Pip's. We want to see if it resembles Nel's tattoo. I'm just not sure how to do this without confusing matters."

"I'll do it," said Verity, taking the phone from Merry. "Wait here."

So they remained just inside Prue's entryway while Verity went to the sofa and sat down and then gently tapped Prue on the shoulder.

They watched as she said something, then produced the phone. Then Merry felt her stomach lurch as she watched Prue grab the device and nod frantically. Prue then looked up and around and spotted them hanging by the door and cried:

"Yes! That's *exactly* like it! Where did you...? How did you...?"

Verity waved them over and so they repeated the story, but Prue was not nearly as sceptical as the others and had jumped to her feet, re-energised, and run to fetch the photo albums.

"I'll show you Nel's! I'll show you how similar they are! That bookshop girl wasn't lying. She did see Nel! I'm sure of it! She saw her alive! I just know it!"

And so here they were, frantically wading through old photo albums, Prue explaining how she used to be so good at getting digital photos printed, but that had fallen by the wayside when John fell ill. "I could go through my phone, I suppose," she said, "but I honestly don't remember photographing it lately. If I've snapped it at all, it will be from the early days when she wasn't so embarrassed by it."

"What age did she get it?" asked Earle.

"It was an eighteenth birthday present. From her friends. I never could forgive them for that."

Then Prue's voice broke as she kept sweeping through the pages.

"Have you got one of Nel in a swimsuit?" Verity suggested. "That would show her shoulder."

Prue grimaced. "She hated being photographed, especially at that age. I'm not sure... ha! Here's one!"

Then she pulled at the plastic covering across the page, her fingers trembling, so Verity took it from her and carefully removed the photo as they gathered around her and stared at the image. It did indeed reveal Nel in a one-piece Speedo swimsuit, half turning away from her mother's lens, one hand out like she was trying to block her, but her tattoo was clearly visible.

Merry produced the photo she'd snapped of Pip's tattoo and held it alongside the image.

The tattoos were identical.

While Prue continued wading through the albums, trying to find more images of that infamous tattoo, Verity drew the sleuths into the kitchen, then turned her eyes to Earle.

"What does all this mean?" she asked. "I'm so confused."

Merry answered for him. "This proves Pip saw Nel *after* she was supposedly abducted. It proves that Crispin Regatta wasn't near her when she walked past the bookshop. The police have that all wrong! They must have!"

Earle held a cautionary palm up. "That may be true, Merry, but it doesn't mean Regatta didn't circle back. It doesn't mean he's off the hook. Not yet."

"So what do we *do*?" asked Verity.

"I need to show this photo of Nel's tattoo to Odetta; she's not gonna like it. Then she needs to check all the street cameras again and triple check Regatta's alibi. Because that's the sticking point. If he really was on a Zoom call at ten that morning, then yes, you might be right Merry; this changes everything. But first…"

He reached for the phone in his pocket. "I'm going to get the others back here. This case is not over. Not by a long shot."

~

Kila had just waved a worried woman away, promising he'd put her "oddly behaving" boyfriend on the strictest surveillance (the guy sounded like he might be gay, but Kila didn't want to break the news to her just yet), when the fresh text came through, and he was filled with red-hot rage. But it wasn't Earle's text he was reading, and it had nothing to do with Nel Chambers.

Dragon Malone's lawyer had tracked him down earlier that day. Catching Kila as he left his house for Balmoral that morning. It was the reason he was running late.

"You ever return phone calls?" said the man, stepping out from the shadows (or from behind Kila's parked car at least).

Kila took a step backwards. "Not from lawyers if I can help it."

Except Sheila of course.

"Look—" The Legal Aid lawyer stepped closer. He was a walking cliché—attaché case, slicked-back hair, ill-fitting suit. All that was missing were the pinstripes and braces. "My client is being fair dinkum, Kila. He's very anxious to meet with you."

"Oh, well we wouldn't want to cause *him* any anxiety…"

The lawyer sighed. "Deaglan just has—"

"Deaglan? Who the hell's Deaglan?"

"That's Dragon's real Christian name. He prefers that now."

Kila snorted. The dipshit could change his name all he liked, but he was still a fire-breathing monster as far as Kila was concerned.

"Look," said the lawyer, quickly, "are you going to meet with him or not?"

"I already gave you that answer."

"Well, he's trying his luck again."

"His luck ran out when he hurt my sister."

"That's what he wants to talk to you about, mate. He—"

"I'm not your mate, Abdul. Don't call me that."

Another impatient exhale. "He's got something important he needs to tell you."

"Is he going to confess to her murder?"

"Well, no, not exactly—"

"Then I'm not interested."

"Come on, Morea, you're gonna want to hear this."

"Mate, all I heard from that turd for the six months of his trial was 'not guilty, not guilty, not guilty.' No, that's right…" Kila stepped towards Abdul then, causing the man to step back and slam into the side of Kila's four-wheel drive. "*You* said those words; that turd didn't have the balls to open his mouth. And he hasn't opened it ever since. And now I've got to waste my time because he finally wants to *talk*?" Kila whipped out his keys and clicked the car open. "Tell *Dragon* that I'm not interested; tell him there is nothing he could say that would change my mind. Not one word."

Then he'd jumped into the car and sped away that morning, leaving the lawyer standing in the gutter, where he belonged.

Now holed up in his office, Kila thought he'd got through to the cretin, thought he'd finally be left in peace, but then the fresh message came through. He glared at the text, but it wasn't from Abdul. It was from the turd himself. Dragon Malone.

Kila had not yet clicked it open—didn't want to give the bastard the satisfaction—but could see the first two lines and they did not bode well.

Dear Mr Morea, I'm sorry about what happened to your sister but…

But?

…I had an abusive childhood?

…I was strung out on drugs and didn't know what I was doing?

…it wasn't me! I'm innocent! Blah blah bullshit blah!

Kila didn't want to hear any more of his lies and excuses. He pushed his chair back from his desk, stood up, and smashed the phone to the floor just as Earle's message came through.

"God damn it," Kila said, then scooped it back up and read Earle's text through the freshly cracked screen, his rage diminishing with every word.

CHAPTER 22 ~
AND SO IT BEGINS (AGAIN)

The sleuths were all gathered again out on Prue's balcony, and you could cut the air with a knife. Half of them believed what Pip had said. The other half thought it was a furphy. And at least one of them could not concentrate on any of this, her mind wafting back to the laneway murder in Kings Cross.

How dare Ruffus hand Spice Boy over to Katie! An amateur! It was infuriating.

Frankie tried to focus on what Earle was saying but just couldn't manage it. Eventually, as they went over and over the case again, she stood up and said, "I need to get a drink."

And headed back inside.

Prue and Verity were missing in action when Frankie first arrived, but the PA had now materialised and was seated at the dining table, going through what looked like photo albums.

"Can I get you anything?" Verity asked, barely looking up.

"Yes, you can get me my scoop back!" Frankie called out to her.

That got her some attention.

"Sorry?" said Verity.

"So you should be! Why didn't you tell me this case was breaking? It's all over the news! I should have been the one to break it. You told me Odetta wasn't going public with it, and I believed you. But now Channel Seven gets the scoop and I'm left looking like a fool in front of my editor!"

"That wasn't my call, Frankie. You'll have to take that up with Detective Soderbergh. And, forgive me, but I thought you were here to help us find Nel, not score yourself a scoop."

"Oh, *semantics*," she spat back, storming into the kitchen.

Why did everyone act like the two were mutually exclusive?

"You okay?"

This was Kila, who'd noticed the commotion and followed her in.

"Fine," she spat back.

"You still angry with me for not getting you in to see Dragon?"

She shook him off. "I'm not on the case now anyway. They want me on this one, full time."

He didn't seem to be listening. He was looking around, opening cupboards. "You find anything strong in here? Whisky? Vodka?"

"Actually, I was going to pop the kettle on."

"Forget that. I need hard liquor."

"What are *you* stressed about suddenly?"

He groaned and told her about the call, about Dragon's grovelling message.

"Why does he keep hassling you? I thought it was done and dusted years ago."

"Good bloody question. It's like an open wound they keep sticking a knife in. Aha! This will do it!"

And he pulled out a bright blue bottle of gin.

"That's quality gin," she told him. "Hundred bucks a bottle."

"Good," he said, reaching for a glass. "It'll be worth every drop."

Back on the veranda, Merry pulled Frankie aside. "Is everything okay?" she whispered. "You don't look happy, and Kila looks like he wants to drown himself in his drink."

"Oh, just more blather about his sister," she whispered back. "I wouldn't mention it."

Merry nodded fervently.

They had all learned about Kila's sister soon after the Burlington case had been concluded. Verity had brought them together one final time to hand out fresh cheques and crack open French champagne. Thank them for their efforts. Then another bottle had been opened, and then another, and pretty soon the Burlingtons had been forgotten and they were learning about each other instead.

It was a lovely drunken evening that went well into the next morning. And perhaps it was all the revelations that night that saw them scatter after that, despite promises to stay in touch.

Merry had spilled the beans on her unfaithful hubby, and Kila had offered to track him down and shove something stinky in his exhaust pipe.

"Don't you dare!" she'd said. "I think he's being punished enough.

I get to keep our lovely kids, and he's all alone with his floozie in some crappy little unit."

And they had all cheered at that.

Then Earle had admitted his daughter was gay like he was confessing she was a criminal, and they'd scoffed and called him an old Boomer and told him to build a bridge and get over it.

"Yeah, Earle," Frankie had said. "That's nothing!" Then she'd revealed the truth about her own background—how she'd promised to keep a politician's secrets, then spilled them in a series of award-winning articles, causing the man to take his own life.

That had them all gobsmacked.

Until Martin declared, "Some men are better off dead!" shocking them further until he revealed the truth about his own background. How he was really Braxton Wicks, a poor little boy from an even poorer fishing village, whose teenage mother had bailed soon after his birth, and whose older, violent father—his mum's high school janitor no less— could very well be her rapist.

And that's when they'd got onto Kila and his sister.

Despite everything that had been revealed that night, Kila's was the story that left them truly heartbroken. His poor younger sister, "sweet little Chili Morea," was murdered by a monster on an innocent date night.

She was only nineteen.

Kila's story had stayed with Merry long after that drunken get-together and was one she pulled out often. It reminded her there were worse things than a cheating husband or an absent child.

And now she needed to shake it all away and focus on Nel Chambers. Because the only thing worse than a murdered woman was a woman who could've been saved if only they'd found her in time.

"We've got to stop flaffing about!" Merry suddenly announced, causing Kila to spill his drink across Prue's outdoor table. "Whether we believe Pip or Crispin or whoever. If there's even the slightest chance we can find Nel—and alive—we need to stay on it!"

Perhaps it was the conviction in her voice that finally brought consensus, but now they were all nodding.

Then Martin said, "But how? What's our next step?"

"We imagine for just a moment that Crispin isn't lying, and neither is Pip," said Merry. "Because if you think about it, their two stories are the only two things that *do* add up. Crispin says Nel banged her head, then walked away, and he left soon after—was spotted driving away at 9:52. Pip says she saw Nel walking back in this direction about twenty minutes later. She was holding her head and looking upset. Maybe she wasn't crying over Crispin. Maybe she was crying because her head hurt! As simple as that."

"If it looks like a duck...," began Frankie.

"...and quacks like a duck...," added Kila.

"...it probably *is* a duck!" squealed Merry, who then thrust a hand to her lips, and tried to quell her excitement.

"So where did she go after that?" asked Martin. "What happened after she passed the bookshop?"

Merry glanced at Earle, who'd been watching all this quietly. He nodded assuredly at her, and so she forged on. "*That* is the question we should be asking. Instead of obsessing about Crispin, we need to look for the man Pip spotted with Nel after ten o'clock that morning. The man with brown hair and wearing yellow, who may or may not be a killer but could very well have all the answers!"

It wasn't a whiteboard, but it would do the job. Merry had scurried inside and found a notepad and pen and was now making a list of every man they knew of who was connected to Nel and matched Pip's description.

The list was annoyingly short.

There was Les Polanski from apartment one. He was the ideal candidate—a little gruff, a little lecherous, not exactly Nel's biggest fan. Problem was, even allowing for Pip's inability to read ages, he was a lot older than "could've been in his thirties," and his hair was partially grey.

There was Mrs Bianchi's grandson Tommo, from apartment two, but he was still in his twenties and wasn't even around at that time of the morning. *Or was he?* They should really check his alibi again.

And then there was the mysterious Japanese man from apartment three, the one they knew nothing about.

"How do you spell Takahashi?" asked Merry, pen poised. "And what age do we reckon he is?"

"Prue said he turned forty last year," said Frankie before spelling out his name. "So that's close enough to thirties. And he's likely to have dark-coloured hair if he's Japanese." She looked at Kila.

"You left your card under his door. Did he ever call you back?"

"Nope, but here's the thing, people," said Kila. "We don't really know Nel. Not at all. She could have a dozen other dark-haired friends who had it in for her. Or it could be a complete stranger who just followed her from the park. Saw that she was wounded and pounced."

"That's a mighty big coincidence," said Martin. "What are the chances that a random psychopath got lucky and happened upon a woman who was dazed and confused? Ripe for the picking? It's not a plot I'd write." Then he held up a finger at Frankie and said, "Don't."

She looked away coyly.

"Maybe it was more luck than coincidence," said Merry. "What if someone had a beef with Nel, for whatever reason, and took the opportunity when it presented itself? We have to work out who wanted her gone, starting with who she was arguing with over the phone on the Tuesday afternoon before she vanished."

They all looked at Earle. "Still not sure, sorry. I've flagged it with Odetta. I guess we'll find out soon enough. But you are forgetting the most obvious suspect, folks. Colin Boyder. He has brown hair and looks thirty-something."

"Ah! The blasé fiancé!" said Martin. "Good. Yes. These cases often come back to family and loved ones."

They'd learned that for themselves last time.

Earle pulled his spectacles off. "I think we should seriously consider him first before we let our imaginations run wild."

"I've got some thoughts if you want to hear them," said Martin, ignoring Earle's words entirely. "If Colin was the brown-haired man Pip saw, it would explain why Nel was crying. Maybe Colin came down to talk her into returning home but instead sees her chatting with a handsome blond kayaker. Maybe that 'chat' was innocent, maybe it wasn't, in any case Colin jumps to the conclusion they're having an affair. Why not? We all did. After Crispin drives off, Colin confronts his cheating fiancée while she's still at the oval. They argue as they walk back towards Prue's place. Maybe what Pip saw was not a woman crying over a sore head—although I'm not denying that happened—but maybe Nel was crying because she'd just had a fight with her fiancé. The guy is like an unlit firecracker. I could see him exploding, couldn't you, Earle?"

Earle glanced up from cleaning his eyeglasses with a clean

handkerchief and shrugged, non-committal.

"Then what?" said Kila. "Colin kills her in broad daylight and somehow disposes of the body? Right in front of a popular beach?"

Martin frowned. "Don't ever consider a career change to writing, Kila; that's nonsensical. No, he's obviously got his car somewhere. Manages to convince her to get in and why wouldn't she? They're engaged. Probably didn't want to make a spectacle, so she agrees. Then he takes her elsewhere, where he does all the above, somewhere private. Has anyone stopped to check *his* whereabouts that day?"

All eyes swept to Earle, and he sighed as he put the glasses back on. "One more thing for Odetta's to-do list."

"You're seriously buying that outlandish theory?" said Kila.

"It's pure speculation," Earle replied. "But it's as good a theory as any, and as I said, most women are killed by people they know."

"Not just *people*," said Frankie. "*Men*. And, worse, men who profess to love them!" Then she slapped all three men with a snarly look that made them feel oddly guilty.

Earle didn't bite. He got enough female angst at home. Knew when to stay quiet. Instead, he now pulled out his phone and scrolled clumsily, trying to locate Odetta's number. Again.

"She needs to apply for a search warrant for Colin's place. And she needs to do it quickly."

"You think Nel could be in Colin's house somewhere?" asked Martin.

"He did take his time to answer the door when we went there, remember?" he replied. "I couldn't see any obvious signs when I searched the bedrooms, but..."

"When did you search the—?" Martin grinned widely. "Prostate problem my foot! You had a look around while I was distracting Colin on the way out!"

He winked. "Nothing like playing the age card to get you access."

"You're not as straight as you make out," said Martin.

The older man smiled. "Just don't tell my old colleagues." His smile dropped. "I still can't understand why the guy took so long to answer the door to us. Maybe there's a hidden room or a basement or something." Then he stroked his beard and chuckled again. "Crikey, you lot are rubbing off on me."

While Earle made the call to Odetta, Martin headed into the kitchen to fix himself a drink. If Kila could knock back gin and tonics in the middle of the day, so could he. Prue was leaning against the benchtop when he walked in and offered to make it for him.

"I need to keep busy," she told him, "and I'm glad somebody is enjoying that gin. It's a gift from a neighbour, but I'm not much of a drinker and Nel wouldn't go near it. She has principles, my girl."

Then her voice cracked again, and he took the bottle from her.

"Just relax, Prue. I can make my own G&T."

He reached for a lemon in the fruit bowl, wondering whether it would suit this particular type of gin, when he noticed something else in the bowl. Something he had forgotten about.

He picked up the long white envelope he'd spotted the day before, the letter from Council, then glanced across at Prue, who seemed lost in her thoughts.

He said, "Sorry to disturb, Prue. But tell me more about this gin."

CHAPTER 23 ~
THE DISHWATER BOYFRIEND
(PART 2)

It took Colin Boyder just twenty seconds to open his front door to Earle this time, and the ex-detective felt a flash of disappointment as he glanced at Odetta, who was now beside him. And maybe a smidge of embarrassment too.

Earle had located Odetta fairly quickly—she was still on the esplanade, now reinterviewing the guys in the bottle shop—and so he told her his theory about brown-haired Colin who may or may not be hiding his fiancée.

Odetta had exhaled wearily at that. She had a suspect. She liked her suspect. She was not thrilled with the idea that her attention would need to be diverted elsewhere. It was bad enough that Pip Dollarway had cast doubt on the missing woman's final movements and they had to rethink everything—reinterview everyone!—but her evidence about the tattoo was very compelling, and Odetta was a pragmatist.

"I'm here now," she said. "Might as well pop in and have a little chat to this so-called fiancé."

And so, as Constable Logan continued the doorstops, Odetta and Earle had driven up the road to Colin's house together. The fact that Colin had opened the door so quickly and was now breezily welcoming them in was not a good sign, thought Earle. But it didn't necessarily mean the guy wasn't hiding something.

Odetta introduced herself, adding, "I believe you already know Mr Fitzgerald."

Colin nodded, eyes narrowing on Earle, but he didn't say anything as he waved them onto the sofa, then perched up against the dining table.

"Any news on Nel?" he asked, as though simply enquiring about the weather. "She's not answering her mobile." Like he was telling them something new.

"Any reason you haven't returned *my* calls?" Odetta threw back at him.

"Sorry, Detective. It's been ridiculously busy at work."

She gave him a sharp look. "Your fiancée is missing, Mr Boyder. We hold grave fears for her safety. Have a suspect in custody. And you're worried about *work*?"

He had the good grace to look contrite. "I'm only just realising how serious this is. I told him"—a quick nod at Earle—"I was sure Nel was just clearing her head. I didn't imagine she'd been abducted! I mean, it's something that happens to other people... not me!"

It's not happening to you, thought Earle. *It's happening to Nel, you bozo.*

"Where were you at ten fifteen on Wednesday morning?" Odetta asked, pulling her notepad out. A nice, neat subject change.

He blinked. "I was here. Working. Like I said, I've been very busy."

"Were you on a Zoom call? Send an email? Anything with a time stamp to prove it?"

His blinking sped up. He reached for a laptop on the table beside him and began scrolling through it. "I don't think so... I... no, nothing. You'll just have to take my word for it."

Odetta smiled serenely. "I'm afraid I can't do that. Would you mind if we searched your property?"

"What?" He looked around. "Why? What are you looking for?" And then, "You can't possibly believe she's here, hiding somewhere?" Then, to their blank expressions, it clicked. "You think I had something to do with it? That I have her locked up in the basement or something?"

Actually that's exactly what Earle was thinking, but Odetta did not answer that.

"What car do you drive, Mr Boyder?" she asked instead.

"A Volvo station wagon." He scoffed. "Now you think she's locked in there?" Another scoff, then he reached for some keys in a bowl on the table and flung them across at her. "Search it yourself. Go on. Search my whole house!" Then, his brain catching up with him perhaps, he quickly added, "But you will find Nel's prints all over the place and the car. She drove it half the time. I just don't understand why I'm even a suspect. I love my fiancée. You should be questioning her neighbour; she's the one who had it in for her. She's a better use of your time."

Now Odetta and Earle shared a look. "What neighbour?" she asked, the question directed as much at Earle as Colin.

Earle sat forward, waiting for Colin's reply.

He shrugged. "I don't know her name. Haughty, frizzy-haired woman who thinks she owns the suburb. Acts like a Good Samaritan, doing odd jobs for them, plying them with expensive gifts. She only does it to curry favour."

"Are you referring to Rachelle Easterly? From the building next door?" asked Earle. "Why would Ms Easterly need to curry favour with her neighbours?"

"Oh, another thing Prudence neglected to mention? That old witch has been trying to get some massive renovation passed by the local council all year, trying to 'beautify' her building apparently. Would have been a terrible intrusion on Prue and the others at Bellavista—builders would have taken over the front footpath for months, their scaffolding was going to wreck the view, and don't get me started on all the dust and noise and commotion."

Odetta held her pen up. "What has this renovation got to do with Nel, Mr Boyder?"

He looked at her like she was dim. "Nel found out about it and put a stop to it, of course. Until she came along, Prue and the others were just going to wave it through without a single objection. Luckily for *them* Nel got wind of it and told her mum to fight back."

Odetta looked wearily at him, clearly believing this was a deflection, but Earle couldn't help wondering if Colin was onto something and Prue's objection to the development wasn't so lucky for her daughter.

~

Martin was outlining a very similar theory to the remaining sleuths as they sat in Prue's living room. The coastal breeze had picked up, and it was too cold and gusty to remain on the balcony, so they were seated around the sofa, nursing drinks and picking at a cheese platter that had suddenly materialised.

Verity had vanished again, but it didn't matter. Prue was like a woman reborn, flitting around them like she was hosting a cocktail party, clearly holding on to this new theory that if Crispin was innocent, perhaps Nel might still be alive.

Kila wasn't sure those two things added up, but he wasn't about to burst the woman's bubble. All she had left now was hope, and he wasn't going to be the one to rip it from her.

After all, he never got a chance to be hopeful for his sister. Didn't even know she was gone until the cops showed up at his door, told him they'd found her body sprawled in a city laneway. Like a discarded hubcap. He'd been out on his own date that night, hadn't given Chili more than a fleeting thought. Now it's all he could think about. Every waking hour and well into the sleeping ones too.

If someone had walked in soon after that first shocking police doorstop and told him "Oops, sorry, we think we got it wrong. Chili might still be alive!" he would have dropped to the floor and kissed the shoes they were wearing. But he never got that opportunity, and he wasn't going to wrench it from Prue now.

"What do you think, Kila?" Frankie said, dragging him from his reverie. She had a worried crinkle in her otherwise flawless forehead, and he struggled for a smile. "Just wondering what you think of Martin's theory. Do you think the woman next door could have something to do with it?"

Kila shrugged. "Nah. She's a she, and she hasn't got brown hair, so…"

"That's a red herring," said Martin. "Has to be. Even Pip admits she wasn't sure Nel was with the guy who was following her. I think he's irrelevant. I think Nel returned to the building, and Rachelle was waiting out the front, saw her opportunity, like Merry said."

"And what?" said Kila. "Arm-wrestled her into her building and dropped her into an acid bath."

"*Kila!*" said Merry, looking around aghast, a finger at her lips to shush him.

"Sorry." He, too, was relieved to see Prue had vanished into the kitchen. Lowering his voice, he added, "I'm just saying, Rachelle didn't look like Mafia to me. I don't think you bump off someone's daughter because they stand in the way of plans to repave the terrace."

"Oh, I don't know," said Frankie, taking Martin's side now. "Don't underestimate the animosity between neighbours. I once reported on a woman who was hacked to pieces by her neighbour of thirty years because he'd finally had enough of her yapping terrier. It can get ugly out there."

"Oh my God," said Merry, eyes wide. "What did he do to the poor *dog*?"

Frankie shrugged and Martin scoffed. "Who cares about the dog? Listen, from the sounds of that development application"—he pointed towards the kitchen—"the renos were a lot more serious than that. Prue told me Rachelle was *obsessed* with them. And she does own half the building. But here's the thing. I asked to see the apartment the other day, you know, the one that's for sale on the right-hand side?"

"I *knew* you went there to check that apartment out!" said Kila.

"Were you looking for yourself or for the case?" asked Frankie, almond eyes narrow.

"Yeah because *you* never think of yourself, Frankie, when we're working a case," Martin fired back. "The point is, I told Rachelle I was an interested buyer, and she turned all coy and wouldn't let me in. Said the unit was now off the market."

"You don't believe her?" said Merry.

"No I do not, and don't forget, that apartment—*Rachelle's apartment*—is the very one that looks directly into the spare bedroom downstairs. The big one. The one Nel was sleeping in until she moved—for no apparent reason."

"So?" said Frankie, now not following.

"So what if Rachelle had been spying on Nel? Either trying to intimidate her or just trying to find some dirt on her? Think about it! She was bringing in their bins. She couldn't win her over with bribes, so maybe she was going through the contents, trying to find something to blackmail her with, get her to convince her mother to rescind her objections to the renovations. Maybe she could never find any dirt. I don't know. But I do wonder whether she approached Nel about it again after her walk that morning. Rachelle's already admitted to seeing her when she was heading out. Maybe she waited at the front for her to return and saw her crying and decided to pounce while she was vulnerable. Or maybe it was more innocent than that. Maybe she offered her a cup of tea or a bandage for her head, then they got into another argument about the renovations and things got out of hand."

The others were all looking at him like he was delusional, so he added, "Okay, I'm not sure about the details, but I can't help wondering if *that's* why Rachelle didn't let me look inside the apartment that was for sale because… I don't know… Maybe that's where Nel is."

"*Alive?*" gasped Merry, hand at her mouth, and he shrugged like it was irrelevant.

Frankie just stared at him, not sure whether to applaud or laugh, while Kila looked almost amused.

"You honestly think Nel is right next door, tied up in that apartment?" This was Merry again, flabbergasted.

Martin said, "Yes! Maybe. I don't know, but it's the ending I would write if it was a Flynn Bold adventure." Before they could scoff further, he added, "Besides, it's easily proven. We just have to get into that apartment. And I think I know how to do it."

"I thought you said she wouldn't let you in," said Frankie.

"No, but there might be another way."

Then Martin pulled out his phone and put a call through to his mother.

CHAPTER 24 ~

KILA'S CRAZY VIBES

As Martin got busy instating his plan, Earle returned from his visit with the fiancé.

He quickly filled them in, adding, "Odetta's brought in a crew to start searching Boyder's property. He's given permission, which is both good and bad. Good because search warrants can take forever to obtain, and bad because it usually means they'll turn up nothing of any consequence. Otherwise, why agree? Meantime, Odetta's gone back to headquarters to face the music. Thanks to Pip's evidence, she now has to release Regatta and widen the search. It's a bit of a public relations disaster, to be frank."

He didn't want to think of how smug Morgan would be, how cruelly he would taunt Odetta about getting into bed with rats (Earle being the rat, of course), but Frankie didn't have a jot of sympathy for the detective.

"Odetta should never have released that information about Regatta so quickly in the first place."

"You're still sulky you missed the scoop," said Kila.

She ignored that and said, "Okay, who else is on this list then, Merry? I'm not really into the Colin angle, and I'm not as convinced as Martin about the woman next door if I'm being honest. I mean it's a great theory—just imagine if the poor darling has been over there all this time, looking in at her old bedroom!" She shuddered a little then. "But I've got my money on Mr Takahashi in apartment three. Why hasn't he called you back, Kila? That's very suspicious. In fact, I wonder if anyone has seen him since Nel vanished." She glanced around. "Where's Prue...?"

Frankie jumped up and headed for the kitchen while Kila continued to look unconvinced.

"You know who else was a bit suspicious?" he said, rubbing a hand across his growing stubble. "The guy who runs the bookshop. We should question him."

Merry sat forward with a start. "*Dougie?* Are you being serious? His hair is more a golden-blond colour, and besides, I'm pretty sure his own daughter would have recognised him if he was the man tailing Nel that morning."

"I'm not saying he was the man with the brown hair. I'm just wondering about him, that's all. Seems suspicious to me that he insisted Nel didn't come into the shop, then his daughter contradicts him and says she did—"

"Ah, no, no, no. He never insisted anything. He just said he didn't remember her."

"Nel dropped in two days before she disappeared. That's not long ago, Merry. How do you forget that so easily? It's not like the shop's packed with customers. And here's the thing, he has no alibi during her disappearance. Pip opened up that morning, yeah? He was supposedly fishing until midday. What if he wasn't? What if he'd taken a fancy to Nel and acted on it?"

"You're talking about bookshop man?" said Frankie, who'd returned and was listening in. "You really think he could have something to do with it?"

"As if!" said Merry, sounding like her daughter suddenly.

"You just have a crush on him," said Kila. "*Golden-blond.*" He snorted, teasingly. "And I saw the way he looked at you."

"I don't! He didn't!" She let it drop. "Look, I'm just saying, if Dougie is somehow guilty—and what motive would he have?—then why drag his daughter out to tell us Nel came into their shop in the first place? It makes no sense."

"That is true," said Martin, who'd also returned. "I didn't get that vibe from him."

Kila said, "I thought we were keeping all options on the table. I'm just saying he's an option. A lonely single parent—"

"Not all single parents are lonely, you know!" Merry spat back, and they all swapped a look that made her feel even more defensive.

Frankie held a hand up. "Let's forget bookshop man for now. It does seem very unlikely. I just asked Prue about Takahashi. She reckons she hasn't heard a peep out of him since... get this— *late Tuesday evening.* Sounds like he might also be missing."

That shut them all up for a moment.

"Okay, now *that* is what I call suspicious," said Merry, giving Kila a sharp look. "Or maybe..." She began clicking her fingers. "Maybe it's perfectly innocent! Maybe Nel and Mr Takahashi were crushing on each other and have, I don't know... run off together?"

There were a few subtle snorts from the group, and Martin said, "Why wouldn't Nel tell her mother that?"

"Maybe she did and Prue forgot, or maybe the note slipped down behind the fridge or something."

"That's a lot of maybes, Merry," said Earle. The voice of reason.

"I know how we could find out," said Frankie, producing a set of keys. "Takahashi gave this spare set to Prue last year when he flew home for his mum's birthday. Needed her to water his plants or something. Who's up for a spot of snooping?"

~

While Earle and Frankie bickered over the ethics of poking about in a stranger's apartment without their permission, Kila ducked downstairs to see if the Polanskis knew where Takahashi might be while Martin headed to Nel's old bedroom. Or the one she had slept in before something—or someone—drove her out.

Merry followed the author down and found him standing by the sliding glass doors, looking up at the neighbouring building, at the unit for sale. The one Rachelle would not let him see.

"What's the plan?" Merry asked. "You really think your mum is going to be able to get in? I mean, if Nel really is in there, Rachelle is hardly going to fling the door open."

He massaged his nose. "It's worth a try. Maybe Nel's not there now, but maybe there's some evidence that she was. I don't know..." He gave her a small smile. "I'm getting desperate."

"You're really worried about Nel, aren't you?"

"Of course I am." He looked offended. "I know I can be a little aloof, Merry, but I do have feelings, yes? They weren't all beaten out of me in my childhood."

"I'm sorry, I didn't mean..." She offered him a small smile. "I'm glad you're in touch with your mum again."

He mirrored the smile. "So am I."

Then their eyes wandered back to the apartment across the way.

"Maybe we should tell Odetta about this?" said Merry. "Get her to apply for another search warrant? Might be safer for your mum."

"Oh, she can handle herself." He was beginning to understand that better now. "But you heard Earle. Search warrants can take ages, and I doubt they're going to give Odetta one for a loosely connected neighbour with no evidence other than my stupid vibes."

"Hey, your vibes are not stupid! They're better than Kila's at the moment. Dougie the bookshop man indeed!"

Martin bumped his shoulder with hers. "If it helps, I don't think Dougie had anything to do with it either. I wouldn't stress about him. Oh look, there she is!"

Merry followed Martin's eyes to the neighbouring apartment and did indeed see a woman walking towards the window, a second woman just behind her.

"That's Mum and Rachelle, quick! Hide!"

They both ducked down behind the bed, then poked their heads up and watched as a small blonde reached the window and stared out. She was clearly talking, saying something to a taller redhead—Rachelle—and then they both laughed as Olivia turned away and was soon out of sight.

All of that left Martin frowning.

"I guess she didn't find Nel in there," said Merry, announcing the bleeding obvious.

"I guess that's a good thing," he added, not sounding like it was.

After waiting five minutes, Martin headed outside to rendezvous with his mother and Merry found herself sitting in Nel's bedroom, the smaller one, the one without the fishbowl glass doors.

She hadn't really wanted Nel's body to be found in Rachelle's apartment, but she couldn't help feeling disappointed too. Nel Chambers had been missing now for two whole days and nights. Where was she?

Was she still alive?

And would she ever get a chance to sleep soundly in this cosy room again?

Merry's eyes danced across the beautifully made bed and the unpacked suitcase and the relationship book that certainly hadn't helped. She picked it up and sighed to herself as she reread the title: *Men Are from Mars, Women Are from Venus.*

Had Nel bought this book with optimism? she wondered. Was she hoping to understand what happened to her relationship?

Questioning whether Colin was the One. It wasn't a new copy, was a little shabby around the edges, and Merry wondered whether it was a gift from somebody. Her Mum, perhaps, or…

Wait a minute.

A tiny prickle ran down Merry's back, and she stared at the cover again, then turned it over and searched for a sales sticker but couldn't find one. There was a momentary burst of relief before she held her breath and opened the hardback cover, finding her way to the front matter, to the copyright information.

And that's when she saw what she didn't want to see.

The book was first printed in 1992. And this was a first edition.

CHAPTER 25 ~
SCROUNGING FOR CLUES

Martin was seated in the deepest corner of the Bistro at Bather's Pavilion, a heritage-listed building down the other end of Balmoral Beach, far from Prue's apartment and the oval, when Olivia walked in, and it took her a moment to find him. When she did, he offered her a subtle nod, like they were spies from a corny novel, and she smiled to herself as she made her way across.

"Braxton," she said, then bit her lip again but didn't bother apologising this time.

He must've been distracted because he didn't pull her up on it, just waved her into a seat and said, "I can't believe you got in!" Then he lowered his voice and added, "I do hope you were subtle."

Olivia cocked her head to one side. "I've lived by my wits my whole life, honey. I'm not a fool."

It was the first time she had stood up to him, and he took it well.

"Of course, yes. Sorry, Mum. So, how'd you manage it?"

She blinked at him for a few moments, then cleared the lump that had appeared in her throat. "Um... well, I just called Rachelle directly, like the agent said—like you asked me to—and she told me to come straight over."

Olivia paused as a waiter came to take their orders, then added, "She seemed thrilled to show me the apartment. I asked if there were any other interested buyers like you said to, and she said, nope, it's all yours if you want it."

He looked outraged by that and then exhilarated. "So she lied to me! Ha! That's *very* suspicious."

Olivia smudged her lips downwards. "Actually I don't think it's personal. I think she has a problem with men in general." Then she laughed. "She nearly saw you and that woman, lurking down there in Nel's bedroom by the way. Lucky I was in front and was able to block you as you ducked behind the bed."

"You get a really good view from there, don't you?"

She nodded. "That's what I'm saying. I think she wants to sell to a woman." She paused again as a bottle of chilled water arrived. Thanked the waiter, then said, "I asked what happened to the previous tenant. You know, just making small talk really so I could have a proper look around? I mean, I figured fairly fast that Nel wasn't stashed in there anywhere."

"Oh, I didn't really think that—"

"No, of course not," she replied, not quite believing him. "Anyway, she kind of skirted around that question, but she did point out that the master bedroom looks straight into the building next door and asked if I'd have an issue keeping the curtains drawn. That's when I spotted you guys. I told her no, no issue at all, and she looked relieved. I got the feeling the previous tenant was a bit of a voyeur, and that's why she wants a woman. *You're* not the problem, Braxton. It's your gender."

He sat back and sipped his coffee, looking disappointed.

She added, "It's not just Prue's apartment you can see straight into. You can also see into the one below, and there's a woman in that one too, if I'm not mistaken?"

He thought about that and nodded. That's right, Tommo's grandmother, Mrs Bianchi, lived directly below Prue. "She's got dementia."

"Really? Well, then I can see why Rachelle wants a tenant who'll respect the neighbours' privacy. I guess it's just safer to rent to a woman."

"Not all men are perverts you know, Mum," he said.

And she nodded, trying to keep her smile in check and the lump from her throat. But it wasn't the comment that had her in a spin. It was the fact that somewhere along the line, Braxton had stopped using her first name and started calling her mum.

~

Les Polanski in apartment one did not look happy to see Kila at his door again but managed a grunting hello before announcing, "We've already been questioned now, officially by the detectives. I'd like to help Prue, but I'm not sure there's too much more I can tell you."

"Just a quick word, promise not to bite," said Kila, not taking no for an answer as he stepped forward, forcing the man to take a step backwards and let him in. He had a feeling if Frankie were with him, Les would have opened his arms and the door wide.

They'd barely got to the lounge room when Les began calling: "Somlak! Sooooomlak!"

His tiny wife appeared from the adjoining kitchen, oven mitts on, eyes wide. "Ooh, hello. I sorry, I not know we have guests. You want drink?"

"No, he doesn't," her husband grumbled back. "It's just about Nel."

So, no sparkly glass of water for him either.

"Oooh, she still missing?" asked Somlak.

"Yes, she is," said Kila. "So is Mr Takahashi in apartment three. It's probably unrelated, but we do want to have a word with him. Any idea where he might be?"

Somlak shot a worried look at her husband, but he shrugged nonchalantly.

"Work, I'd say," said Les. "Poor bloke gets worked to the bone. I hope he's charging for overtime or on a bloody good package. The only time I ever see him is on the way to or from the office."

"What's he like? This Takahashi fellow?"

Les scratched his scaly skin. "Polite enough, not rude like Nel could be, but I wouldn't know the first thing about him. Could be a drug dealer for all we know. He's never bloody here. Bit suspect, you ask me."

"He not a drug dealer!" said Somlak, giving her husband a playful tap. "He always nice to me."

Kila smiled, wondering whether Somlak was ever going to work out that her husband should also be nice to her, not just her neighbours. He said, "When did you last see him? Can you recall?"

Once again, Somlak was staring at her husband as though waiting for him to answer.

Les said, "My wife saw Mr Takahashi last weekend when he was putting his bins out. I saw him the same day Nel disappeared if you must know, in the car park, around ten thirty. But I really can't see how all this is related to Nel."

"Still," said Kila. "It would be helpful to find out what he was like, whether you have any idea where he was heading."

"Back to work! Where else? The guy's a workaholic. As for what he was *like?* Well, not too happy that morning, I can tell you that. Said he'd forgotten his car keys and had to head back in."

Kila looked at Somlak for verification, but Les quickly said, "Somlak wasn't with me. She's got her cleaning job on Wednesdays, don't you, Sommie?"

The woman smiled stiffly, and Kila wondered why she had to work as a cleaner when they lived in a multi-million-dollar apartment.

"I was alone that morning," Les was saying. "I spoke to Takahashi for a few minutes, just a casual chat about Body Corporate business, then I got in my car, and that's the last I saw of him."

"So this was what time exactly, Les?" asked Kila.

"Like I said, ten thirty, bit before. I had my skin check-up at the cancer clinic at eleven, and it's a thirty-minute drive, so it would've been around then. I don't like to get there early, waste of my precious time, but I won't keep a specialist waiting. I'm not rude. Not like some."

And Kila knew his mind was back on Nel. He really didn't like the woman. But Kila was more interested in why a workaholic was heading into the office so late on a weekday morning.

"Oh, I gather Takahashi works late nights so goes in late most mornings," explained Les. "I think it has something to do with the time at his head office in Tokyo. They're a few hours behind."

Kila nodded. That made sense. "So what was your casual chat about?" Then to Les's burgeoning frown he added, "Again, *every little detail helps.*"

"Like I said, just boring Body Corp stuff."

"Such as? It could be important."

"I don't see how it will help Nel in any way, shape or form, but if you must know, it was about the renovations next door. Takahashi's been on the fence over the whole thing, and I wanted to convince him to get on board."

Kila tried to think back to what Martin had said about all that. "You're in *favour* of the renos?"

"Of course I am! I'm not a blasted fool like some! They're adding genuine value to that property, and I want to do the same thing here. This old building could do with a proper makeover. And we can't very well object to their development application and then ask if we can do the same, now can we?"

Kila rubbed a hand through his curls. Was Martin right about that? Did this all come down to a dusty building job? "I thought those renos had been rejected by Council?"

"No, just stalled is all. And only because Prue let her meddling daughter talk her into voting against it at the last Body Corp meeting. Mrs Bianchi is away with the fairies, so she abstained, or at least her grandson had the good sense to do it for her, so it all came down to Takahashi."

"So what'd he say?" asked Kila. "When you asked him?"

"Oh, he sounded very positive, like he might vote in favour." Yet there was something about Les's pinched lips and Somlak's sudden look of surprise that gave Kila pause. He was sure the man was lying.

"Then what happened?" asked Kila. "He drove off to work?"

"Eventually I assume, but like I said, he'd forgotten his keys, so he went back inside and I got into my car and headed off. Haven't seen the fellow since."

Then he sat back like that was the end of the subject.

Kila sat back too, his brain ticking over. This was interesting information. If Pip's sighting and the timelines were correct, this meant Takahashi went back indoors around the time Nel would have been returning to the building, if indeed she did return. Had the two met inside, in the hallway or stairwell perhaps? Was that when they hatched a plan to run away? Or did something untoward happen?

Or, even more interestingly, did Les circle back and meet them in there himself? Was there another *casual chat* about the renovations, and had that escalated into violence?

~

Earle was so concerned about Frankie's proposal that he insisted if she were searching a stranger's apartment illegally, he would accompany her.

"If you're going down, Frankie, I'm going down with you."

"Fine by me," she said as they made their way across the landing to apartment three. "You've got Odetta in your pocket; she'll waive the charges."

"Er, no, that is not how it works. Entirely unethical."

"Oh Earle, lighten up." Frankie placed a fist at the door and gave it a good loud knock. Just in case.

They waited a few minutes, but there was no response.

"Okay! Better go in and water the plants for Mr Takahashi!" said Frankie, voice booming in case a neighbour was listening in.

"That's our defence is it?" said Earle, more softly. "We were watering the plants for a man we've never met?"

"Not at all." She placed the key in the lock. "We're doing it for Prue." Then, as the key turned, she added, "Prue Chambers is so distraught over the disappearance of her daughter she can't remember whether Mr Takahashi was going away or not. Vaguely recalls him asking her to give the plants a drink. We're just helping the poor woman out."

Then she winked as the lock unclicked and the door swooshed open. That's when they spotted Kila's business card lying on the carpet just inside the entrance.

Exactly where Kila had left it.

~

"Relationship troubles?" came a voice behind her, and Merry looked up from her lap to find a young man standing behind her, an old lady clad completely in black and the size of a sparrow beside him.

It was Tommo and his grandmother from the apartment below Prue's. Tommo was staring down at the book in Merry's hands and smiling. Or perhaps it was the enormous jam donuts she had just bought from the nearby café that gave the game away, one of them half-eaten.

Some people turned to alcohol for courage. Merry turned to food.

Soon after finding this first edition, she'd thrown the book in her handbag and dashed up the road to confront Dougie, but all she'd managed to do was stock up on sweet treats and find her way to the nearest park bench looking out over the water. And she'd been sitting there for some time, staring blindly at the view, trying to find the gumption to ask a man about a book.

Because Kila was right, damn him, she *had* quite liked the bookshop-keeper. He was so sweet and cute and friendly. But more than that, he was the first man in years who had looked at her— actually *looked* at her, and that felt nice. To be seen. But all she could think now was how he'd lied about seeing Nel. Kila was right about that too—how could Dougie possibly sell a book to someone just before they went missing and not remember them? The shop clearly had few customers, and Dougie wasn't eighty, like Tommo's grandmother. He didn't have dementia.

"Tommaso has relationship troubles," said the old lady, echoing her grandson's words and shaking Merry from her reverie. She had a thick Italian accent and beady green eyes.

Tommo smiled patiently at his grandmother. "No, Nonna, I *used* to have relationship troubles, remember? Now I'm lucky to have a girlfriend at all." He looked suddenly wistful, his own eyes back on Merry. "Broke up with my girl about two years ago." Smiled sadly as he added, "Two years, two weeks and ten days. But who's counting?" Then he laughed lightly and said, "It was probably just as well. We weren't well suited. In the end."

"Relationships can be hard," Merry told him. "Believe me, I know. I'm divorced, trying to work out whether to take him back."

"Hence the book?" Tommo said, eyeing it off again.

She glanced down and then shoved it into her handbag. "So, what broke you and your girl up?"

He nodded towards the old woman, who now seemed fixated with a one-legged seagull.

"Being on dementia duty is not much of an aphrodisiac. Soon as you mention it to girls, they usually charge for the door."

"The door," said the old lady, smiling serenely now at Merry. "Got to keep the door closed."

"Yes, Nonna, keeping you safe, hey?" Now he smiled at Merry. "She wanders. Found her at the top of Raglan Street the other day, trying to catch a bus. God knows where she was heading."

Merry tried not to laugh. "It's a beautiful thing you're doing, Tommo, looking after your grandmother. One day you'll find a girl who thinks that's an attribute." He smiled sadly, like he did not believe her. "How long *have* you been looking after her?"

A cloud crossed his face then. "Two years, two months and... twelve days." The wistful smile was back. He took a heavy breath and said, "My mum's too busy, and there's no one else to do it..." He exhaled softly. "Okay, we better get on. Just giving Nonna a bit of fresh air and then we're going to pick up something from the bakery, hey Nonna?"

"Nonna very hungry," said the older woman.

"Here!" said Merry, holding out her second jam donut. "I haven't touched this one. It's all yours if you want it."

The older woman looked offended. "Yuck!"

"Sorry!" said Tommo, blushing. "She doesn't really know what she's saying."

"No worries, I just thought she had a sweet tooth," sad Merry. "They are pretty disgusting." She smiled.

Then she took a punt, remembering that they hadn't fully investigated Tommo properly (or perhaps she was just trying to shift the blame from Dougie). "Before you go, Tommo, do you mind if I ask you something? And it's going to sound a bit rude."

He rubbed his stubble. "Go on then."

"You told us you came in after midday on Wednesday, well after Nel had vanished." He nodded. "You don't happen to have an alibi before then, do you? It's just—"

He laughed. "You sound like the cops."

"I'm sorry."

"Nah, that's cool. I was home with my flatmate, Sergio. I think they gave him a buzz, but I can give you his number too if you like?"

"No, no, that's fine. I was just checking."

He smiled. "It's a beautiful thing you're doing too. Looking out for Nel." His smile faltered.

"You really like her?"

A shrug. "She's sweet. Nonna loves her too." Then he smiled mischievously and said, "And don't you go pinning it on Nonna either." He winked. "The cleaner came through after eleven that morning, so she would've noticed if Nonna had stashed Nel in the cupboard, isn't that right, Nonna?"

But Nonna was no longer listening; she was wandering off towards the water's edge, so he yelped and said, "Sorry, I better—" and raced after her.

"Okay, bye!" she called out, then stared at the treat glumly before she brought it to her lips and took a giant bite.

No point confronting Dougie on an empty stomach.

~

Mr Takahashi's apartment looked like something from a real estate brochure, everything clean and shiny and in its place. And like the brochure, there wasn't a living soul in sight.

Earle didn't like it, and he wasn't just talking the décor (another place that could do with a bright Beryl makeover!).

"It's too quiet," he told Frankie.

"He's obviously gone away," she began, but he held a hand up.

There was quiet, and then there was deathly quiet.

"Wait here," he said and began to move through the space.

"Bugger that," she replied, following fast.

"Just don't touch anything then."

He pulled his sleeves down to cover his hands as he slowly opened first the master bedroom door—bed perfectly made, not a dropped garment in sight—then through to the adjoining en suite bathroom—a small selection of grooming products, all with lids on, no toothpaste splatter on the mirror, the towel on the rack bone dry.

Together, they backtracked and walked through the living room, glancing about.

"Prue wasn't wrong about his passion for dead authors." Frankie was pointing at a glass case full of hardcover novels by the likes of Jane Austen, Charles Dickens and the Brontë sisters. "How many copies of *Pride and Prejudice* does one man need?" she said as they continued on to the kitchen.

That room, too, was neat and tidy except for a lone bowl in the kitchen sink, a few specks of muesli dried up at the bottom and a white mug with the remnants of coffee.

"If he did go away, it's only recent," said Frankie, sweeping a hand across a healthy-looking fern sitting in a pot on the kitchen bench.

Earle stepped across and opened the fridge doors. There were some fresh leafy vegetables, a few green apples, a plate of smoked salmon and a carton of organic coconut milk.

"It's healthier than my fridge," said Frankie, but Earle was growing worried.

"This stuff is fresh," he told her. "And you don't buy expensive salmon, then head off on a trip."

"So what are you saying?"

"I'm saying I don't like it. Let's keep searching."

~

"You hungry?" said Dougie the minute Merry stepped into his bookshop.

"Sorry?" she said, smiling automatically at his sweet, dimpled face.

"No, I'm sorry, that was a bit abrupt. It's just... well, Pip's just been collected by her mother. They have to report to police headquarters, give a statement."

"Oh, right." She felt a flash of guilt.

"I could have taken her of course," he added. "I do have wheels, you know? But Felicity says I've done enough damage, getting our daughter mixed up in police business, and she's taken her for the night, even though I'm cooking a giant pot roast and now it'll go to waste. I wondered whether... I mean, I know this is a bit cheeky, and I know you're busy with the search and all, but then a girl's gotta eat, right?" He smiled, blushed. "Sorry. I'm really botching this up! I'm just wondering, if you get some time, whether you'd like to drop back for an early dinner?"

Then, as if on cue, the scent of minted lamb began wafting through the shop.

"Certainly smells delicious," was all Merry could think to say.

"Comes through the rickety old floorboards from my kitchen above. I've been known to scare customers away with my burnt porridge! But I can assure you I won't burn the roast tonight!"

He laughed at that, and for the life of her, Merry couldn't help laughing along. And before she knew it, she was agreeing to return and he was beaming like she'd accepted a marriage proposal.

As she went to leave, he said, "Did you pop in for anything? More questions about your friend?"

Merry placed a hand into her bag where she'd slipped the book earlier, but she couldn't find the courage to ask him about it now, or perhaps she just didn't want to know the answer, so she shook her head innocently and told him she'd be back later.

Then she scurried out before her brain kicked in and she realised that she'd just accepted a dinner date with a potential murder suspect.

~

Earle was relieved Merry wasn't with them when they opened that cupboard door under the staircase in apartment number three. It felt like weeks since Merry had done a similar thing on the lower level of Prue's place, half expecting to find Nel lurking there, giggling when they found little more than old suitcases and storage boxes.

Merry had been both disappointed and relieved, but she wouldn't be feeling either of those things now. She'd be gasping like Frankie at the thin Japanese man who was crumpled around a Dyson vacuum cleaner inside, his tailored suit as tidy as his house.

Except for the bloodstains on the back, of course, where he'd been stabbed more times than was necessary.

CHAPTER 26 ~
A CAUTIONARY CALL #2

Merry was just closing in on Bellavista when she heard the first siren. Like everyone else on the esplanade that sunny winter's day, she looked around curiously, and then her heart plummeted.

Oh no!

Oh no, no, no!

She picked up her speed and got to the entrance just as the first police car was arriving. Earle was standing out the front, a grim look on his face, but he held a hand up to grab her as she rushed towards him.

"It's not Nel," he told her, reading her distress. "It's the fellow in apartment three. He's dead."

Merry blinked, trying to understand. "Mr Takahashi? How did that happen?"

Earle looked past her and held a hand up to wave.

It was Detective Soderbergh, and she did not look happy.

~

It took just ten minutes for the building to turn from a luxury seaside residence to a brightly lit crime scene. Police tape had been strung up everywhere, and forensic officers were streaming in and out, clad in top-to-toe plastic jumpsuits.

After initially phoning the police and being briefly questioned by Odetta—"Stay close. I'm not done with you yet!"—Earle had retreated to Prue's apartment with Merry, where the others had now gathered.

The discovery of Takahashi's body was shocking, and they were only just digesting that when Merry casually mentioned Dougie's dinner invitation. It was like she'd just told them she was dining with the devil.

"You're doing *what*?" said Earle, expression aghast.

"Over my dead body!" said Kila.

"Or yours if you're not careful," added Earle.

"Oh, leave her alone," said Frankie. "Merry can handle herself. Besides, she *has* to go to dinner with bookshop man. You know what we found in Mr Takahashi's apartment?" All eyes were on Merry now. "A full collection of... wait for it... *first edition* novels. Half of them by Jane Austen would you believe?"

Merry winced. "Did they have price tags from First Chapters?"

Frankie looked disappointed as she shook her head no, but then Martin said, "Well he wouldn't use price tags on precious first editions. Could ruin the dust jacket. But there is one way of finding out where Takahashi got them, and I agree, it would be helpful to talk to Dougie, Merry. I'm not saying he had anything to do with it, still can't see it myself, but he might know more about Takahashi and his link to Nel, if he's spent so much time in his shop."

Earle looked wary. "We assured Odetta we would now step back."

"No, *you* assured Odetta," said Frankie. "I did no such thing. I'm about to get a report through to my boss—if I still have one— and the rest of you need to keep moving forward with this. Things have just got a whole lot murkier, but that's no thanks to Odetta. If it wasn't for us, she'd have Crispin before the courts and they never would have found Takahashi's body."

"I think the stench would have caught someone's attention eventually," said Martin, who knew from his own research that it didn't take long for the smell of rotting flesh to start emanating outwards and the flies to start moving in. "How did you explain it all to Odetta?" he asked Earle, remembering the man's strict views on accessing premises illegally.

Now Earle looked disappointed, but more with himself. "We used Frankie's nonsense excuse about Prue being confused and wanting us to water his plants."

"Hey, she bought it, didn't she?" said Frankie.

"No, she did not," Earle replied. "She's just pretending to for her sake and mine. She's going to get a lot of heat from Morgan over this. She really should have warned us off from the very beginning. It's one thing to help a worried mother; it's quite another to start poking around in people's houses. I just hope we haven't contaminated the crime scene."

"We barely touched a thing. Take a chill pill, Earle," said Frankie. Then checking her phone clock, she said, "I better tap something out for the paper before Ruffus sacks me. And I can't see why Merry shouldn't go and enjoy a lovely pot roast with Dougie. It's not interfering; it's a date, right? Didn't I hear he was ogling you earlier?"

Merry blushed behind her pink glasses.

Frankie smiled. "See! Perfectly innocent. Then while you're there, you can ask a few innocent questions, have an innocent little poke around and see if you can find any link to Nel. If not, we can scratch him from the suspect list."

"You can use the word innocent all you like, Frankie," said Kila. "Doesn't change the fact Dougie could be guilty. He's definitely a common link. I think it's dangerous."

"Oh, Kila," she replied. "Merry's not a child. She's part of this investigating team. I'd do it without question. So would you—if only Dougie were gay and liked moody private dicks."

"But what exactly is Merry supposed to do?" Kila shot back. "Woo the information out of him? Sleep with him to get to the truth like y—"

He stopped as Frankie's smile turned frozen, quickly held a hand up and said, "I didn't mean anything by that. Shit. Sorry, Frankie."

The journalist looked fit to burst, and the others shared a frown. They all knew the story of the drunken politician, and it was not something to joke about.

Desperate to break the tension, Merry leapt to her feet and said, "Where's my lippie? If I'm going to have dinner with bookshop man, I'm going to need to look half-decent."

~

Detective Soderbergh didn't smile at Earle as he opened the door to Prue's apartment for her. She wasn't really angry with him, but it didn't hurt to keep these old guys on their toes.

"Mrs Chambers here?" she asked, not waiting for a response as she marched in.

"She's in her bedroom. Takahashi's death has really thrown her. I can get her."

"Do that please."

When Prue appeared, soggy tissues clenched in both hands, Odetta drew her away from Earle and his buddies on the couch and over to the dining table where she immediately put the woman's worst fears to rest.

"No news yet on your daughter, Mrs Chambers. And we found no indication that she's linked to Mr Takahashi's homicide."

Not yet at least.

Prue slumped into her chair, relieved, as Odetta knew she'd be.

"Of course we're going through the apartment now very carefully." (If only we'd thought to go through it earlier!) "But, as I said, it is a homicide, and in the light of your missing daughter, we can only assume that a connection may very well soon arise."

Might as well start getting prepared, she thought as Prue looked distraught all over again.

Odetta continued, "I know it's a very difficult time, but I do need to ask you some more questions."

"Of course, yes, anything."

"First of all, did your daughter have a relationship of some kind with the deceased?"

Prue looked surprised by this. "No. I mean, only to say hello to."

"So there's no connection that you know of? They never—"

"No! Absolutely not!" Prue's fear was making her feisty again.

Odetta gave her a moment, then said, "We're trying to track Mr Takahashi's final movements. I've already spoken with the other tenants." Or Les Polanski at least. His wife wasn't much use, and neither was Mrs Bianchi, although at least she had a loving relative by her side, which was more than Somlak had. "When was the last time you saw your neighbour? Can you remember?"

"Um... I don't think I've *seen* him since last weekend—just a friendly wave in the corridor on Saturday. But I definitely *heard* him come home on Tuesday, late, as he usually does."

Her voice was rattly again, her expression back to panic mode, because if that had happened to her neighbour, what state was her daughter in?

"His door always makes a loud click, and my bedroom—well, it's just near my front door, which is across from his, so I do tend to notice. But I'd never complain! He was always such a sweet man."

Odetta nodded again at that. It seemed to be the general consensus although the dinosaur in apartment one had suggested he might also be a drug dealer. The *eejit*.

"What time was that, Mrs Chambers?"

"About midnight? I was in bed, watching a movie. It reminded me I should be sleeping, and so I turned it off."

"Did you hear any voices? Any idea if there was someone with him?"

She shook her head. "And I never saw him the next morning. I just assumed he went to work. I didn't realise..." Then a startled look. "How long has he been in there?"

"The forensic investigators are still working that out." She closed her notepad and stood up. "Thanks again for your time, Mrs Chambers, and I do wish I had some better news for you."

Prue didn't appear to be listening; she was now sobbing quietly into her bedraggled tissues.

~

The bookshop smelled delicious when Merry stepped inside to the aroma of minted lamb. She could also make out roast potato, sweet pumpkin and a trace of cinnamon and apple. A pie perhaps?

It was past opening hours, but Dougie had left the door ajar and was in the back, sorting through boxes. Her heart was in her chest, but just one sniff of the air and glance at his sweet, dimpled smile and she felt her nerves dissipate.

If this man was evil, then she should hand in her resignation from the group immediately.

"Welcome, Merry!" Dougie sang out as he pushed the box back and waved her in. "I'm about to lock up, and we can head upstairs for some tucker. I do hope you're hungry. I went a bit mad in the end. Oh, and do you drink red wine? Because if not, I can pop to the bottle-o next door and grab something else."

"Oh, red wine would be great!" she said, ignoring Kila's final comments to her: Have your wits about you, and for God's sake, don't drink! He could spike your glass!

"Goodoh, I'll just..." He indicated he needed to get past her to the front door, and she giggled and stepped back, then felt her throat drain dry as he slammed it solidly, then turned the dead bolt.

If Kila did need to come to her rescue, he was going to have difficulty breaking through that lock. Trying not to think about that now, she followed as Dougie slowly switched off lights and then waved her up the internal staircase to his lodgings upstairs.

Once they got to the top, she felt her nerves ease again. The space was full of light, large glass windows catching the last of the sun's rays as they reflected off the nearby water. Before she knew it, Merry was admiring the view and his snug furnishings and forgetting everything else.

Dougie had done such a beautiful job with the place. Traces of frilly pink bedding could be seen from one room (had to be Pip's), another had a desk, files and books everywhere (surely his office). And his bedroom was at the farthest end, all muted browns and greys. While it was clearly a very old building and slightly run-down, he had decorated it with so much love and care. There was a mix of plump, mismatched lounge chairs and warm lamps on rustic side tables, framed photos in every direction. One wall was devoted to old books, another to old albums, and she stepped across to check them out while he checked on the cooking.

Merry had no idea what Dougie's ex-wife's place was like, but she could see why Pip loved living here.

"Wine?" he said, handing her a goblet.

She hesitated for just a second, then took it, clinked his matching goblet and took a large gulp. Then another. It was only as she was taking her third gulp that she noticed a set of car keys sitting on top of a Christina Stead novel on the coffee table.

The insignia on the keys looked familiar, and her throat suddenly drained dry again.

"You drive a Jeep?" she said, and he glanced up from the Stan Getz album he was about to put on the turntable.

"Yes. Why?"

"Oh, no reason."

Merry slowly placed the goblet onto the coffee table as her heart dropped into her stomach.

CHAPTER 27 ~
ONE SUSPECT DOWN...

Detective Soderbergh had wrapped up her interview with Prue and was just stepping back into the stairwell when she turned and gave Earle a look.

He'd been pretending not to listen in, didn't dare speak to her directly. He knew a cranky woman when he saw one. Had learned that the hard way from Beryl.

But now Odetta looked amiable. Almost friendly.

So he excused himself and followed her out. And that's when her face turned grumpy again, and he braced himself for a tongue lashing, but it was herself she was beating up.

"I cannot believe this has happened! I am such a fool!"

"Now, now, Odetta, you weren't to—"

"Morgan will have a field day with this one! I should never have jumped to the conclusions that I did about Regatta. I should have interrogated him better, got that flying surfboard story out of him a lot earlier than I did. I've wasted such valuable time."

"Do you know when Takahashi was—"

"I'm not saying I could have saved *him*. Pathologist thinks the man was likely killed sometime between midnight on Tuesday, when Prue heard him come home, and late Wednesday. Which was well before we got involved. We'll know more once he does the autopsy. I just feel like I've spent too much time obsessing about Regatta that I never even followed up on the missing neighbour. It's very sloppy police work."

"Go easy on yourself, Odetta," said Earle. "Regatta was a credible lead. Nel called his number that very morning, and he proceeded to lie to you about exactly what had happened during their exchange. Then you found the blood in the back of his vehicle, you made a logical conclusion, the same one I would have made—and Morgan if he could ever admit his own failings."

Because to Earle, getting it wrong was not a sign of weakness or even poor policing. Not *admitting* you got it wrong and correcting the course was so much worse. And so much more dangerous. The Burlington case was proof of that.

"So Regatta's off the hook now?" he asked.

"Looks like it." She was disappointed. "We found Nel's blood on the underside of one of his surfboards, just as he said we would. Also, luckily for him, half the posh houses in this area have their own security cameras, including the monstrosity across the road from him. We can only make out the corner of his Jeep's tail light, but we do see that it arrives at his home just on ten that morning, as he told us—in time for his Zoom call—and does not budge for twenty-four hours. In fact, the next time it moves is not long after you and I paid him a visit. That must have been when Mrs Regatta drove it to see the private investigator at the zoo."

Then she looked even more dejected and said, "Needless to say, Bob Taylor confirms what he already told your friends. Emma Regatta did hire Taylor to tail her husband, but he never once saw Crispin anywhere near a woman fitting Nel Chambers' description. What's more, Nel's number doesn't appear anywhere in Crispin's phone records. It wasn't him arguing with her at four p.m. the day before, like you suggested—it was a travel agent, by the looks of it—and his number only appeared on hers once. At 9:40, the morning she vanished. So I think the lost mobile phone story pans out. Damn, if only I hadn't been so narrowly focused!"

"What about this brown-haired fellow then?" asked Earle, keeping her on track. "The one young Pip spotted following her. Could it have been Takahashi?"

She waggled a hand in the air. "Her evidence on that wasn't very convincing. Her mum brought her down to the station—God, talk about bossy! Pip's mother's a nightmare—anyway, we tried to get an identikit picture of the man from Pip, but all she could give us was 'ordinary' and 'boring'." Odetta shook her head. "But definitely not Japanese. She was adamant about that. Says she's into J-Pop and K-Pop or something, so says she'd notice *that*." Another cranky headshake. "I'm not dismissing it, but I'm not letting it send me down another rabbit hole, that's for sure. I'm keeping all options open at this stage. What I did find interesting was the way Pip described Nel Chambers' appearance that morning. It sounds to me like Ms Chambers might have been suffering from a concussion."

"That'll happen if a surfboard lands on your head," said Earle.

"Exactly. Get this: Regatta now admits the woman was knocked unconscious *for a few minutes*, and when she came to, was very woozy."

"And he just let her walk away?"

"Says he couldn't convince her to stay, insists he tried to call an ambulance. I don't believe that hogwash; there was certainly no triple zero call made from his phone. Any case, he says he assumed she lived close, because she was using the oval, but I think he was in a hurry to get home to his Zoom call, and so he let her stagger off. Insists he never saw her with anyone else and doesn't recall any brown-haired man lurking nearby. I think Nel was badly concussed and probably didn't know whether she was Arthur or Martha at that stage, so who knows where she ended up."

Earle felt a flash of fury. "If Regatta had done his due diligence, called an ambulance or had the decency to walk the poor woman home, none of this might have happened."

"Ah yes, but then you and I would never have met," said Odetta. "At least there's one silver lining."

He looked surprised. "I thought you were grumpy with me and my lot."

"Yeah, well, I never could keep a grudge for long."

"So what now?"

"First light, we're starting a full-scale search. I should have done it days ago! Checking all waterways, crevasses. Who knows where the poor woman ended up? There's a bloody great ocean out there. Maybe she walked into the water."

Earle rubbed his beard. "You think that's all this is? A case of misadventure?"

"Well, I was starting to… until you found Mr Takahashi's body! But like I said, I'm keeping all options open. Maybe the bully in apartment one is right and it's completely unrelated? But I can tell you this for sure, Earle. As soon as I find Nel Chambers, if indeed I do, I'm going to slap Regatta with charges of hindering an investigation so fast he'll be the one left holding his head."

"I thought you didn't hold grudges."

"Yeah, well, there's always an exception for douchebags."

~

"Everything okay, Merry?" Dougie called out through the bathroom door, the dulcet tones of *The Girl From Ipanema* streaming behind him.

"Yes! All good!" she called back, one hand over her phone.

Soon after discovering the man drove the same vehicle as Crispin Regatta, she'd excused herself and headed to the bathroom where she promptly locked the door in case he'd spiked her drink and she was about to pass out. Then put a call through to Kila.

"I'm coming straight up!" he'd announced. "I'll have you out of there in minutes."

"No, wait..." She gave her head a shake. She felt fine. What's more, she was thinking more clearly now, and she realised that Dougie owning a Jeep wasn't really proof of anything.

Surely it was just a silly coincidence.

"The blood was in Regatta's car, remember?" she told Kila. "He's already explained what it was doing there. I'm just jumping at shadows."

"I'll come and get you anyway. You're obviously on edge."

"No, no, I'm here now. And I haven't even asked about Mr Takahashi."

"Forget Takahashi if you don't feel safe."

"But I *do*." She glanced around the bathroom. The space was clean, smelled of Ajax, and she noticed he'd placed a small cup of wildflowers by the sink and a fresh towel on the hanger. You could still see its crease marks. "I'm not going to give up now. Frankie wouldn't and neither should I."

"Frankie doesn't have three kids to worry about—"

"Two. I only have two kids at home now."

"Doesn't mean you're not worrying about the third. All Frankie cares about is Frankie and her bloody job. So, do what you feel is best. Forget bloody Frankie."

She was surprised by his animosity but didn't have time to question it. Dougie was calling out again, and she'd been hiding out long enough. If he'd poisoned her, surely she'd be feeling something by now.

"Dinner's on the table," she told Kila. "I'll keep the phone close in case I need you."

Then she hung up before he could object further, straightened her hair and glasses, and opened the door to face him.

"Everything okay?" Dougie asked again as she stepped out into the hallway.

"Oh, yes. I was just feeling a bit funny, but all good now." She inhaled. "My, that smells so tasty!"

As they sat at the tiny, beautifully decorated dining table just near the record player, Merry tried to work out the best segue into the case while Dougie made small talk.

"So how's your teenage daughter?" he asked, then at her surprised expression, he added, "You mentioned something about her when we first met."

"Oh, Lola. Yes, well, she's fine. She's babysitting my fourteen-year-old tonight. Just don't tell Archie that."

He smiled. "Let me guess, he's too old for babysitters."

She nodded, then realised she hadn't asked about his daughter. "How did Pip's formal interview go? With the police?"

His dimple disappeared. "She called me just before you got here. Said it was fine, but her mother… Well, Felicity's furious with me, like it's all my fault. Don't know why."

"She's just being protective," said Merry.

"That's one word for it. So, I heard all the police sirens earlier. I hope that wasn't about your missing woman."

"No, but it might be related." She let him finish his mouthful before she said, "A man in the same building was found murdered."

Merry watched Dougie's face for traces of guilt, but he just looked shocked and then worried. For her, it seemed, and his daughter.

"This is a very dangerous business you've got yourself mixed up in, Merry. Are you going to be okay? Do you think Pip is? Maybe Felicity's right. Pip's a witness. She could be in danger."

"Oh, I'm sure she'll be fine!" Merry said quickly. "The police are all over it. I just know they're close to solving this thing." But she didn't know that at all, didn't have as much faith in Odetta as Earle did. "I did want to ask you something though, if you don't mind."

"Of course, anything if you think it will help."

Merry pushed her chair back and made her way to the top of the staircase where she'd dropped her handbag earlier for a quick getaway. She pulled Nel's relationship book out of it and returned to the table.

"This was in Nel's bedroom," she told him, holding the book out.

"I'm wondering if she bought it from you."

Again, Merry braced herself for something—guilt? Fear? *Menace?*

Dougie just looked delighted. "Ooh, yes, this *is* one of mine!" He took it from her and lovingly stroked the cover. "So she *did* come into my shop. Pip was right. Fancy that."

Merry frowned. "And you didn't remember her?"

"Oh no," he said breezily. "I have an appalling memory for faces."

Her frown deepened. "It was only a few days ago, Dougie. We think she bought it from you two days before she vanished."

"Oh yes, yes, she did. I do remember now." His eyes were on the book, and he was leafing through it. Then, sensing her scepticism, he quickly added, "I have an uncanny ability to remember books, but not faces." Then as her frown turned to confusion, he placed the book down and sat back like he was about to confess to a crime.

He cleared his throat and said, "I have a mild case of what's called prosopagnosia—face blindness. Drove Felicity batty. Pip too. I'm not sure they always believe me, but it is a condition, I can assure you. And a very unhelpful one when you own a local business. People get quite disappointed when they pop in and I don't remember them even if they'd been in the day before and I chatted to them for twenty minutes."

"Are you for real?" she said, sounding like Lola again.

He nodded. "All faces blur to me, and it's hard to remember them the second time around, especially if they're wearing a different outfit or have done something different with their hair, which they usually have, just my luck! But books. Ha! I never forget a book. So I always ask what book they've purchased, and then it all clicks into place. Eventually, I begin to remember their faces. But never at first."

Merry had never heard of that condition, wished she could google it now to see if he was being honest, but he was now inspecting the book and smiling again.

"Okay. Now I remember this woman. She was sad, that's right. Said she was struggling with her boyfriend, was it? He wants to settle down or something. Her mother can't stand the fellow and was trying to talk her out of it. And she really wasn't sure how she felt. She asked me all sorts of questions, mostly about men and how they behaved and whether it was normal for men to scoff at romance. I told her it was not. I told her if I had a woman I liked, I'd be smothering her with flowers and gifts and cooking her pot roast every night." Then he glanced down at the meal and blushed a bright crimson red.

Merry blushed too, and they both grabbed their goblets and swallowed large gulpfuls. Then Merry forged on; there was no time for flirting! "So... the book?"

"So I pulled this one out from the shelves and told her it might help. Men are a bit like an alien species sometimes, or at least that's what Pip tells me. Maybe I should keep this book and read it myself!"

They both laughed at that, and it felt like such a release for Merry, but again, she had to stay focused. She said, "So, here's the thing, Dougie. The guy who was murdered, the guy across from Nel's place. He... well he had a bunch of first edition books too. Mr Takahashi?"

Another vague look from Dougie, so Merry added, "Seemed to have some fixation with Jane Austen."

Dougie's face lit up. "Oh, Katsu! Yes, he loves his classic English literature!" Then it hit him. "Oh no, *he's* the chap who was murdered?"

She nodded, again watching him for signs of guilt.

But now Dougie just looked crestfallen, and she was the one feeling guilty for ever contemplating that this sweet bookshop man could be a murderer.

It was only after they'd polished off most of the roast and half the apple pie (turns out Dougie was also a comfort eater), and he'd walked her safely back to Bellavista, that Merry felt a fresh flutter of doubt. As they stood outside the building, she thanked him profusely for dinner, and he'd blushed and said she was welcome, then looked for one terrifying moment like he might lurch forward and kiss her before thinking better of it and offering his hand to shake.

"I do hope you find that poor woman," he said. "But you know where to find me should you have any more questions or want to... you know, drop in or buy a first edition of something."

Then he'd blushed the most delightful pink again before adding, "It was such a pleasure to meet you, Meredith Kean." Before turning and walking away.

And that's when it hit Merry, like a book to the face.

If Dougie really did suffer from face blindness as he claimed, how come he remembered her so easily? And had done so from the beginning?

~

Earle couldn't remember if he'd told Beryl he'd be home for dinner, but the house was deadly quiet as he stepped inside, and it was too late for apologies, so he hung his car keys gently onto their hook by the front door and then slipped his shoes off and padded softly into the kitchen.

It reminded him of the old days when he'd return late from a breaking case and Beryl and young Tess were fast asleep. Beryl always left him some dinner in the fridge, a plate of something wrapped in plastic, ready to be microwaved, but he wouldn't use the noisy contraption, terrified the beeping would wake them. So he'd sit at the kitchen table and eat the meal cold, then head off to bed, but not before stopping in Tess's room to check if she needed covering with a blanket or, in later years, if she'd fallen asleep again with her headphones on.

He'd gently remove them and bend over quietly, giving her the softest kiss on the forehead, before heading in to Beryl.

Now he wasn't feeling hopeful Beryl had even left him leftovers, and he sure as hell wasn't padding into Tess's bedroom. She might still be awake.

Stomach rumbling, he opened the fridge door and peered inside. There was a dinner plate with two chops, a large dollop of mashed potato and some broccoli covered in plastic, a slice of pecan pie beside it.

His heart leapt as he pulled it all out, grabbed a fork from the drawer, glanced quickly at the microwave, then began to eat it cold...

~

When Merry returned to Prue's apartment, all that remained was Kila, who was out on the veranda staring up at the moon, and Verity, who was just leaving.

"Prue's tucked into bed," Verity explained. "She was a wreck. I've just given her a sleeping tablet, so let's hope it does the trick. And speaking of wrecks, I want to check in on George, see if he needs more Irish stew."

"You're a very good PA," Merry told her. "You go above and beyond."

"He's a very good boss. I'd do anything for him. And there's no one left now to look out for him, so…" Then she squeezed Merry's arm and left her to it.

Out on the deck, Kila had a bottle of shiraz on the table beside him. It had hardly been touched, and she recognised it as the same bottle Martin had bought from the bottle shop next door to First Chapters.

She dropped her head to the side and said, "You were lurking outside the bookshop, weren't you?"

He had the decency to look sheepish. "Only after you rang me. I just wandered up, hung around, just in case. I cleared off when I heard you two coming down the back lane."

Merry was touched and gave him a hug. "Where are the others?"

"Frankie took off, said something about her boss and needing to 'square the ledger,' whatever that means, and Martin was taking his mother out for dinner."

"Really? Oh that's lovely!"

He smiled. "He might be growing up on us, young Marty."

And she knew what Kila meant. Martin was a little like Frankie. Full of ego and not a lot of concern for anybody else. Although she could see that was changing.

"You need to go easier on him," she said, dropping into a seat.

"Oh, he can handle himself." Kila held out the bottle, but she shook her head.

"Got to get home. I just wanted to fill you in on how it went."

And so she did, feeling traitorous as she finished up with her concerns about Dougie's memory. "If he really has face blindness, or whatever it is, how come he remembered me? And don't say it's because I'm so memorable. Because I'm not."

"Merry—"

"Don't!" She raised a palm to shut him up. She could stomach false flattery from her ex-husband, but not from Kila. She respected him too much. "So what do you think? Could he be fibbing about the Prosecco-face thingie? It is a very handy excuse."

Kila shrugged as she reached for her phone and began to google the condition. It didn't take long to learn that prosopagnosia did exist, and she felt heartened until Kila pointed out something.

"Just because it's a real condition, doesn't mean he's got it."

And so her heart plummeted all over again.

CHAPTER 28 ~
AND NOW FOR DAY THREE...

Waking up on Saturday morning used to fill Martin with joy. And that's because he treated his writing like a job, sitting at his desk Monday to Friday, then giving himself the weekend off. But this week he hadn't written so much as a word of his new novel. And he couldn't exactly blame Nel Chambers for that. Truth was Martin hadn't written for months, hadn't even finished the first chapter. Kept rereading his words and then pressing Delete.

And his agent was already circling.

Lizzie hadn't liked the idea of a literary novel, warned him his readers would be even more disappointed, but she'd made so much commission from Martin's murder mysteries she had no choice but to let him get on with it.

And yet it was going exactly nowhere. He hadn't earned himself a weekend off in months, and that's why Saturdays now filled him with dread.

But not this Saturday. Not this morning.

This morning, Martin felt great, and it had a lot to do with last night. As appreciation for her help, he'd taken his mother out to dinner, choosing a restaurant close to her house that he knew whipped customers in and out fast. He wanted to thank her, but he didn't want to drag it out.

And yet it had dragged, for hours, and he'd loved every single minute of it.

For the first time since they'd reconnected, they'd had a genuine conversation. One that went beyond mere small talk. First Olivia told him all about her current life—how she fancied a man who lived three doors down, how her beloved hairdresser had just been diagnosed with dementia—"and she's only forty! *Forty,* Martin, imagine it!"—then she'd moved on to her dreams for the future.

Turns out Olivia was pining to become a midwife, and failing that, a nurse. And finally, most interestingly, she'd opened up about her past. Martin was surprised to learn she had a loving family but had turned her back on them when she got mixed up with the wrong crowd. The wrong man. That's when she went off the rails.

But before he could enquire further, they were being kicked out of the restaurant and were back at her place, opening that bottle of shiraz he'd given her. And the rest of it was a blur. And now here he was, waking up in her guest bedroom with its spotted curtains and soapy smells and pretty, floral sheets. Not even his thumping headache could detract from that.

"Martin! Breaky's ready!" came her voice through the door, and he staggered up to tug on his jeans and T-shirt (this one read "ME? SARCASTIC? NEVER!"), grinning despite his hangover. But it wasn't another delicious cooked breakfast he was grinning at.

Martin! She'd finally started using his new name, his happy name. The name that didn't make him feel like a failure. *And* without equivocation. He wondered when that had happened.

"I'll just be a sec!" he called back on his way to the bathroom. There, as he scraped fingers through his freshly dyed hair and rinsed his mouth out, something began to niggle at the recesses of his brain, and his grin began to waver. He turned the tap off and stared at his reflection.

What was it his mother had said last night? It was something important, he was sure of it. But it had nothing to do with her childhood or a violent high school janitor.

It was about the case, he knew that for certain. If only he could remember...

Two eggs, three rashers of bacon, and a large latté later, and Martin's memory had not kicked in, despite asking her about it.

"Are you sure it's something I said last night?" asked Olivia as she went to refill his cup. "We didn't really speak about the case if I remember rightly. In fact..." She bit her lower lip. "I'm so sorry if I freaked you out about your father, Martin. You seemed to be so confused about him. So muddled. I wanted to set the record straight, but... well, I promised myself I wouldn't dwell on the past with you, would only move forward."

"That's fine," he said, but the truth was he couldn't remember any of that either. Nor could he dwell on anything—he was already late to meet the others. So he thanked her for the breakfast, then surprised them both by giving her a hug before he headed out.

~

Frankie couldn't help smiling as she updated the *Herald*'s online news site on the Nel Chambers story first thing that morning. Then created a fresh, related story, all about the unexpected murder in a neighbouring apartment and how she was a star witness.

Suck eggs, Tagger, Frankie thought. I scooped you big time!

Tagger probably still thought Regatta was the primary suspect in Nel's disappearance. But she already knew from an early call to Earle that Odetta had released him and would likely slap him with his own set of charges.

"Regatta's silence hindered the investigation. If he'd confessed to the flying surfboard incident immediately, she might have found Takahashi earlier."

"Do they have any fresh leads?" Frankie had asked, as much for Nel's sake as the paper's. "Any idea how Takahashi ended up stabbed under his own staircase?"

"No, and I don't think I'm going to be hearing from Odetta on that one. She's been patient with us, but…"

"Oh, she'll have to do a media conference first thing," said Frankie. "Press will be all over it. Probably start bandying the words *serial killer* around before we know it."

The only thing more exciting than a murder victim was the potential for more corpses.

She was just sending it to the sub-editors when Katie strolled in, bright and bushy-tailed.

"Hey, do you know where Ruffus is?" Katie asked, taking the desk across from Frankie. "He's usually in well before me. Even on a Saturday."

Frankie's top lip curled. "Probably yelling at his wife or kicking his dog or something." She noticed today's paper in the junior writer's hands and tried to keep the delight from her voice as she added, "Your Phillip Weaver follow-up didn't make the front page."

Katie didn't hide her disappointment. "Yeah, they buried it on page seven! But, you know, there wasn't much more to say, so…"

I'm not so sure about that, thought Frankie. If *she* were still on that story, she would have found a fresh new angle, interrogated Weaver's old cell buddy, dug a little deeper. No one had yet been able to explain how Weaver ended up with $5,000 cash in his hands and who exactly had relieved him of it.

But Frankie wasn't on the case and no longer cared. The Chambers story was growing legs, and she couldn't wait to get back to it. Speaking of which... She jumped up and grabbed her handbag.

"I've got to head off. If you see Ruffus, tell him I'll phone him later from Balmoral."

Katie nodded and then turned dispirited eyes back to the front page of the newspaper.

CHAPTER 29 ~
A CAUTIONARY CALL #3

The five sleuths had a mix of emotions writ large across their faces. Takahashi's murder had brought a new level of urgency and desperation to the case. Frankie was exhilarated—another layer to unravel! Merry was deeply worried—this did not bode well for Nel. Both Martin and Kila just looked dejected, like they were somehow failing. As for Earle? Well, he was wearing his "back off" expression again.

"Don't say it," said Frankie, exhausted by the man's trepidation. "No one can stop us investigating, Earle. Why do you always try to put the brakes on?"

"I'm not trying to put the brakes on anything," he shot back. "But we aren't here on an official basis; you have to remember that."

"Yes, we are! The mother of the *still* missing woman hired us," said Frankie. "And if you really are going to set yourself up in private practice like you said you were, Earle, then you're going to have to learn how to sidestep the police and break a few rules for the sake of your clients. Like Kila does."

"Hey, I don't break the rules," Kila said. "At least not lately."

Even Earle rolled his eyes at that one. "I'm not saying we can't still investigate. We're here for Nel, not Takahashi. So it's Nel we have to focus on."

"But they have to be connected, surely?" said Merry.

"That may be so, but I got a call from Odetta first thing. Morgan's laid down the law, like I knew he would. We're not to interrogate any witnesses regarding that homicide and, once again, are to give this building a wide berth, outside of Prue's apartment. That includes the other tenants."

"Okay then, scratch what I just said," said Kila. "I've already interrogated Les and Somlak about Takahashi."

Merry bit into a thumbnail and said, "And I might have mentioned something to Dougie at the bookshop last night. Sorry!"

"Oh, I forgot about *that*," said Frankie. "How d'your hot date go, Mez?"

"It wasn't a hot date!" Merry's blushing cheeks made a lie of that. Then before they could tease her further, she filled them in on what she'd learned, of her initial panic over Dougie's Jeep, and his apparent memory problems.

"I have heard of prosopagnosia," admitted Frankie, "but *you* don't look so convinced."

"She's right to be worried," said Kila. "I was with you, Festive, the day after you met Dougie, and he had no trouble remembering your name and face. He remembered your full name, in fact. So why didn't he remember Nel?"

She bit into her thumbnail again, now just looking worried.

Martin listened to this exchange and still wasn't buying it.

"What would be Dougie's motivation?" he asked. "Why would a guy in a bookshop want to hurt anybody?"

"Just because he works with books, doesn't make him a saint," said Frankie.

"It certainly puts him in a higher class than journalists," he replied, only half joking. But the question remained and they all considered it.

"Maybe Dougie's a sexual predator," said Kila, ignoring Merry's look of distress. "If Nel really did tell him all about her boyfriend troubles, maybe he took advantage of that. We know he was supposed to be fishing alone that morning, didn't return until lunchtime, right? Well, where's the proof of that? His alibi is wide open. He could have been heading out when he saw Nel walking past the shop, crying. So he quietly invited her upstairs for another supportive chat or to give her another sad little self-help book. Except he couldn't keep his hands off her and she fought back. One thing led to another and, well…" He sat back with a bleak, knowing look.

"But his daughter was just downstairs in the shop that morning!" spluttered Merry. "Pip would've seen them. *Heard* them at the very least, through those thin floorboards!"

"Not if he'd taken her up via the back stairway. Pip could've been wearing earbuds, and it's not like the shop has any customers who'd notice," said Kila. "If he did hurt her, Dougie could have easily carried Nel's body down to his old Jeep. It's parked out of sight behind the building."

"You were poking about behind the shop last night while I was upstairs with Dougie!" said Merry, aghast.

"Just checking for evidence. Wouldn't be the first time there was blood in a Jeep down at Balmoral."

"And?" said Frankie, eyes twinkling.

Kila smudged his thick lips downwards. "Looked clean to me but that doesn't mean he didn't use it to transport her out of there or to his boat maybe. He could've dumped the woman anywhere off the coast, and no one would even have noticed."

"And Mr Takahashi?" demanded Merry. "How does he fit in to this crazy theory?"

Kila gave it some thought. "Takahashi would have been driving near the shop at around that time on his way to work, not long after Les saw him at ten thirty, yeah? He might have spotted Dougie talking to Nel on the street or down the laneway. Timeline fits perfectly. After Dougie kills Nel, he realises he has to silence the witness who saw them together. So he pays Takahashi a late home visit on Wednesday evening. Takahashi probably hadn't heard about Nel at that stage, so he happily opens the door to the lovely bookshop man who gets him his first editions. Then, once they were safely in Takahashi's apartment, Dougie stabs him to keep him quiet."

Merry looked even more horrified than she had before, but Earle and Frankie were nodding along, and it did make an awful kind of sense to Martin. And yet... there was a piece of the puzzle missing or in the wrong place or something. Kila didn't have it quite right; he knew that. Just didn't know which part was mixed up. Wished he could remember what his mother had told him, the thing that had been bugging him.

"What about the neighbour, Rachelle Easterly?" Martin asked. "Are we off that angle entirely?"

"Actually, I've got another theory if you want to hear it," said Kila.

"Is Dougie innocent in this one?" asked Merry.

He winked and said, "Oh yeah, you're gonna like this one better."

As Kila explained his second elaborate theory for the morning, the others listened with dubious expressions. He described how he'd recently learned that Les supported Rachelle's renovation plans and how he'd bailed up Takahashi in the carpark for a casual chat that fateful morning.

"Maybe Les lied to me about that and Takahashi told him he was *not* going to support the renovations under any conditions. That would have made Mr Polanski see red. Maybe they were arguing in the group stairwell, and that's when Nel walked in and a fight broke out. Or maybe Les followed Takahashi back to his apartment—he was fetching his car keys, yes? And that's where the fight escalated into violence. Maybe Nel caught him coming out of Takahashi's apartment soon after—again, the timing fits—and so he had to get rid of her too, to cover his tracks."

Kila was right. Merry much preferred this theory, but Frankie was looking sceptical and Earle seemed confused and asked him to repeat everything.

As he did so, Martin began nodding his head. He liked this theory more too. It linked in with his own suspicions.

"Do you remember when we first spoke to Rachelle?" Martin said. "She mentioned chatting to Les that morning, but he never said a word about it initially. Maybe they were discussing the renovations."

"That's right," said Kila. "Why didn't he mention it earlier? What's the big secret? Maybe he didn't want us to head down this path because he knew we'd put two and two together."

"And get twenty-six," said Frankie, eyebrows high again. "Neighbours can come to blows, sure, but you don't kill to defend *someone else's* renovation plans! Why would Les bother? I'm sorry, Kila, but it's all a bit..."

And then she opened her arms and stretched widely. Kila found a cushion on the lounge and lobbed it towards her head. Martin caught it before it got to her and gave Kila a frown.

"How are we going to find out?" he asked, returning the cushion.

"Somlak knows something about all this," said Kila. "I could just *feel* it. I need to get her alone. Away from Les."

"Oh, so you can *charm* it out of her?" said Merry, half joking, half smarting over his comments about Dougie. "I know what you're like with the *ladies*."

Kila frowned, shooting a glance at Frankie. "No, not like that." He shifted in his seat. "She clearly doesn't want to contradict her husband, but if I ask the right questions without him breathing down her neck, I might just get the truth this time."

"Er, no, folks, I think you're forgetting something," said Earle. "We're not to interrogate any potential witnesses, especially regarding Mr Takahashi."

"Oh bugger that—" began Frankie just as they heard a loud chopping sound coming from outside.

They all raced to the balcony in time to see a blue-and-white police helicopter swoop down and past the building, then head south along the beach towards the oval, whipping the sand and trees up as it went.

"Cavalry have arrived," said Earle.

At least he hoped it had this time. And he hoped this time they would find something.

~

As the sleuths stood down on the esplanade, watching the choppers scan the beach around Balmoral and then circle the oval and surrounding nature reserve, Frankie said, "What do they think they're going to find from all the way up there?"

Kila didn't care. The choppers were a godsend as far as he was concerned. They'd brought most of the locals out onto the street, including the tenants of Bellavista. All except one. He noticed Les Polanski standing between Mrs Bianchi and Tommo on one side and Prue and Rachelle Easterly on the other. They were all staring skyward, so Kila's eyes turned back to the building.

This was his chance. He might not get another.

Ignoring what Earle had just said—Kila didn't take orders from anybody—he dashed back through Bellavista's open doorway and straight up to apartment one, rapping loudly on the door so as to be heard over the sound of the helicopters.

A minute later the door swung open and Somlak stood there with a smile.

"Hello, so sorry, Les downstairs," she told him. "Want me get for you?"

"That's okay, Somlak. I'm here to talk to you."

Then her smile flickered as he stepped inside.

CHAPTER 30 ~
CONNECTING THE DOTS

Martin watched the helicopters and had to agree with Frankie. It all felt like a staged public relations exercise. It looked and sounded impressive, but what could they possibly hope to achieve?

"Martin Chase?" came a voice beside him, and he looked around to find Rachelle standing there, arms crossed, a stern look in her eyes. "I've got a bone to pick with you, young man!"

"Oh?" he said as the others dissolved away.

"Yes," she replied. "If you're really that desperate to see my apartment, you should have told me so yourself. Not send your mother in to sneak about on your behalf!"

He was gobsmacked. "How did you know that was my mother?"

"You're like two peas in a pod! Didn't anyone ever tell you that?"

"No." He almost smiled. "But if we're bone picking, Rachelle, then I have to say, I think your policy of not selling it to a man is extremely sexist."

Rachelle looked taken aback now. "I'm sorry about that, Mr Chase, but I've rented the unit for years, and it's caused me so much grief in the past it seemed like a sensible policy."

"What kind of grief?"

"Just nagging comments, mostly from Nel, to be honest." She sighed. "Look, my last tenant liked to walk around his bedroom naked. She could see straight in. Asked if he could remember to keep his curtains closed, but he never did. And I don't exactly blame him. It's not *her* apartment. It's Prue's. Still, that's why I was offloading it, trying to find a permanent buyer with a little more tact than that."

"Was he provoking her, this tenant?" Martin asked. "Sexual harassment maybe?"

Rachelle laughed uproariously. "Lordie! Hayley's gay! Ended up moving in with his lovely boyfriend. It just made Nel uncomfortable,

211

that's all. Me? I would have sat back and enjoyed the show!" She winked. "But seriously, I was also trying to ingratiate myself with the Chambers if I'm being honest. Trying to meet them halfway. I thought if I could do one good deed—sell the place to a lovely conservative lady who kept her clothes firmly on—they might see their way to agreeing to my renovations. Quid pro quo." Sighed again. "Your mother would have been perfect, Martin. She's not really in the market for a new apartment is she?"

"No, she's not. But I am. And I can assure you I would never strut around the place naked. I'm a stickler for my privacy and far too lacking in body confidence for that."

"Is that right?" said Rachelle, giving him the once-over.

~

As the crowds watched the choppers perform their work, Merry was watching Dougie, who had come out of his shop and was now walking towards Bellavista. He wasn't looking upwards either. He was scanning the crowd, looking for something. When he caught sight of Merry, he smiled and waved at her, and she went to return the wave but couldn't quite lift her hand.

What if he was the killer? What if Kila was right?

"Are you okay?" Dougie asked as he got closer.

She blinked. Blinked again. "You remembered me," she said, her voice barely audible.

He looked at her, confused, so she added, "How can you have this face blindness thingie when you only met me once and you remembered my name? And not just my name, Dougie. You remembered my full name, Meredith Kean!"

Dougie's face contorted then, like he'd been caught out, his expression mirroring Pip's from yesterday. "I... I don't know what to say, Merry."

"Don't say anything," she replied. "I'm not sure I can believe a word you say."

Then she turned and rushed away.

~

Somlak was determined to fetch Kila a cool drink, and there was nothing he could do to dissuade her, even though he knew Les could walk in any minute. So he followed her into the kitchen and fired his questions at her while she did that.

First he asked about Mr Takahashi and who might have wanted to hurt him, but she seemed genuinely baffled by his murder, and tears sprang into her eyes as she pulled a bottle of mineral water from the fridge.

Pouring it into a glass, she said, "It so sad. Katsu so nice!"

"And it's a pity too, because he was so in favour of the renovations next door," said Kila, his tone casual. "Now your husband will have to try to talk Prue into supporting it."

"Oh, Katsu not like renovations!" she said, catching him by surprise. "Silly Les! I think he say little fib to you! He just wishful thinking."

Yep, that's what Kila thought. So if Les lied about that...

"I know you were cleaning on Wednesday morning when Nel went missing, Somlak, but I wonder whether you might have noticed something unusual before you left for work, or..."

If she was willing to dump her husband in it on the renos, maybe she'd confess to witnessing an altercation between him and Takahashi?

And for a few shocking minutes he thought she was going to.

The woman held a finger to her lips, then handed him his glass and ushered him out to the balcony, closing the sliding door behind them.

Only when they were standing at the furthest edge, looking down on Les's bald spot and the other tenants around him, did she relax and offer him a look—but it was full of contrition.

"Okay, I also do some fibbing," she said. "I usually clean house on Wednesday morning. But last Wednesday they no need me, tell me go away, so I have free morning! I go see my sister. We go to movie! But shh!" She nodded down to Les again. "Don't tell Les, hey? Les say I too lazy. He still think I working."

Then she giggled like that was hilarious, but Kila was not laughing.

He didn't know where to start with that. He wanted to tell Somlak she didn't need to be married to a controlling bully who not only called her "lazy" but made her clean other people's houses when he didn't work and they clearly didn't need to. But there was a bigger issue at hand, a more pressing one, that was setting off his alarm bells.

"Whose house do you usually clean on Wednesdays, Somlak?"

he asked. "Who told you to go away that morning?"

She went to answer, when she noticed some movement down on the street and began pointing. "There!" she said. "Down there! You see!"

And he followed her gaze back to the locals on the esplanade below them.

CHAPTER 31 ~

LIES AND LOCKED ROOMS

Rachelle whipped her frizzy hair from her face and unlocked the door to the vacant apartment, then waved Martin through with a flourish.

"I'll let you inspect the place," she said, "but you better not be lying about being a prude, Martin."

"Oh, I'm not lying to you, Rachelle," he told her. "I make the Queen look like a slut."

She laughed heartily at that, but he wasn't being entirely honest with her. Yes, he was a prude—just ask his ex-girlfriend Tamara—but he also had his sleuth's hat on. Still felt like the case all came back to this apartment.

There was something his mother had said...

"I'm hunting for clues," he'd whispered to Earle before he followed Rachelle inside. But that wasn't strictly true either, and as he walked around now, he couldn't help admiring the unit's sunny outlook and decorative cornices and lovely high ceilings, and... Stop, he told himself.

Focus!

"And through here," Rachelle was saying, "is the room in question. This is the master bedroom with a simply lovely dressing room and en suite bathroom, complete with a spa bath you don't often see in apartments from this era. And this"—she stepped towards the window—"is the view that's caused all the drama. As you can see, it does look straight into Prue's bedroom. Hence my trepidation."

"That's not Prue's bedroom," Martin said. "Hers doesn't face your building; it faces the back. That's one of her spare bedrooms downstairs, the one Nel was first using."

"Oh, okay, whatever," said Rachelle, like it was inconsequential, but Martin wasn't so sure about that. He stepped closer and stared across at Bellavista, first at Prue's apartment and then down to Mrs Bianchi's below that.

He knew the old lady's place was a direct replica of Prue's two-storey apartment upstairs. And like Prue's, he could see straight into what must be Mrs Bianchi's largest spare bedroom on her lower level, but he couldn't see much as she had her curtains drawn. Unlike yesterday, it seems, when his mother spotted her down there.

Or did she?

Finally he remembered what had been niggling at his brain all morning!

~

Kila could not get down to the street fast enough. He looked left and right, left again. All sleuths but one had vanished.

"Everything okay?" said Frankie, perched on a low brick wall, tapping away at her device.

"Where's Earle?" he asked. "And Martin and Merry?"

"They took off," she said. "Everybody's in such a flap today, and I'm the one who has to bang out five hundred words in the next five minutes."

Then she caught the troubled look on his face and said, "What's going on? Kila?"

He shook his head, his eyes now searching further afield for Detective Soderbergh or Constable Logan. Somebody! But all he could see were the Balmoral locals or what was left of them, some staring his way, one of them with eyes narrowed.

~

Olivia was surprised to see Martin back at her front door so soon and behind him an older gentleman with a white beard who looked a little like a very worried Santa Claus.

"Oh, Martin," she said, "is everything okay?"

"This is my colleague Earle Fitzgerald," Martin said. "Have you got a minute?"

"Of course, come in. I'll fire up the espresso machine."

"No time for that, Mum. We're just here to ask you an important question."

Martin drew her to the sofa. Held her hands—another surprise—

and said, solemnly, "You need to tell me exactly what you saw yesterday when you were in Rachelle's apartment."

Olivia was confused, so he took a breath and explained. "When you did your home inspection with Rachelle, remember? You walked into that bedroom that overlooks Prue's building, and you said you saw Merry and me through the window, watched as we ducked behind the bed, yes?"

She nodded.

"You also said something about the apartment underneath. You said something about seeing a woman in that one. Do you remember?"

She nodded again and looked more certain. "That's right!" she replied. "And you said she had dementia, which I thought was strange, but then I remembered that my hairdresser got dementia very young. Remember I told you? She was just forty, and I couldn't see the woman clearly so…"

She stopped talking as Martin's jaw dropped. He shot a look at Earle, then back to her, gripping her hands even tighter.

"What did the woman look like, Mum? The one you saw in the guest bedroom?"

"Um…" Olivia gulped, trying to remember. She had a feeling her son's case relied entirely on her next words. Wanted to get them right. For his sake. "She was quite young, maybe in her thirties? Other than that, pretty ordinary, really. Long, dark brown hair, I think, but that's about all I could see."

It was clearly enough. Now both men were gaping back at her, then, as the older man grappled for his mobile phone, Martin said, "What was she doing, Mum? Tell me exactly!"

"Nothing," she replied. "To be honest, she looked just like Sleeping Beauty."

CHAPTER 32 ~
ALMOST A FAIRY-TALE ENDING

Nel Chambers did have a touch of the sleeping beauty about her when Odetta finally broke in. But she was a sporty-looking Sleeping Beauty, and Odetta wasn't sure she was sleeping.

She was laid out on the double bed in Mrs Bianchi's lower bedroom, her hair spread out around her, her body on top of the covers in the exact walking gear she'd worn when she'd gone missing—minus the cap and sweatshirt. There were flowers strewn across the pillow and, on the bedside table, a can 'of Coke, a half-eaten chocolate bar, and medication made out to Maria Bianchi. Nel's yellow sweatshirt had been folded neatly and placed at the foot of the bed.

The detective held her breath as she stepped across, while Logan held on to Tommo who was now at the doorway, crying and wailing and telling them to "leave my beautiful girl alone! She's mine! I'm looking after her! She's *mine*!"

Odetta turned back and roared, "Get him out of here!" Then she rushed to the woman's side and tried to feel for a pulse. If it was there at all, it was worryingly light, and she wasn't taking any chances, so she began resuscitation while she waited for the paramedics to arrive.

And all the while Tommo could be heard wailing about his girl. His beautiful, beautiful girl. And how he finally had something pretty to look after.

~

By the time Earle and Martin returned to the esplanade, there were two ambulances, a forensics van, and police cars in every direction.

The crowd on the street had quadrupled, visitors milling with locals, all eyes lit with horror and excitement, while the other sleuths stood just under the awning in front of Rachelle's building.

"They found her," Kila called out as the men drew near. "She's alive, but only just. Your tip was spot on, Earle. Tommo took her."

Soon after Somlak had pointed to the Bianchis on the street below, Kila had rushed down to get some help and was just considering smashing the Bianchi door down by himself when Odetta's car came to a screeching halt in front of him.

"I think I know where Nel is!" Kila had yelled, but she was already out of the car and heading straight for Tommo Bianchi.

Turns out Odetta was on her way back to Balmoral when she received Earle's frantic phone call, and she wasn't waiting for a search warrant this time. She'd got to the esplanade in record time and forced Tommo to show them into his grandmother's apartment, where Nel had been captive the entire time.

"Wasn't my tip," said Earle now. "Martin's the one who worked it out first. He's today's hero."

Martin wasn't feeling heroic, kicking himself for not catching his mother's clanging clue earlier. "It was a team effort," he told them, but Kila was having none of it.

"You did well, man. Be proud of that."

"Yes, exceptional work, Marty," added Frankie while Merry just grabbed him in a bear hug.

The author wasn't sure anyone should be hugging anyone just yet. "How's Prue? How's *Nel*?"

"Not too sure about Nel," said Frankie, "but we were with Prue when she got the news. She was utterly shocked. Speechless. Verity had to hold her back from rushing down there. That's the last we saw of her before they kicked us out. Which is ridiculous really because if it wasn't for us… if it wasn't for Martin…" Then she blinked and said, "Speak of the devil."

They turned to see Odetta striding out of Bellavista, pulling off her gloves. She spotted the sleuths, said something to a police officer standing guard at the front gate, then headed towards them.

Merry held her breath as Odetta approached, only releasing it when she heard the detective say the words, "Nel's going to be okay. She's not in great shape. The paramedics are stabilising her in there and then getting her to North Shore hospital when it's safe. But... well, I think she's very lucky that five zealous sleuths happened along." She scratched her short white hair and added, "I can see why DI Morgan loathes you lot."

Earle gave her an apologetic smile and asked, "So, how'd she look when you found her?"

"Freaky, to be honest." Odetta described how Tommo had laid Nel out on the bed. "I didn't see obvious signs of abuse—she's still in the same gear she was in when she was abducted—but we'll know more once she gets to hospital. Of course, she may not remember much. She was loaded to the eyeballs, we believe, with antipsychotics, his grandmother's dementia medication. Nel is so drowsy she's barely coherent. I guess every time she started to come to, he gave her another hit."

"But why?" asked Frankie. "Why keep her there?"

"We'll need to get a psychological assessment, but the man clearly has serious issues," Odetta replied. "The way he'd laid her out, the way he responded when we found her. It's like she was his doll or child or something. He kept saying how much he loved her and just wanted to look after something pretty for a change. Said if he had to get stuck caring for an old lady, why not someone young and beautiful too? Someone to make it all worthwhile."

"Oh no," said Merry, hand to her lips. "I wonder if that's what Mrs Bianchi was trying to tell me yesterday? When I saw them near the beach, she said Tommo had relationship troubles and he laughed it off, said that was in the past, but maybe she was talking about Nel? Maybe she knew Nel was down there and thought Nel was his girlfriend? She also said something about keeping the door closed. I can't believe I missed that! Maybe she meant the door to that prison bedroom!"

"Maybe," said Odetta. "But you weren't to know."

"And Mr Takahashi? Did Tommo kill him too?" asked Frankie.

"One crime at a time, please people," she shot back. "We've taken Tommo into custody. We'll get to that one next. But I suspect he's responsible. Takahashi was probably just in the wrong place at the wrong time, saw Tommo dragging Nel into his apartment—"

"The brown-haired man," said Earle, and she nodded.

"We think Tommo realised Nel was hurt and took advantage of the opportunity to abduct her. Maybe he'd been stalking her for a while? Any case, he followed her inside and then somehow got her into his grandmother's apartment. It wouldn't have been hard if she was badly concussed. I suspect Takahashi saw them together and had to be silenced. We now know from his employer that he never came in that Wednesday morning. I suspect Tommo killed him to shut him up sometime soon after."

"The poor man," said Merry. "Why didn't his boss report him missing?"

"His boss is in Japan. His colleagues in the Sydney office just assumed he was taking a well-earned break. They had no idea. Sadly. We'll find out more once we interrogate Mr Bianchi formally. I'm just so relieved Nel is alive, and I know we have you lot to thank for that." She glanced at her phone. "I have to get back, but I just wanted to give credit where credit's due."

As Odetta returned to Bellavista, Merry spotted Dougie in the crowd of onlookers and blushed profusely.

Frankie noticed. "Go and say hello!"

"I couldn't possibly. I'm mortified that I ever believed Dougie could do such a thing!"

"But you didn't believe," said Frankie. "You stood up for him over and over when Kila kept pointing the finger. Because that's what I heard, Merry. Okay, maybe for a scary second you entertained the idea, but your initial instincts were spot on. And he is a sweetie. Look at him, giving you a bashful little smile. Go on, say hello. Invite him for dinner. Shag his brains out."

"Frankie!" Merry slapped her playfully now and then offered him a bashful smile back just as a well-dressed man with a microphone appeared, pushing through the crowd, a stocky cameraman behind him.

"Oh, goodie, it's my favourite newsman!" said Frankie, offering the shocked Tagger a smile of her own. But hers wasn't bashful. "Now watch this," she said to Merry as two of the police officers rushed up to Tagger and blocked his entry.

Frankie giggled and said, "That was so satisfying."

When Merry looked around again, she saw that Dougie had vanished.

Earle watched as one of the paramedics appeared from the building, then jumped in his van and drove it down the steep driveway that led into Bellavista's underground carpark. Earle was glad of that. It meant these lechers with cameras would not capture Nel being rattled out the front door on a stretcher and piled into the back of the ambulance.

After all she had been through, it would be a final indignity she did not deserve.

He was just looking back at the lechers when he spotted a familiar figure breaking through the police line. It was Colin Boyder, and he looked like a man possessed. His hair was tufted up, his crumpled shirt buttoned incorrectly. For the first time since Earle's visits, he looked like a concerned fiancé.

"I only just heard!" Colin said after spotting the ex-detective. "Why wasn't I told? Where's Nel? I've been worried sick!"

Earle held a hand up to stall him, thinking, *You never looked very worried to me.*

"She's being assessed by paramedics now," Earle said. "They're taking her to the Royal North Shore Hospital. I suggest you wait for her there."

"No! I want to get inside! I want to see my fiancée!"

"And you will," said Earle as Kila stepped forward, ready to intervene. He waved Kila back. "Now is not the time, Mr Boyder. No one but family is allowed in there right now."

"I *am* family!"

"Not yet you're not," said Earle. *And hopefully you never will be.*

He thought about his own family then and his unreasonable dislike of Tess's partner Fiona. What *had* he disliked about her, exactly? Sure, she was bossy and scared him a little, and he had no clue why she'd fallen out with his daughter—Tess never told him anything—but he did know that if Tess had vanished for three days without a word, it would not have taken Fiona three days and an afternoon to show up and start asking questions. Like Mrs Chambers, she would have organised a search party within hours.

Colin Boyder was a lousy partner, and if anything good came from Nel's near-death experience, Earle hoped it was her waking up to that fact.

Not long after Colin had taken the hint and headed off, the ambulance reappeared from inside the carpark, and Frankie watched as the TV reporters all scrambled to get the shot. Yang was amongst them, and she watched as he scrambled too. That's why she loved being a feature writer so much. You didn't have to scramble with the best of them. Could stand back and make notes like a civilised human being.

And that's exactly what she did, tapping all the colour and chaos into her smartphone.

She was just wondering whether to find a quiet spot to compile it into a longer piece for the Sunday edition when she received another call from her boss.

She picked up, saying, "Yes! I'm at Balmoral! I've got the answers to your questions and I'll get the inside story to you, pronto!"

"Don't care about that," he replied, his voice, well, *odd*. "Get back to the office. Now."

And with that he hung up, and she was left with a few questions of her own.

CHAPTER 33 ~
FRANKIE'S FINAL COMEUPPANCE

By the time Frankie got to the *Herald*, she was feeling, frankly, pissed off. The scoop of the century was happening back at Balmoral, and Ruffus was dragging her away! How could he be so stupid? Now was not the time to chastise her about not being a team player! Who cared about reporting in and playing happy families when a major story was breaking?

She had reached his internal office when the glass door swung open and he stepped outside.

"You won't believe what's happened!" she told him. "We've located the missing woman. Alive! Police have a suspect. I'll whip a quick story out and then— I'm sorry, but I really do need to get back."

He had a hand up to stall her, a flinty look in his eyes. And that's when she noticed a woman standing behind him who looked vaguely, *ominously* familiar.

"Step into my office," was all he said before they both turned and made their way back in.

Frankie locked eyes with Katie, who'd been watching from her desk. The junior reporter looked suddenly stricken, glancing away and then down, her gaze now locked to her keyboard.

"What's going on?" Frankie asked the sports reporter who was also watching, but he just looked disappointed. Or something.

So Frankie frowned and followed Ruffus in, remembering then who the woman with her editor was—it was Dimity Peters, head of the Human Resources Department.

Oh God, she thought. Okay, okay, I'll attend the next after-work piss-up!

Dimity waved Frankie into a chair and then closed the door behind them.

"What's going on?" Frankie asked her just as Ruffus cleared his throat.

"Know anything about this?"

Frankie glanced around to find him holding a crumpled double-page spread in one hand and a plastic bag with something brown in the other.

She blinked, almost chuckled. "What is this?"

"For once in your life, Frankie Jo, just answer the fucking question," he said, his tone curiously low.

"Easy now," Dimity said to Ruffus, confusing Frankie further.

"Fine." Frankie crossed her legs. "That's page six and seven of today's edition—I can see Katie's lame follow-up to the laneway murder there on the right—and that..." She stared at the bag. "Is that a rock or something?"

Ruffus dropped the bag to the table with a thud and gave Dimity a pointed look. She stepped forward and then produced a small recorder, which she placed on the edge of his desk, facing Frankie, then perched beside it.

"I'd like to advise you that I will be recording this conversation."

"What?" said Frankie.

Dimity pressed the Record button, then said, "Interview with Francesca Josephina," before adding her and Ruffus's full names and the time and date. Then she said, "I'd like to inform you that you are entitled to union representation—"

"Union? I don't want the union! Why would I want them here?" A glance at Ruffus. "What's this about?"

"You tell me, Frankie," he said, his voice still eerily subdued. "Please, I just need you to be honest."

And that's when Frankie knew she was really in trouble because Ruffus was a barker. He made a lot of noise. Now he sounded like a mouse, and he, too, looked so very disappointed.

Dimity reached for the plastic bag and held it up again. "This rock was wrapped in that particular page of today's newspaper. It was thrown through your boss—Mr Jones's—living room window at around six this morning. Do you know anything about that?"

Frankie glanced at Ruffus, but like Katie, he suddenly couldn't meet her eye. "You don't think...," she began. "I mean, surely you can't be saying...?"

"Please just answer the question," said Dimity.

"Oh my God!" Frankie was on her feet and noticed that Ruffus was now leaning backwards, like he feared she was going to charge. She tried to take deep breaths, but her lungs were suddenly constricting. "W-why? Why on earth would you think I would trash your house? Ruffus?"

Ruffus continued to avoid eye contact while Dimity picked up a folder from his desk and then began leafing through it. She produced a large photo and held it up for Frankie to see.

"Do you know anything about the vandalism to Mr Jones's vehicle three days ago?"

Frankie stared at the photo of Ruffus's baby-blue vintage Chrysler Valiant, with an ugly scratch etched down one side. She felt a similar scratch run through her spine. Shook it off. Couldn't think straight.

Dimity added, "Are you responsible for this vandalism?"

"What? No!" Deep breaths. In and out. "No, I am not!"

Frankie could not believe what she was hearing.

Dimity placed the photo back, then pulled out a sheet of paper and began reading from it. "Yesterday afternoon, soon after your editor removed you from the Phillip Weaver story, did you threaten him with the following words: 'You are going to be so sorry!'?"

Frankie stared at him. "Oh for goodness' sake! I didn't mean anything by it!"

"We'll take that as confirmation," Dimity said into the recorder, then began reading from the page again. "And did you, earlier that same morning, tell one of your colleagues that someone ought to teach Ruffus a lesson?"

Frankie felt her blood run cold and glanced back towards the door, towards Katie's desk, then sank into her seat, bewildered, as her future imploded before her eyes.

~

"You guys are doing it, aren't you?" said Martin, smiling wickedly at the group.

The remaining sleuths had decamped to Ballo's, the café next to the bookshop. The forensic team were still crawling through Bellavista, and Prue was at the hospital with her daughter. Verity had suggested they hang close as she needed to talk to them, and so those who could made their way down, Merry with her heart in her mouth, both excited and nervous about the prospect of seeing Dougie again.

But First Chapters bookstore was closed, and now she felt relief and disappointment.

It was only after they'd quietly raised their coffee cups to toast another case resolved, and Kila had lamented the fact that Frankie was absent, that Martin made his declaration.

"What guys? Who's doing it?" asked Merry, sipping from her mug, hoping he wasn't referring to her and Dougie because everyone was getting way ahead of themselves there, thanks very much! They'd only had one date, and you'd hardly call it a date, really. She went to interrogate the poor fellow, and he'd probably worked that out by now, would likely never forgive her for thinking he could be responsible...

"Kila and Frankie," he told Merry. "They're a couple."

"*Really?*" she said, sitting forward and staring at Kila.

The fact that he was shrugging nonchalantly, not furiously denying it, made her realise Martin was onto something.

"How long?" she asked him, and he shrugged again.

"They got together straight after the last case," said Earle, surprising even Martin. "I noticed it at Seagrave when we all returned to collect our cheques and celebrate. Remember that very boozy evening? Kila and Frankie couldn't keep their eyes off each other." Then he laughed at their collective surprise and added, "And you lot call yourselves detectives."

Yet Kila wasn't laughing. He was glancing up and down the street, his eyes furtive. "Okay, steady on people," he told them as they continued to snicker. "Frankie doesn't want it broadcasted. Just keep it on the lowdown, yeah?"

"Why exactly *not?*" said Merry, feeling offended for her friend. If Kila was her boyfriend, she'd be shouting it to the rafters. Of course the two of them would have made a terrible match. She was far too straight for the rule-breaking PI. Dougie was more her style with his sweet, dimpled smile and his lovely bookshop and...

She gave herself a shake and tuned back in to what Kila was saying.

"We think Frankie's crazy ex has been stalking her. Frankie doesn't want to add any more fuel to the fire."

"What ex?" asked Martin. "I didn't know Frankie was seeing anyone back then."

"She wasn't," said Kila, his face clouding over. "I'm talking about her ex-*best friend*. Remember Jan? The Boss? Big hair, even bigger personality? She crashed Seagrave one day, all huffy that Frankie had been neglecting her."

"Oh that's right," said Merry. "She had the giant handbag and stole half the pastries? She was a bit nutty."

"*Nutty?*" He looked around, then back. "That woman is a sociopath."

~

It was only as Frankie was dumping her box of office possessions into the boot of her car, the official dismissal letter resting on top, that she finally understood what had happened.

It all clicked into place.

Frankie's Audi didn't have a single scratch along the side, like Ruffus's, like Kila's, but she almost wished it had. Her boss and her boyfriend had got off lightly.

As for Frankie? She'd just learned the hard way what happened when you dumped an old friend who thought they owned you.

And that you owed them everything.

Now it wasn't just Frankie's future that was flashing before her eyes. It was her distant past and the ugly consequences that were catching up with her at last.

CHAPTER 34 ~
TOASTING THE SLEUTHS

When Verity finally joined the group at Ballo's, she was surprised to see Frankie still absent. "I thought our investigative reporter would be the first one here, demanding to know every minute detail."

"We haven't heard a peep from her," said Earle. "It's just us for now. Can I grab you a coffee?"

"I'll get it," she said, waving the young waitress over.

Order complete, she reached into her handbag and produced her cheque book. Or, rather, George Burlington's, because few people under the age of seventy used cheques anymore. As she signed the cheques herself—"George has made me a co-signatory; he just hasn't the energy for business anymore"—she thanked them for their service.

"How is George today?" asked Merry, but Martin waved that off.

"I want to know how Nel is! And Prue. How are they holding up?"

"I just saw them in hospital with Odetta, and they're much better now that Nel's out of that man's clutches." Verity shuddered and shook her head. "Dear girl is very weak and dehydrated. She's going to be attached to a drip for a while and going to need quite a few weeks of rest after what she's endured. Her executive functioning is shot. Her speech disjointed—partly from the concussion and partly from all the drugs he fed her. Odetta says that Nel was lucky to get any sustenance at all. Just a can of Coke and a few bars of chocolate."

"The groceries!" said Merry. "I spotted all that sweet stuff that fell from the bag when we first met him, and he said it was for his grandmother. I can't believe I fell for that. Hell, I fell for all his horrible, horrible lies."

"Don't beat yourself up, Merry," said Verity. "We were all sucked in by his Good Samaritan act. Prue thought Tommo was adorable, helping his dear old grandmother. If only we'd known he was so unhinged. I hope he doesn't get found not guilty by reason of insanity."

"Even if that happens, Verity, he'll be confined to a secure psychiatric prison for some time," said Earle. "At least I hope he will."

Verity hoped so too. "Odetta thinks he'll claim the stress of looking after a very high-needs grandmother. Apparently no one else in the family would step up, so he felt he had no choice."

"That's bullshit," said Kila. "It's not an excuse."

"No," said Earle. "But it is an explanation."

"What's useful," said Verity, "as horrendous as Tommo is, he appears to be owning up to everything. Seems *proud* of what he'd done, like he'd rescued Nel and was keeping her safe at Nonna's place. Thought he was very clever too, feeding you lot that false clue about the Tuesday four p.m. phone call. And his fake alibi."

Merry blanched, then told the others, "The snivelling liar told me he was with his flatmate on Wednesday morning, said the cops had checked that."

"They hadn't got around to it," said Verity. "Hadn't checked that Tuesday phone call properly either. There *was* a call to Nel around three thirty, but it was from a local travel agent, and no one told anyone to get lost or leave them alone. If they'd double-checked all that, they would have realised Tommo was a consummate liar. It was pretty sloppy police work."

"Hey, we all dropped the ball on that one," said Earle, feeling for Odetta suddenly.

"If it helps," added Verity, "you were right about the crime being opportunistic. Tommo *was* in the area early on Wednesday, and according to him—so take this with a grain of salt—he just *happened* to notice Nel looking woozy up near the oval that morning, soon after she'd been hit by the surfboard."

"He was stalking her for sure," said Kila.

"Any case, Tommo says he didn't notice the cap, but he did see that she'd dropped her yellow sweatshirt, so he followed her back, just to hand it to her, apparently."

"Pip saw that too!" said Merry, eyes on Kila. "When she first described the brown-haired man to us, she said he might have been wearing yellow. Maybe it was Nel's sweatshirt she remembered.

He must've been holding that when he walked past."

"Highly likely," said Verity. "He told Odetta he tried to give it back to Nel, but she was acting strangely, and that's when he realised she needed 'looking after'—his creepy words, not mine. So he somehow managed to shepherd her into his grandmother's apartment. Told her he'd get her a headache tablet."

"He gave her a lot more than that," said Earle, and she nodded.

"Doctors say Nel is lucky to be alive. They believe she suffered a traumatic brain injury from the surfboard. There would have been swelling, dizziness, loss of memory. Which is partly why she doesn't remember much after it happened. According to Tommo, he'd just got her to his grandmother's apartment door when Takahashi came in from the parking garage to fetch his car keys and spotted them together. One moment of forgetfulness and the poor man's life was over."

"So Tommo followed Takahashi to his apartment?" asked Martin.

"Yep. Popped Nel into the guest bed, apparently without any objections, then grabbed Takahashi as he was coming back out with his keys this time. Said he needed to borrow a vacuum cleaner of all things, convinced Takahashi to go back in, then stabbed him while he was opening the downstairs cupboard."

"Dreadful," said Merry.

"And bloody lucky for Somlak," said Kila. "She turned up to Mrs Bianchi's door at exactly eleven for her regular cleaning job. If she'd got there any earlier, she might have gone the way of Takahashi. Somlak told me she thought Tommo had only just arrived when she saw him and was so surprised when he sent her away. So off she went to the cinema, without a second glance."

"Hang on," said Martin. "Somlak cleaned the Bianchi place *every* week? Why? Surely the Polanskis aren't hard up for cash?"

"I was wondering the same thing myself," said Kila. "So I had a quiet word with her about that later." He smiled. "Somlak's savvier than we give her credit for. Told me she enjoyed the work—she cleans about five other units in the area, apparently. Says it gets her away from 'silly Les', and when she gets enough cash together, she's going leave him and move in with her sister." His smile turned mischievous. "I informed her she didn't need to get the cash together. She could take him for half that apartment any time she liked. Told her to get in touch with my lawyer, Sheila. She'd sort her out. Somlak loved the sound of that."

"I do too!" said Merry, raising her cup again.

They toasted Somlak and lucky escapes, then Earle asked about Colin Boyder.

"Was the fiancé lurking at the hospital?"

Verity shook her head. "Prue sent him packing. Said he hadn't earned the right to see her daughter but could call Nel in a month or two. When she's stronger."

"Let's hope she's strong enough to tell him to bugger off," said Earle, and they were surprised by his vehemence but happily toasted that too.

Then Merry held her cup up one last time. "I'd like to toast young Pip Dollarway," she said, her eyes flicking to the shop next door. "If it wasn't for her insistence that she saw Nel with a brown-haired man *after* Crispin Regatta had left the beach, we might all have stopped looking."

"Good point," said Earle. "Pip was a much better witness than I gave her credit for."

"Goodness! You all need to stop beating yourself up," said Verity. "Prue thinks you deserve medals for your work! And so do I. I'd ask my assistant to look into that but she'd probably botch it up."

"Why do you keep her if she's so hopeless?" asked Martin.

Verity shrugged. "I took her on as a favour to George." She smiled. "Don't ask." Then she drained her coffee and stood up. "I'd better make tracks. Have hired gardeners to get stuck into Seagrave tomorrow, so I need to get over there, break the news to Sir Grumpy."

"I noticed that place was a bit of a mess," said Merry. "What's going on with the old guy? It's like Sir George has given up."

"That's because he has." Verity dropped some cash on the table for their coffees. "Tells me he wants to fade away and let Seagrave fade away with him. But I won't allow it. Over my dead body, I say!"

Then she thanked them again and left them to it.

As the sleuths continued reviewing the case, marvelling at how fortunate—how convenient—it was that Tommo Bianchi had confessed to everything, Kila's mind drifted back to another criminal who never had the decency to confess to anything: Dragon Malone. A man whose own fixation with a woman had also led to murder.

Except…

He pulled out his phone and read the start of Dragon's text again. Or at least what he could make of it through the cracked screen:

Dear Mr Morea, I'm sorry about what happened to your sister but…

But?

He shook his head. Nope. There was nothing that bastard could say that would assuage his guilt. He switched the phone off and pushed his chair back with a scorching screech.

"You heading home?" Merry asked, looking up from her coffee with a start.

"Nope," he replied. "Just taking this party up a notch."

Then he pulled out his credit card and headed next door to the bottle shop.

~

By the time Earle got home, it was late, and he kicked himself again for not phoning. Then he performed his dance of the light foot—slipping off his shoes, tiptoeing down the hallway and into the kitchen.

"In the fridge," came a voice from the table, and he was startled to see Beryl sitting in semidarkness, a mug of something chocolatey in front of her. "Couldn't sleep," she told him when he flicked on the light and glanced up at the clock.

It was just after eleven, well past her usual bedtime, and his, too, since retirement.

"Sit. I'll warm it up again," she said, pushing her chair out.

"I can do that, love. I'm not really very hung—"

"Sit," she said again, her voice firmer now, and he realised this wasn't about dinner.

So he let her zap the casserole and waited until she'd placed it before him, adding a fork beside it, noting that she didn't slam either of them down and feeling emboldened by that.

"Everything okay? Tess all good?"

He should have kept his gob shut.

"*Of course* she's not good, Earle. Her father thinks she's a bitter disappointment."

"No, I do not," he replied.

"Then why does she think that? You've barely been able to look at her since she came home, and she needs our support now,

Earle Thomas Fitzgerald, not our judgement."

"I'm not..." He picked up his fork. Smashed it back down. "It's me I'm disappointed with, damn it! It's *me* I'm judging!"

Beryl would normally tell him to keep his voice down, but she just looked astonished.

"Why would you say that?" she whispered.

He lowered his own voice. "Because it's true."

Then he told her how he felt about his daughter. How he'd let her down as a child and how he was sure he'd let down his grandchild too. "I was a terrible father first time around. I don't want to stuff up again."

"You weren't a terrible father," came a voice from the doorway, and they both looked around to see Tess standing there in flannelette pyjamas, her round belly poking out. "You were a terrific father!"

He looked away, swallowed the lump in his throat. "Not true," he managed. "I was working all the time. I was never home."

"You had an important job," said Tess, now waddling across and pulling a chair out for herself while Beryl just watched them, eyes wet with tears. "I was so proud of you for that! Have you ever asked Fiona about her dad?" Then she shook her head. "Of course not. You barely spoke to my partner. Well, her dad left when she was a teenager. Is living on the streets, or so she thinks. Fi reckons she's seen him a few times, not far from our apartment."

Earle sat forward and looked at Beryl, who just sighed. She clearly knew the story.

"Oh dear," he said. "I'm sorry. I never realised. So, did Fiona speak to him? Approach him?"

Tess smudged her lips downwards and looked like she was about to cry. "Fi doesn't want anything to do with the poor man. Reckons he's a loser not worth knowing! But... well, I think that's crap. It's a cop out! I mean, you don't end up homeless on the street for no reason, right? You always said that, Dad, that we shouldn't make assumptions, that we need to try to understand everybody's story."

"Is that what you've been fighting about?" he asked.

She nodded. "It's *her father*, for God's sake! But she doesn't want a bar of him. I... I can't have our child around someone who thinks the homeless are not worth knowing!"

Earle placed his palm over hers. "I'm sure Fiona doesn't really think that, honey. I suspect she's a very scared daughter, terrified of approaching him. She's probably still trying to come to terms with it, that's all. You need to be patient with her, give her time."

Now Tess was smiling. Giddily. "See! You have such a good heart." She looked at her mother and smiled. "You've been good parents, both of you. But sure, you haven't been perfect, and neither have I." Now her eyes were back on Earle. "I know we've struggled since I came out. I know it's something *you* still need to come to terms with. But, well, I haven't been very patient with you either, have I? We've both got to work on that."

"We will," said Earle, voice raspy.

She smiled again. "But here's the thing, despite it all, I've always known you loved me, Dad, and I've always known that I can count on you. Fiona never had that. I do. And that's why I'm back here. Not because I *can't* take care of this little one on my own. It's because I don't *want* to. I want you beside me, Dad."

"But... what if I stuff it up?"

"You won't! You can't. It's not in your DNA."

Then she reached over and hugged him, and he never wanted to let her go again.

Later, after she'd waddled back out, her own mug of hot chocolate in hand, Beryl gave Earle a look, and he said, "What?"

"Why do you have to make life so damn difficult, Earle?" Then she smiled to show she still forgave him. "So, I gather the case is over. I'm hoping that means you found the poor child in one piece?"

He nodded. "But she's got a long road ahead of her. It was a traumatic experience."

"Yes, but she's alive, and that, my dear, is partly thanks to you." She sat forward. "That's why you have to set up your business, Earle! You have to put up a shingle. Hire your services out. That girl is not the only one who needs you. And I'm not talking Nel Chambers now."

A small smile snaked across his lips. "I might have myself a few partners."

Then his mind drifted back to the café he'd just left, the other sleuths still there, coffee long ago replaced with something stronger.

About twenty minutes after Kila had returned with two bottles of that tasty shiraz and the waitress had brought fresh wineglasses,

Frankie had appeared with a dark and sullen expression. She thrust a spare glass out to be filled, then told them about her sudden dismissal.

"Is that even legal?" asked Martin. "Shouldn't they give you an official warning first?"

"And you didn't *do* any of that stuff, right?" asked Merry because she wouldn't put it past the woman.

Frankie looked offended. "Of course not, Merry! I'm zealous, but I'm not violent! No, at first I thought one of the junior writers might be sabotaging me. Katie, she's... well, she's a lot like me to be honest. But now I think it's Jan. My old university mate. Has to be."

"Kila told us about her," said Earle.

"And we know about you guys too," added Martin, causing Frankie to scowl at Kila, then shoot her own furtive glances down the street.

"You honestly think that woman has been following you? Keying Kila's car?"

"Left a dog turd on my doorstep too," he confessed, and now Frankie looked mortified.

"Why didn't you tell me?"

"Knew you'd worry. I can handle a bit of random faeces."

"It's not random at all," she shot back, turning her eyes to the others. "The woman's psychotic. It's been going on for months. Every time I stay over at Kila's place, he gets a little 'gift' from Jan in return." She sighed irritably. "But she never crossed the line when it came to my work. Now... now she's upped the ante, and I can only hope this is game over. She might not have scared Kila off, but she has managed to destroy my career. As far as I'm concerned, there's nothing left to burn."

"Oh, you'll get another job," said Earle, but she shook her head.

"It's not like in your day, Earle. There's not a lot of full-time jobs left in this industry, at least not the jobs I like. It's all moving online, all vacuous clickbait. I loved my work! I loved that I got to write decent, in-depth articles, and it wasn't just about the byline, although yes, of course, I loved seeing my name in print too. I liked that my articles probed real issues, helped real people, that I was helping make sense of all the darkness out there."

"I know how else you can help people," said Merry, giving Earle a conspiratorial smile.

And so as day turned into night and the streetlamps came on, followed quickly by the café's twinkly fairy lights, more alcohol was purchased and then large pans of pizza to soak it all up, and the sleuths hatched a plan to set up a detective agency together.

Merry said she needed purpose beyond playing her favourite board game and pining for her old life. "Since the case started, I haven't found myself back in Otis's room once, haven't called him, making him feel guilty. And that's because I've been working with you guys on something that really matters. I know you're not supposed to say it, but I've loved every minute of it, and I want to do more like it."

"Say it all you like," said Frankie. "Nothing wrong with loving your job, even when your job involves the dark side of life. And you're right. It has been an enjoyable process, sleuthing with you lot." She dropped her blond locks to one side. "You know it's ironic, really. Ruffus always says I'm a terrible team player, always thinking of myself, but it's because I was such a good team player that I lost my job in the first place. Jan wanted me all to herself. But you guys bring out the best in me."

"God, if that's Frankie's best, you're in trouble, Earle and Merry," said Martin, giving the journalist a sly smile.

"Shut up, you smug author, and tell us you'll join our agency," said Frankie, but he wasn't buying in, not yet.

"I do like the sound of that. I have to say, you'll be a formidable force. But I've got a book to finish first. Actually, starting the blasted thing would help."

"Is this your new novel?" asked Merry, and he shook his head.

"Got a whole new idea for a book, and I can't have any more distractions. Not with this one. But what about *your* writing, Frankie? Are you really willing to give it all up so quickly?"

"I'm not sure I'd have to give it up entirely, would I?" She glanced across at Earle. "Writing articles is nothing like writing a book. I could pick up the odd freelance piece from time to time, couldn't I? When things are slow?"

That's when the last of Earle's doubts fell away, and he realised this idea was gold. With at least three of them in the agency, it would free them all up when things got busy in their respective lives. Take the pressure off entirely.

"I don't see why not," he told her. "When my Tess has her baby, I could step away for a bit, and you too, Merry, when your kids need you or Otis is visiting or whatnot."

"What about you, Kila?" asked Merry. "You've been very quiet. Are you going to sign on the dotted line too?"

He pushed a stray curl from his eyes. "I don't know, Festive. This all feels far too warm and fuzzy for me." He winked to lessen the blow. "Plus I do have my own PI business, yes?"

Merry pouted, and he grabbed her hand and squeezed it.

"Tell you what," he said, "when you get in a pickle, when you can't see the wood for the trees, when Frankie here starts acting like Princess Bitchface—"

"Hey!" shot back Frankie.

He chuckled. "I'm just saying, call me anytime you need me. Or even as a last resort."

That's when Merry sat forward with a start.

"That's the name!" she declared. "That's what we should call the agency! The Sleuths of Last Resort."

Frankie's button nose crinkled. "At risk of sounding like a princess"—a glare at Kila then—"doesn't that sound a bit, well, *desperate*?"

"Yes, it does," said Earle, "but then it's the desperate cases we want, or at least I do. I want to assist people who really need our help, who have no other options. Who've been ignored by the police or tried all other avenues and just can't find the answers. Don't you?"

Frankie gave it some thought and was soon nodding fervently. "I think you might have just nailed our business brief, Earle. Our *raison dêtre*, so to speak. No offence, Kila, but you can keep your desperate housewives."

Now it was his turn to look offended, but Merry was nodding along. "Absolutely! That's our point of difference. We should only take on really serious cases, help the genuinely needy."

Then she leapt to her feet and held her hand out, palm down in the middle of the table, just as she'd done six months ago in the Burlington case. "Come on then, let's make it official."

And just like then, Earle chuckled and stood up first, then pulled his hand back and reminded her that it would be a long hard road ahead.

"Setting up a new business is not easy, folks, and we can't expect

Sir George to keep furnishing us with clients. He's going to run out of friends and family eventually." He half smiled. "We'll have to pool our resources, and it may take some time to get on our feet."

"Oh, we'll be *great!*" Merry shot back, eyes now down to Frankie.

The journo stood up, palm out. "Of course I'm in. When have I ever said no to anything?"

Then they all gave Martin and Kila a final, expectant glance, and Martin shook his head and Kila heard his own words echoed back to him: "You look like a pack of idiots, you know that, right?"

Laughing, Merry pushed the others' palms downwards and yelled out, "It's official. The Sleuths of Last Resort are now in business!"

EPILOGUE

Martin checked the speedometer on his Aston Martin, then released his foot slightly from the accelerator. He was anxious to get started on his new book, but he was in no hurry to get where he was going.

He thought back to his last dinner with the sleuths and how he'd told them he was writing a new story. But it wasn't just any story, and it certainly wasn't literary fiction. It was something else entirely.

Halfway through a similar dinner, a night or so earlier, he'd had his first real light-bulb moment. As his mother waxed lyrical about her extraordinary life, Martin realised it wasn't more fiction he needed to write and certainly not another Flynn Bold adventure. It was *Olivia's* story. A story that actually mattered! Turns out Frankie was right. Fiction did pale in comparison.

Problem was Olivia wasn't buying it.

"You need to stop looking outwards," she told him when he turned up after Ballo's to reveal his brilliant new plan, drunk on both shiraz and excitement. "You need to write your own story. And sure, my story is part of that, but it's not the whole story, and you know it. You can't complete the picture—you can't move on with your life—until you speak to your father. Don't you think, Braxton Wicks?"

She had thrown his given name back in his face, and he didn't want it, didn't like it, felt a flash of fury.

"Don't call me that!" he'd yelled at her then. "I don't want to be associated with that monster!"

Then her eyes had widened and she'd said, "Why do you keep calling him a monster? You said that the other night."

"Because he was violent! Abusive!" Martin reached a hand to his nose, once broken by his father during a fight on a fishing trip. Stroked it. "*Wasn't he?*"

Olivia looked surprised. "Not to me he wasn't. And I'm sorry if he ever hurt you, Martin, but he was my saviour back then.

He rescued me from a violent boyfriend. He never told you that?"

Martin collapsed into a chair then, didn't know what to think. She leant down beside him and now took his hands in hers.

"This is what I'm talking about. Somewhere along the line you've got your story mixed up, your wires crossed. You need to go back and see him. Talk to him directly. Hear it from the horse's mouth."

And so here he was, driving towards the shabby fishing village and his old stomping ground and a father who might not have done as much stomping as Martin remembered.

Where had that violent image come from? Why had he despised the man so much?

And would his father still be alive and willing to set the record straight, let alone forgive him for what he'd accused him of that dreadful day in the dinghy? No wonder he broke Martin's nose in three places.

Martin didn't know what was true anymore and what could be trusted, but he did know his mum was right, and it was time to sort fact from fiction.

~

"Where are you going?" asked Frankie, voice croaky, one arm stretching out across the sheet towards Kila. "Come back to bed."

He was perched on his side, staring blankly into his lap, and he glanced back at her and smiled.

"Anyone ever tell you you look beautiful in the mornings?"

"Yes, you, every morning!" She propped herself up on one elbow, rubbed some sleep from her eyes. "Now stop deflecting. It's six a.m. Where are you off to at this ungodly hour?"

He shrugged and stood up. Grabbed some jeans from the floor and tugged them on, then reached for a shirt, smelt it, reached for another. "Got an appointment," he said as he buttoned it up.

Frankie groaned and flopped back down again. "What appointment? You didn't tell me about any appointment."

"Nothing to worry about. Go back to sleep. I just have to see a man about a dog."

But it wasn't a man he was seeing. It was a low-life criminal lawyer. And it wasn't just any dog he was referring to. It was his sister's killer. At least, he thought it was.

Until very late last night.

Frankie and Kila were just tumbling into bed when Dragon's second text came through. How the bastard even got hold of a mobile phone, not once, but twice, was beyond Kila, but it didn't matter now. All he could think about was the message that had been playing like a loop in his head all night and into the morning. This one was shorter, more succinct, not so easily hidden beneath the scratched screen, so Kila couldn't help but read exactly what Dragon wanted to say:

I let her go.

They were four tiny words, but it felt as though a claw had grabbed Kila's heart and crushed it like it was made of tissue.

Until then, until those four words, there had never been one scintilla of responsibility from the evil cretin. Not so much as an acknowledgement that his sister had even existed. Dragon's defence had always been that the two had never met. That Chili had stood him up on the blind date, and someone else was to blame for her murder.

But now...

If the bastard was telling the truth, it sounded to Kila like Dragon was not only confessing to meeting his sister, to *hurting* his sister, he was saying he released her afterwards—like a fish from a hook, a mouse from a trap, an angel from the devil's lair—and that meant something else entirely.

Something far more disturbing.

Because if Dragon let his sister go, then she must have been alive and breathing, right? So how did Chili end up *not breathing* in a filthy city laneway just a few hours later?

As he gently closed the front door and headed for his scratched-up four-wheel drive, Kila had a feeling another door was opening and Chili's story was only just beginning.

~

Merry couldn't help humming happily as she laid the picnic blanket down on the soft sand of Balmoral Beach, then grinned across at her daughter, who looked bored beyond belief but knew better than to complain and simply offered her a lukewarm smile in return.

At least Archie looked happy to be here.

"Can I hire one of the kayaks, Mum? Can I?"

Merry glanced across to the boat rental shed at the wharf and several kayakers milling about, her mind on Crispin Regatta now. She wondered if he was amongst them, whether he'd ever show his face at Balmoral again. She knew Detective Soderbergh was furious with the man, and she understood why, but the fact remained, despite initial impressions, the only thing the fool was guilty of was letting a badly concussed woman walk away without medical assistance. It was negligence at worst.

"Sure, Arch," Merry said. "Run over and see how much they cost."

As he did that, Merry looked back towards the esplanade, towards First Chapters bookshop and a man who should not have forgiven her for thinking he could be a monster.

Yet he'd waved that off without so much as a grimace.

"You were deeply worried about young Nel," he told her when he'd popped his head into Ballo's just as the sleuths were leaving that final night.

By then they were all stonking drunk and had sniggered as they headed off in respective taxis, leaving Merry with a man determined to have his say.

"I really do have prosopagnosia," he said. "I didn't lie to you about that. And it is strange that I remembered your face; completely unexpected. But the fact is, Meredith Kean, I did! I do! From the moment we met, I haven't been able to forget your sweet, open smile and gorgeous little giggle and those cute cat's-eye spectacles."

As Merry blushed crimson behind those glasses, he added, "I don't mean to embarrass you, but the truth is I want to keep seeing you, Merry. If you'll let me."

And now here he was, walking towards her, instantly recognising her in the crowd once again.

Merry turned back to Lola then and said, "They're here now, sweetie. Remember what we talked about, okay? Please, just try to play nice."

Lola rolled her eyes and followed her mother's gaze across the boardwalk and up to where a man who looked a little like a blond Ronald McDonald was shuffling along, grinning like a fool, a cool chick with blue-tipped hair behind him, a picnic basket in hand.

The man stopped and waved with gusto towards Merry while the girl performed an identical eye roll to Lola's before they continued walking. Then Lola shot a quick look back at her mum and was surprised to see her face had now lit up like... well, like it was Christmas.

And for the life of her, Lola's face lit up too. Because she might be a "self-obsessed teenager" (or whatever her mother had thrown at her when she tried to get out of this super-corny "meet the kids" moment), but even she understood that sometimes she wasn't the centre of the universe, and it was time for her mother to be happy.

~

Earle held the newborn in his arms like she was made of eggshells, then looked up at Beryl, who was glowing as only a first-time grandmother can.

"She won't break, Dad," said Tess, like she was the expert and he'd never held a baby before.

But he had held a baby and he'd brought her up right. Done a good job, Beryl and him, as it turns out. And he suspected he might do okay the second time around too. Especially now he had some business partners to share his workload with.

Which was just as well because the Sleuths of Last Resort had their first official client!

A distraught woman had called him just as Tess was going into labour, and so he'd flicked the call straight to Frankie. And she'd called Merry, and he knew they were meeting with the client later that day.

He wondered what this case was about. A missing child? An unexplained death? Murder?

Something important, he hoped. Someone who really needed their collective expertise and experience.

But he wasn't going to call the sleuths to find out, not yet anyway. This was not the time for crime and misadventure. This was the time for family and new beginnings.

And so he drew the baby closer to his heart as Tess and Beryl clucked like a couple of old ducks beside him.

~~ *the end* ~~

ACKNOWLEDGEMENTS

Before I start handing out gold stars, I'd like to apologise to the good people of Balmoral Beach in Sydney's lower north shore. Yes, Balmoral is a real location and a very beautiful one at that, but it's actually a peaceful spot and I did take poetic license with some aspects. Bellavista and Rachelle's neighbouring apartment block do not actually exist, and nor do the shops where much of the action happens, including Dougie's lovely little bookstore, First Chapters. Sadly, there is no such store on the esplanade, but gee it'd make a lovely addition, don't you think?

Now to some people who do exist and to whom I owe more than just gold stars. Firstly, thanks to my parents, Dianne and Michael, for being such good sports about the fact that I was bringing murder and mayhem to their doorstep.

Thanks also to Christian, Felix and Nimo (who gets an extra pat on the back for his beautiful cover design), to Annie Sarac at the Editing Pen and to Elaine Rivers, my wonderful editor, reader and friend.

And, finally, thanks to all of you—my friends and family, fans and first-timers—for reading my stories and thereby encouraging me to write more. You only have yourselves to blame!

If you'd like to receive news, views and the odd free eBook, just sign up to my author newsletter: **calarmer.com**